The Intrusions

STAV SHEREZ

FABER & FABER

First published in this edition in 2017
by Faber & Faber Limited
Bloomsbury House,
74–77 Great Russell Street,
London WC1B 3DA

Typeset by Faber & Faber Ltd
Printed and bound by CPI Group (UK) Ltd, Croydon CR0 4YY

A CIP record for this book
is available from the British Library

ISBN 978-0-571-29725-2

FSC
www.fsc.org
MIX
Paper from
responsible sources
FSC® C020471

2 4 6 8 10 9 7 5 3 1

THE INTRUSIONS

Stav Sherez is the author of *The Devil's Playground* (2004), which was described by James Sallis as 'altogether extraordinary' and was shortlisted for the CWA John Creasey Dagger Award; *The Black Monastery* (2009), described as 'spectacular' by Laura Wilson in the *Guardian*; and two novels in the Carrigan and Miller series, *A Dark Redemption* (2012), a #1 Kindle bestseller, and *Eleven Days* (2013), both of which were shortlisted for the Theakstons Crime Novel of the Year Award. You can find him on Twitter @stavsherez.

For Lesley Thorne,
who pulled this one out of the fire
more times than I can count.

Whither shall I go from thy spirit? or whither shall I
flee from thy presence?
If I ascend up into heaven, thou art there: if I make
my bed in hell, behold, thou art there.

Psalm 139:7–8

Prologue

It happens when she leans in to talk to her best friend. It is quick and practised and she doesn't notice. Fifteen minutes later she starts to feel sick. The room wobbles. She almost falls off her stool. Her friend catches her just in time and wants to know what's wrong. She tries to answer but discovers she no longer remembers how to use her mouth.

Bowling balls collide against wooden pins, flinging them across the glossy floor and into the gutter. Players whoop and cuss and crane their necks to check the score on overhead monitors. The song changes, crashing chords shake the room, people scream into each other's ears and gulp down beer. London. A Friday night. In a bar in a bowling alley in Bayswater, a young woman clutches her best friend's arm and tries not to throw up as the klaxon announces another strike.

She realises she's drunk too much when she forgets her best friend's name. She looks at the girl she's known since they were seated together on the first day of school, the girl she's confessed her darkest secrets and wildest fears to.

She can't remember her name.

This scares her far more than the sudden churning in her stomach. She leans on the bar for support. Everything is too loud and too fast as if the room with all its noise and chatter is being poured into her skull. She turns and the room turns with her, people smearing into carousel horses, their faces thorny and beaked. Her friend is calling out her name but she doesn't hear it. She shuffles off the stool, tries to regain her balance, sways forward and collapses to the floor.

The sudden warmth of an outstretched hand snaps her back to the bowling alley bar. Her friend helps her up and wipes the hair from her forehead and she still can't remember her name. She looks around and there's a hundred eyes raking her body, people pointing at her, laughing and taking photos and she briefly sees a beach in another country and another girl fleeing the cruel mockery of drunks.

She looks at her glass; the dark, sticky rum. She's sure this is only her second but that can't possibly be right. The phone in her pocket vibrates. She turns it on and plays the message, the receiver pressed tight against her ear, hoping it's that Sicilian boy she met last weekend – but it's not the boy, it's a man's voice, cool and careful. She assumes it's a wrong number because he's talking in a foreign language but, as she listens closer, she realises it's not a foreign language – it's English – only the man is speaking backwards. He makes a strange sibilant sound halfway between a hiss and a clearing of the throat and then she hears the beep and feels someone tugging at her arm.

Her friend asks her who the caller was. She shrugs and points to the exit and her friend laughs and mimes sticking two fingers down her throat. She can't explain so she simply walks away, leaving her handbag on the floor and her best friend staring in surprise.

The door is only a few feet away but it takes an eternity to get there. She squeezes and staggers between men ordering drinks or checking the heft of bowling balls. They wink and snicker as she passes but she's too far gone to notice, her only goal the door, the door with the bright green neon spelling *EXIT* as if it were a promise.

She climbs the stairs and finally she's out on the street, the rush of cabs and cars howling in her ears. She thinks about the message on her phone – a technical glitch of some kind or is it just this, the way she's feeling, her brain mixing up the words and hearing them backwards?

A man calls out to her from across the street. He smiles and points to his car and says *Taxi?* but she doesn't like the look of his hands and quickly turns in the other direction.

She walks these streets daily but they seem different tonight, as if every surface were alive, faintly throbbing. She hums songs to herself to stop her mind from dwelling on all the crap she doesn't want to think about but the bad thoughts keep coming and she can't make them stop.

The streets all curve and twist and double back on themselves. There are several ways to get from the high street to her room and many more ways to get lost in between. The stiff-necked Georgian townhouses frown at her as she passes them, the trees sway and scratch the sky. Everything spins. She clutches a lamp post, bends over and vomits. The nausea lifts momentarily as she wipes her eyes. The curb looks so tempting, all she wants to do is curl into a ball and wait for this to be over, but instead she uses the curved tops of parking meters as support and slowly makes her way towards the junction.

She sees the men before they see her but it's too late to turn back.

She reaches the corner and considers taking the long way

round, through the gardens and across the playing fields, but that would mean another ten minutes and she's not sure how much more of this she can stand.

There's no choice, she'll have to walk past them.

They're squatting on the opposite curb, bare-chested and covered in plaster dust, passing around a bottle of vodka, their eyes glazed and starved. One of them lifts the bottle up in a gesture of hospitality. She can see the streetlight reflecting off his teeth and knows it won't be long before he feels the need to approach and make conversation.

She closes her eyes, forces her legs and arms to obey, and strides past them, deaf to their entreaties and blind to their stares. She feels the skin around her neck constrict at the very thought of their crude square hands and she holds her breath for the entire time she's passing them, willing her feet to propel her safely out of their reach.

She looks back once, but they're not following, and she's furious at herself for being thankful for something so basic as the right to walk down a street without being molested. She stops to catch her breath and that's when she hears the baby crying.

It's the oddness of the sound that raises it above the cacophony of a Friday night, above the arguments and music and smack of hot stolen kisses seeping from high windows and idling cars.

There it is again. A sharp, plaintive plea emerging from the darkness to her left. She tilts her head and traces it to a small alley – but she can't understand what a baby would be doing there.

She feels a tight little contraction in her stomach as the baby continues its lament, the tone increasingly urgent, a panic obvious even without words. She glances across the street towards the windows of her room and she can almost feel the pillowy embrace of her duvet, but when the baby cries again she turns in the opposite direction.

It's only once she's halfway down the alley that she wonders what kind of person would leave a baby in a place like this but, by then, she's already committed, swallowed by darkness and concealed from the cold comfort of cameras.

She lets her eyes slowly adjust to the dark but all she sees is trash and gloom. She calls out – first, normal words, then baby talk – but the only reply is the distant complaint of cats. She is about to turn back, chalk this up to whatever's running riot through her system, when the baby screams again and this time there's something different about it, something metallic and clipped and wrong and she understands she needs to get out of here but, before she can make a move, a man emerges from the shadows, holding a phone. He pushes a button and the crying stops.

I

I

We believe in the certainty of numbers the way we used to believe in God, Geneva thought as she watched the accountant point to a row of flickering digits on the monitor in front of him. He stopped halfway down and tapped the screen.

'Could you please explain why a night in a four-star hotel was deemed necessary for the investigation?'

Geneva squinted, squirmed and tried to remember. The numbers squiggled and slid across the spreadsheet. She turned and focused on the still space of the wall, trying to stop the room from spinning.

'Detective Sergeant Miller?'

'It was for an informant.' She cleared her throat. The taste of last night's tequila stung her lips. She was desperate for a cigarette and some hot tea. Her eyes kept drifting, lulled by the rows of columned numbers and less than four hours' sleep. A little better than the night before, but still. It had been going on for two months. Lying in the dark, gazing at the ceiling, then waking up at two, three, four in the morning, sweat-soaked and riddled by dreams. She glanced over at the accountant. He had the face of a man who slept well, alert and conscious of his own good luck. At that moment, she couldn't help but hate him a little bit. 'We needed to put her up for the night. She hadn't finished giving her testimony.'

The accountant scrutinised Geneva from behind thick

Coke-bottle lenses and double-clicked the mouse. 'And she couldn't have simply gone home and come back in the morning?'

Geneva placed both hands on the table, leaning in towards the accountant, knowing it made him uncomfortable. 'She wouldn't have come back.' She felt a momentary dizziness and pressed her fingertips hard against the wood. 'You don't understand the situation or the context. He would have got to her.'

'£145 seems rather excessive?' The accountant double-clicked the mouse again, a maddeningly precise rhythmic tick that poked at her hangover. She felt like shoving the device down his throat but instead took a deep breath and reached into her pocket.

'What? To solve a murder? Which we did, incidentally. I'd say that's a pretty good return.' Geneva pressed down on the stress ball nestled in her pocket.

The accountant's lips twitched as he clicked the mouse. 'That's not your decision to make. You're not the one paying the bills.' He clicked several times and highlighted the figure in red. Half the screen was red. He clicked again. 'What about this? £280 per month. That seems an awful lot to spend on coffee, don't you think?'

Geneva squeezed the stress ball until she felt the plastic rip. 'You'll have to ask my boss about that.' Her phone vibrated against her leg. 'I'm going out for a cigarette.'

The accountant looked up from his screen and checked his watch. 'You went for one only an hour ago.'

'Exactly.'

'You do know they're bad for you?'

'Really? Where did you hear that?'

*

She waited for the lift, a cup of tea in her hand, the Styrofoam burning her fingers. She was dizzy and tired and sick of answering questions from myopic accountants who wanted her to justify every investigative lead and expenditure. Each time she blinked, snaky black squiggles wobbled across her vision. It was as if the numbers themselves were swimming in her eye. If this was the future she wanted no part of it. The people upstairs thought they could control crime with flowcharts and spreadsheets but they didn't understand that policing wasn't about the financial viability of pursuing a particular lead – it was about that sudden bolt to your stomach, the sizzle in your teeth as patterns began to emerge out of the chaos.

The lift shuddered, depositing Geneva on the ground floor. She checked her watch, wondering how long she could stretch the smoke break for. The longer she was down here, the fewer questions she would have to answer upstairs. Her iPod was fully charged, the tea was hot and exactly what she needed to get her through the rest of the day. The thought of later tonight sent a blush of heat through her chest as she headed for the back door. Seeing Jim again. Maybe later going for . . . Her phone buzzed, its sudden intrusion startling her wrist, the tea splashing across her shirt and down the front of her jeans. She quickly wiped her hands then answered.

'I thought you said you'd call on Friday?'

Two more hours with the accountants suddenly didn't seem like such a bad idea. 'I'm so sorry. I totally forgot.' She'd got home Friday evening after a mind-numbing day of number crunching and immediately headed for the sofa, a bottle of warm tequila and a schlocky slasher DVD.

'I waited all night.'

'Mum. You could have called me.'

'You know I don't like to disturb you.' At these moments her mother's voice always slid into its previous incarnation, heavy with middle-European vowels, lengthy pauses and oblique sighs; a hidden lexicon of intonations from a century that had gone up in flames.

'Sorry. It's this stupid audit. Feels like I left my brain back in the office, minute I walk through the door.'

'You're still on that? I thought you were going to talk to him?' Her mother had a special way of saying *him* when she meant Carrigan, squeezing more syllables into that one word than Geneva would have thought possible.

'I will. I just haven't had the chance.' She touched the cigarette packet in her pocket, reassured by its familiar shape.

'You think he's punishing you for something, don't you?' The slightest of pauses. 'Don't deny it, I can hear it in your voice. I always said you were wasting your talents and look what you're—'

'Jesus! Can we not have this conversation every single time?' Geneva took the first right and continued down the central corridor, walking past areas thick with the shuffle of handcuffed bodies and clacking keyboards.

'We have this conversation every time because I pray and hope maybe one day you'll listen. I know you, Genny—'

'Mum, I'm in the middle of something. I have to go.'

'Will I see you tonight?'

Another thing she'd forgotten. Christ. She took out her cigarettes. 'I can't. I'm meeting someone.'

'A date?' Her mother's voice rose a half-note.

'Mum, I really have to go.'

She put the phone back in her pocket, wishing she could smash it against the wall instead, be able to go for a cigarette or walk in the park without its shrill alarm yanking her back into the world.

She was halfway there when she heard it.

She could see the back door, a slice of sunshine slanting across the glass, two constables smoking outside. The woman screamed again and Geneva cursed, put the cigarettes back in her pocket, and turned around, the noise becoming more distinct the closer she got – chairs crashing against the floor, raised male voices, a baby bawling.

She turned the corner and didn't know where to look. The entire reception hall was in motion. The duty sergeant emerging from the booth, sweat dripping down his forehead. A man sitting on the floor filming with his mobile phone. The young couple running with their pram towards the door. They were all watching the girl.

She was on the floor, in the centre of the room, wrestling with one of the uniforms, a frantic blur of elbows and hands. The girl bit into the constable's jacket and broke free of his grip. She scanned the room, her eyes stricken and cornered. She saw the uniform getting up, coming towards her, the desk sergeant following close behind – and ran.

Before Geneva could react, the girl slammed into her. Geneva felt gravity briefly disappear then snap back as they crashed to the floor. Her spine cracked against the concrete, pain so bright it made her eyes roll back. The girl landed on top of her, her breath and hair hot in Geneva's mouth. She grabbed Geneva by the shoulders.

'Please. Help me.'

Her accent was Australian or Kiwi and her eyes were like empty swimming pools. Geneva tried to extricate herself but the girl's bony fingers were sunk deep into her flesh. The girl lowered her head until they were so close they could have been kissing.

'He took Anna.'

Before Geneva could reply, two uniforms pulled the girl off. Geneva got up, rubbed a sore spot on her knee and collected the scattered papers. The tea was all gone, she'd have to smoke the cigarette dry.

'He claimed her.'

Geneva looked up. The girl had managed to get one arm free from the desk sergeant's grip and was reaching out as if trying to stop herself from falling. Her hair was stuck to her face, her clothes ravelling from her body, her eyes beseeching Geneva.

'He said he was coming back to claim me.'

Carrigan could tell Branch was in a bad mood because the pipe was back in his mouth after two months of surly abstinence. The super was on the phone, arguing and apologising, his jaw tightening over the pipe stem, the words emerging through clenched teeth. He glanced up, acknowledged Carrigan, and went back to his call.

Two pigeons were fighting on the window ledge outside. An explosion of noise and dust, the scuffle-fright of flying feathers and flapping wings. What did birds have to fight about? Carrigan wondered. The same things we did? Or did they fight over stuff we couldn't even begin to imagine? He rubbed his head and checked his watch. He was running twenty minutes late. He'd been heading out for his appointment with the doctor when the super had called to say he needed to see him urgently.

The cold Glaswegian accent of the newly appointed chief constable crackled through the earpiece. Carrigan heard her admonishing Branch, her voice clipped and broaching no disagreement. Branch mumbled another apology and ended the call. Carrigan waited for the super to say something but Branch ignored him, making notes in a small leather-bound diary.

'If it's about the audits . . .'

'It's not about the audits.' Branch looked up. 'The audits themselves I couldn't give a fuck about. That's not what I called you in for.' He placed the pipe beside his laptop. 'But,

I'm curious, so humour me – why is it you think we're facing an audit now? At this particular time?' Branch peered over the frames of his glasses, his eyes neatly bisected.

Carrigan had no idea what he was talking about.

'You think it's a coincidence we get picked for a random audit less than six months after you mess with the assistant chief constable?'

Carrigan blinked, his mouth suddenly dry. It took him a moment to register what Branch was saying. 'Are you talking about the nuns?'

'Of course I'm talking about the nuns. You didn't think Quinn would let you get away with it, did you? I didn't take you to be that naive. Actions have consequences and now, because of you, this entire department is under scrutiny.'

Carrigan flashed back to the burnt-out convent in Notting Hill and the eleven bodies they'd discovered inside. The nuns had taken the law into their own hands and Carrigan had been forced to go up against the diocese in his investigation. But ACC Quinn hadn't seen it that way. Quinn was connected to the diocese and the church and he'd taken it as both a religious and personal affront.

'He can't touch us,' Carrigan said. 'Fuck his audit. The numbers add up. I put my best detective on it.'

'It's not the audit I'm worried about.' Branch pointed to a slim blue folder on his desk. 'It's that.'

Carrigan took the file and opened it. The first page was a memo from the DPS, the Met's internal affairs directorate, to ACC Cooper and DSI Branch. Carrigan read it, his fingers gripping the paper, trying hard to focus as the words began to slip and slide off the page.

Branch tapped his pipe against the keyboard. 'Quinn means to crucify you and that there is the cross.'

Carrigan flipped the memo over. Three subsequent pages of typed depositions and statements. He scanned names and saw people he'd shared a drink with, a hushed conversation in lulls between cases – people he knew, people he worked with every day. How had Quinn managed to get to them? He put the folder down. 'Jesus Christ.'

'Only going to save you if His second coming is as a shit-hot lawyer.'

'That serious?'

'Depends what they can prove and how far Quinn's prepared to take it.'

Carrigan looked at the file. He couldn't tell if the super was secretly relishing this but suspected he was. 'You haven't asked me if I'm guilty of what it says?'

'Don't need to. I already know you are. Quinn wouldn't have instigated this unless he was a hundred per cent sure.' Branch took off his glasses and rubbed the pouched flesh beneath his eyes. 'You only have yourself to blame. If you hadn't done anything out of order, Quinn wouldn't have been able to touch you and we wouldn't be in this mess. Policework's changed. The things we used to get away with – that's ancient history. I may be able to turn a blind eye provided you get results but the computers won't.'

'You're enjoying this, aren't you?'

Branch smiled lopsidedly. 'Oh, believe me, I would if I could. But this shit flies right back at me. This happened on my watch. Certain people will come to the conclusion I was behind it.'

There was something else beneath Branch's words, another layer of meaning Carrigan sensed but couldn't quite interpret. He looked at the blue file. He'd been a cop his entire adult life. It was all he knew and the only thing that had ever made sense to him, yet – for a very brief window of time – there'd been another life. A part of him had always known this day was coming, that eventually he'd be found out for what he was, a pretend cop, someone who would never fit in, and he'd assumed that when the moment came he'd react in a certain way, but now it was here he was surprised at how wrong he'd been.

'You think Quinn's really going to bother going all the way with this? Over a minor infraction?'

'It's not the infraction,' Branch replied. 'Your investigation put the diocese in an embarrassing position. You fucked with a man's religion.'

Carrigan was about to say something but quickly changed his mind. 'How do you suggest we deal with this?'

Branch shook his head. 'There's no *we*. I've done what I can but Quinn means to take you down. I've got the new chief constable wondering what the fuck's going on and I can't tell her without putting the blame on Quinn and, since the two of them are best fucking friends, I can't do that without putting myself in the grinder. I'm sorry, Carrigan, but I need to do what's best for the team.'

'What's the worst they can do to me?'

A dry chuckle emerged from Branch's lips. 'You know as well as I do, no matter how bad things are, they can always get worse. You want my opinion? You could well be looking at several months.'

'Prison?'

'No, a fucking beach resort. Christ, Jack, you need to start taking this seriously.'

Carrigan ran his fingers along the blue file. 'Do you have any advice?'

'Retire.'

'You're joking?'

'Hand in your resignation. If you're no longer in the job, they can't touch you.'

'That's exactly what Quinn wants me to do.'

'You prefer risking jail time?'

'This is bullshit. Stupid personal bullshit.'

'That's as may be, but both you and I know that facts and truth have nothing to do with the real world. Your naive and innocent act won't wash.' Branch picked up a smartphone and pecked out a text message. 'What have you got on at the moment?'

Carrigan rubbed his head and tried to remember. He'd taken the pills an hour ago thinking he was on his way out. The first tingle ran down the back of his knees and made it feel as if he were floating a few inches above the chair. 'A couple of things coming up in court but those are all assigned. Several minor arrests happening today but nothing I have to be there for.'

'Good.' Branch scratched the bridge of his nose. 'Not that I need to say it, but obviously I do because you're not fucking listening, you need to focus all your attention on this.' Branch pointed to the blue file. 'That said, there's fuck all you can do about it today except stress and fret, so go home tonight and relax. Eat something nice, take Karen out for a stroll . . .' Branch stopped. 'I surmise by your expression and lack of response that things are not well?'

'It's just so bloody hard,' Carrigan replied before he had a chance to think, unaware, as the words came rushing out, how much he'd needed to say them. They'd broken up eight days ago and he hadn't told anyone yet. They'd been seeing each other for six months and, at first, everything was great, and then it wasn't. 'We gave up too easily. I think we both saw the way it was heading and fell into this awful, predictable pattern. Coming home from work so tightly wound up from the day's hassles that the smallest thing – a dish in the wrong place, a stray comment or neglected chore – and we'd explode at each other and end up sitting at opposite ends of the room, watching TV shows neither of us had the slightest interest in.' Carrigan looked away. The pigeons who'd been fighting were now standing side by side. 'I'm sorry. I should keep my mouth shut. Talking about stuff only makes it worse.'

'Don't be silly.' Branch took off his glasses and rubbed his eyes. 'It's all hard. What the fuck, right? That's the world we live in – but relationships, shit, that's like having to carry twice the load. Your problems become their problems and vice versa, all the daily frustrations and slights double up. It's why I live alone and why I'll die alone. Life's complicated enough. You're better off by yourself.'

'Thanks,' Carrigan said as he picked up the blue file.

'What for?'

'The inspiring pep talk.'

3

'Sit down, please.'

They were in one of the smaller interview rooms. A cup of tea and a double espresso on the table. Geneva was sitting, her fingertips drumming against the plastic cup. The girl who'd collided with her was pacing up and down, muttering to herself and pulling at her own hair.

'I can't.' The girl's eyes swept the room and fixed on Geneva. 'He'll get me.'

'Not here, he won't.' Geneva sighed, already regretting her decision. 'You're safe here, but if you don't sit down you'll drive me nuts, so please?'

The girl stopped and stared at the chair. Her hair and clothes were dishevelled and torn as if she'd run through brambles. Two of the fingernails on her left hand were broken. She wore a pair of ill-fitting horn-rimmed glasses that kept sliding down her nose. She pulled out the chair, looked underneath it then checked below the table. When she was satisfied she sat down, shifting and fidgeting as if the seat was too hot.

Geneva took out her notebook and pen and wrote down the time and date. There was no point in activating the digital recorder yet, the girl – these days Geneva thought of anyone under twenty-five as *girl* or *boy* – would probably thank her for it later.

Geneva cleared her throat but the girl was transfixed by the hatchwork of scratches and gouges inscribed upon the table. Generations of criminals had sat and whiled away the uncertain hours by using their nails, buttons, or anything else they could find, to mark their passage through this room. The tables were never changed. Suspects often avoided looking down. It reminded them they were nothing special, only one of many to pass through here.

But not this girl. Her entire body was focused on this one task, her fingers tracing arabesques of signature, curse and football chant, a faint hum dribbling from her lips.

'Fascinating, isn't it?'

'What is?' The girl's head shot up. She looked at the ceiling then back down to the table. 'What do they mean, these words?'

'Nothing. Forget it. What's your name?'

The girl blinked twice. 'My name? Why do you want my name?'

'You said you had something to report. We usually begin by taking your name so we know whom to contact.'

The girl stared at the door. 'Madison. Madison Carter.'

'Good. Now, Madison, you need to tell me what drugs you've been taking.'

'What? I didn't take anything.' She crossed her arms, her fingers twitching to a silent beat.

'I see girls like you come in every weekend,' Geneva said. 'Girls who've taken too much and need something to bring them back down.' As she spoke she could hear a low rasping sound in the room, as if a fly had got itself trapped behind one of the walls. 'I know what it feels like too, you know. I wasn't always a policewoman.' Geneva smiled and tried to impart a sense of trust or friendship, anything but the unease she was feeling, her clothes sticking to her skin in this humid room, the tickle of sweat running down her cheek, the cold lost eyes of the girl in front of her. The rasping sound resumed. Geneva scanned the room, the door, the video equipment. She thought maybe it was the camera but it wasn't. The sound was coming from some-where close. It stopped. It started again. Geneva caught a flicker of movement and her eyes settled back on the girl.

Madison's hands were crossed at the chest, the palms facing inwards, and she was scratching the inside of her elbows – small, efficient strokes that left bright blushes of cherry-coloured flesh.

Geneva reached for the stress ball in her pocket and gave it one hard squeeze. 'Please, don't do that.'

Madison shrugged, stopped, then couldn't resist one more scratch.

'If you tell me what you're on, I can get a nurse to give you something to calm you down.'

'I don't want to calm down.' Madison thumbed her glasses. 'I want my friend back.'

Geneva took a sip of cold tea and sighed. They'd been seeing this more and more. It was like the sixties all over again, except that instead of frying their brains on LSD, kids today took whatever was going – bland white pills that could contain any-thing and often did, a mixture of who knows what as long as it got you high. Geneva had seen teenagers bleeding from the eyes after taking a pill called Boost, a girl who'd clawed the skin off her own legs while high on Meow Meow and, once, a group of boys on a stag night who'd snorted Bath Salts and promptly thrown themselves into the Thames.

'I think he put it in our drinks.'

Geneva snapped out of her thoughts. 'Who?'

'The man who took Anna. He did something to our drinks.' Madison pointed to the wall. 'She's out there right now. What's he doing to her? Please. You need to do something.'

'I need you to calm down. Drink some of that coffee. It's good. My boss's special blend. It'll sober you up, I guarantee it.'

The girl's arm shot across the table. She grabbed Geneva by the wrist, her grip surprisingly strong. 'Every time I close my eyes I hear Anna scream. No one else will listen to me. She's out there somewhere and I can't stop thinking about what he's doing to her.'

Geneva gently pulled her hand away and checked her watch. She should have detailed a uniform to do this but the accountants were waiting for her upstairs with a long list of petty queries and snide remarks. She texted the desk to send over a nurse then switched on the interview room's embedded recorder and stated her name and the date.

'Your friend? What's her full name?'

Madison scanned the room, floor to ceiling, then scratched her elbow. 'Anna Becker. The man came and Anna . . . Anna she couldn't . . .'

'Please. Start from the beginning. When did Anna go missing?'

Madison moved her lips silently, her forehead scrunched tight. She looked as if she were trying to work out a particularly complicated maths equation. 'What day is it?'

'Monday.'

Madison shook her head. 'It can't be. How can the drugs still be in my system if it's been three days?' She started scratching again. She caught Geneva looking and stopped. 'What did he give me? Why won't it wear off?'

'Someone's on their way to look at you. Whatever you took, it'll soon leave your system and you'll be back to normal. I promise.' Geneva glanced down at her notebook. She had to keep the girl anchored in facts – as long as Madison was trying to recall details she seemed fairly lucid but the moment she stopped talking her eyes started to drift and the sound of scratching filled the room. 'Did you know Anna from back home?'

'Uh-uh. She was from some tiny village in Germany. Somewhere with mountains, I can't remember the name.'

'That's okay,' Geneva said. 'She was here on holiday?'

'Nah, she'd come back from travelling. She wanted to settle down and get work as an actress. She'd auditioned for a place at RADA.'

'Did she get it?'

Madison looked down at the ingrained squiggles, her fingers sinking deep into the grooves, rubbing up and down the channelled depressions, and shook her head. There was an intensity to her that unnerved Geneva. She wanted to open a window but there were none in the room.

'Is that how the two of you met?'

Madison pushed her glasses back up and sipped her coffee, grimacing at the taste. 'We share a dorm. She was the first person I knew in London.'

'What was she like?'

A faint smile momentarily transformed Madison's face. 'She was great, you know? You don't meet many, well, you meet so many people travelling but most of them are gone before you get to know them or are assholes from the start. Anna was so great. That first day, I just knew we were going to be good friends – which is funny, because she was everything I wasn't. So sure of herself, confident, bursting with all these big dreams. But she was also kind. Not spoiled like most kids who can afford to travel these days. She always stood up for me.' Madison pulled something from her pocket. Geneva braced herself but the girl was only retrieving her wallet. She opened it and carefully removed a small photo and passed it to Geneva.

The two girls couldn't have looked any more different. Anna was pale and ethereal while Madison was all curves and smiles, a sly suggestion of sex and electricity in her dark eyes. Geneva looked up. The girl sitting opposite her looked ten years older than the one in the photo, though it had obviously been taken recently. Geneva promised she'd return the original once she'd made copies and clipped it to the file.

'Do you remember what happened on Friday night?'

'Everything.' Madison laughed softly. 'I can remember everything so clearly. That's the worst part. Details I'd never normally notice – the stairs, the sound of cars braking, the way Anna . . .' Madison looked down. 'Aren't these drugs supposed to make you forget?'

'I think he may have given you something a little different – but it's good you remember. It'll help us.' Without being aware of it, Geneva had taken the stress ball out of her pocket and was pumping it with her free hand. 'Where did this happen?'

'The Last Good Kiss.'

Geneva recalled passing the subterranean nightclub several times on the way to Carrigan's favourite Chinese restaurant. 'The two of you go there regularly?'

Madison scanned the wall as if she expected to pluck the answer from its surface. 'We hadn't been for a while but yeah, we used to. There's a long happy hour. Best thing about it. The plan was to have a few drinks, dance a bit, then go into town for the night. We were on our second drink . . .' Madison stopped and used both hands to grip the edge of the table. 'I started to feel sick, like one moment I was okay and the next the lights and music were way too much. Anna was looking at me all funny, her mouth hanging loose. She said she was feeling terrible. I suggested we go outside for some fresh air and silence – the club was rammed, lights strobing, music so loud you could feel it rattling your ribs, this song . . . oh God, if only they hadn't played that song—'

'How did you feel out on the street?' Geneva interrupted.

Madison shook her head. 'It wasn't the street. After a certain hour you can only leave through the back. There's a little alley where everyone goes to smoke.' Madison closed her eyes. 'We had to hold each other steady to make it up the stairs.'

Geneva flashed back to all those times she'd had one too many in a bar, the bright lights and spinning ceiling – it could take you by surprise – one minute you're feeling as if this is the best night of your life and a sip or two later everything turns into a funfair ride. 'Did the fresh air help?'

'No. God, no. I felt worse. The entire alley started to spin. Anna dropped to her knees and puked. I tried to help her but my heel snapped and my leg buckled and I fell over. Bright white light flashed across my eyes. Everything was extremely fast and extremely slow at the same time. I saw Anna on her knees being sick and then I heard the van door slide open.'

'Did you see him?'

Madison scraped her chair back and shook her head. 'He was wearing a cap of some sort. It was dark. I'm sorry.' Hot tears splashed down her face. She did nothing to wipe them away. 'I could hear the sound his shoes made, slapping on the pavement as he got out of the van. It was like someone had turned up the volume on the world. Anna was still on her knees, saying *Something isn't right*, over and over again. The footsteps were so loud they hurt my ears. He passed in front of me and there was nothing I could do. He crouched down and I saw him take out a syringe and plunge it into something. I remember it flashing in the light and, as he slid the needle into Anna's shoulder, I thought for a moment that someone had sent for an ambulance, that he was a paramedic here to help us, but then he gently took Anna's hand and helped her up and led her towards the van. As he walked past me, he stopped and said: *Don't feel bad. I'll be back to claim you.* I heard the door slide shut and, for a split second, I saw Anna on her knees in the back of the van, being sick again, and then the engine started and the van was gone. Anna was gone.'

4

Carrigan sat at his desk and stared at the blue file. He'd forgotten about his appointment with the doctor, the calls he had to make and bills to pay, the slow accretion of the day's chores. There was always too much to do and too little time and every day the debt increased as more hours were subtracted from your life. He straightened the stack of incoming files and squared the keyboard and mouse. He put the pens away and tidied the cable cords. He was becoming less tolerant of clutter as he got older, or perhaps just less tolerant.

'Look, I know what you're going to think and I know what you're going to say but—'

Carrigan glanced up. He hadn't heard her come in. 'Then why bother asking?'

'You might surprise me yet.'

There was almost a smile on Geneva's face, though he could tell she was doing her best to hide it. Her morning hair swirled around her shoulders, unruly and with a mind of its own, deep black pouches sinking her eyes. He gestured for her to sit down but she was too hyped up for a chair or any piece of furniture to contain her. She paced and fidgeted as she recounted Madison's story – the drinks, the dizziness, the alley, the van.

Carrigan put the blue file to one side and reached inside his desk drawer. He took out a strip of pills and snapped two from the blister pack. The foil rasped as he dry-swallowed them.

'What exactly do you think we can do for her?'

Geneva stopped pacing and sat down. 'I don't know. Maybe nothing. Probably nothing. Maybe none of this even happened and it's just another case of taking the wrong drugs, or too much of the right ones – but there's a terrified young woman in the room downstairs and that is real.'

'Is she high now?'

'Yes. But she says she was spiked. Three days ago. Says they both were.'

'A lot of people say that because they don't want to admit they've been taking drugs or because they're embarrassed they got so blotto on booze and need to blame it on something else. Besides, any drug would have worn off by now.'

Geneva pressed herself up against the table. 'I know all that, but her account of the abduction is far too detailed, it's not like something you'd make up.'

Carrigan frowned. 'That's the nature of drug hallucinations. People construct incredibly detailed realities. And what's more, it doesn't make any sense. Someone this slick at performing an abduction wouldn't leave an eyewitness. And that stuff about coming back to claim her? Who says that kind of crap? If he was going to take her, he would have done it there and then.' Carrigan glanced out the window, the sky grey and misted with drizzle. 'Have you considered the possibility she saw her friend go off with some guy and the drugs warped it into this?'

'Of course I have,' Geneva replied. 'But her fear's real. That's not an hallucination. She witnessed something. Something which scared her badly.'

Carrigan could tell Geneva wasn't about to give up. He wanted to go back to the blue file. He needed to call the doctor, write up several reports, an endless list of chores running like a ticker-tape at the back of his head. 'What exactly do you want me to do?'

'I want to take her statement formally.'

'The last thing we need right now is a new case. We don't have either the time or the remit to look into every missing person. Let the uniforms deal with it. If it turns out to be anything more than a bad trip they'll pass it back on up to us.'

'They'll miss something, you know that – and if what Madison says is true, it'll be too late for Anna.'

'If you hadn't been downstairs at that particular moment this wouldn't have even reached us.'

'But I was.'

'I'm sorry,' Carrigan replied. 'But we're halfway through an audit. People are watching us and I can't allocate resources to something this flimsy.'

'That stupid bloody audit.'

Carrigan sat up. 'The audit is bullshit, yes, you'll have no argument with me on that, but if we don't complete it we're going to miss out on some of next year's allocations. There've been enough cuts as it is.'

'That's not a reason to neglect a potential murder.'

Carrigan sighed. There was nothing he could say to change her mind. She was right and she was wrong but it was too early in the day to disentangle one from the other. 'Okay, fine. Go ahead and look into this girl's story – send her back to the hostel and reinterview her when the drugs have worn off but I don't want this distracting you from the audit.'

'Someone else can do that. I don't see why I had to be pulled off rotation.'

Carrigan noted the downslope of jaw and clenched muscle, the resolute simmer behind her eyes. 'You think I put you on this as some kind of punishment?'

Geneva nodded.

'Really? Jesus. You know that's not . . . shit, I put you on this because I don't trust anyone else to do it right and because, like it or not, this is crucial to how we go about our job in the next twelve months.'

Geneva looked down at the floor. 'I'm sorry. I didn't know.'

'It's okay. I'm sorry too. It's been a crap day all round.'

*

Carrigan took off his jacket and draped it on the back of the grey plastic chair. For a few minutes he did nothing but watch her breathe. The mounded sheets swelled and ebbed and he was surprised that such a frail body could create even this small disturbance.

His mother's condition hadn't changed. A stroke had crackled through her brain five days ago. Her heart stopped and was restarted but by then she'd slipped into a deep coma. He'd talked to two different specialists and they'd both explained that due to her advanced-stage dementia and the severity of the stroke, the chances of regaining consciousness were almost zero. They began to talk about options and he'd zoned out.

He'd had a brief conversation with her consultant in the alarm-shriek and body spill of the A & E ward an hour ago, but there were no new developments. The consultant told him there was little point being in the room. Carrigan bought a coffee and a stale croissant from the hospital cafe, a stilled silent place of permanent suspension, each customer lost in their own private anxieties and newly cancelled futures, then took the lift to the seventh floor.

In the room it was different. In the room there was just him and his mother and the circling array of machines that did what once only God and prayers could. No one could reach him here. The grey chair was hard and cold and focused his thoughts. The file in his hand honed and sharpened them. He reread the statements, depositions and accusations. Quinn had done his homework. Everything in the file was true.

Carrigan drained the sludge of undissolved sugar at the bottom of his cup and got up. He approached the bed and stood over his mother and pressed his lips to her forehead, shocked by how cold and dry her skin felt, like kissing a stone.

'Please wake up,' he whispered into her ear, its delicate labyrinth so familiar from childhood confidences in dimly lit rooms. The machine beeped, her constant companion in the land of suspended time. Soon, he knew, she would be only memory and a gap that could never be filled. It had been five years since he'd stood graveside and watched Louise plunge into the earth. He'd never imagined he'd be back here so soon nor that the decision, this time, would be his to make. Life was the process of learning to live with less and less. You lost everyone close to you or they lost you. There were no other alternatives. Death had been his career but he'd never been this close to it since Africa, unshielded by the job, here in the raw daily panic and prayer.

His knees ached against the cold floor but this was an important part of it, he knew, and as he looked up at the bed he began to recite a jumble of prayers and entreaties, half-remembered words and mangled verses. He bowed his head and shut his eyes tight. He pressed his palms together and made desperate bargains. He waited, but no light came. He stilled his breathing but there were no thunderbolts or ecstatic visions – perhaps he wasn't trying hard enough, or maybe once you gave up on God, God gave up on you?

And then he felt a change, a slight shift in the room's current. His body tensed. A breeze rippled against the back of his neck. Something creaked.

Carrigan turned just in time to see the door closing, a flicker of black hair disappearing into the hallway. He was immediately up and running. He rounded the bed and crossed the room and opened the door and looked both ways down the corridor, but it was empty all the way down to the gaping mouth of the lift.

5

She'd been looking forward to this all day but now the rain was ruining her hair. Geneva tried standing under the awning but had to keep stepping aside to let people by. Couples with arms wrapped around each other broke out of love's delirium to look at her, small and drizzled, then rushed inside for popcorn and beer. She ignored their stares, the feeling in her gut, and checked her watch again.

The film was due to start in ten minutes and Jim was late. Geneva scanned the rain-sprayed street, hoping to catch a glimpse of him alighting from a bus, running towards her, a look of contrition on his face and a bunch of flowers in his hand. But there was only the ragged march of workers heading home like defeated soldiers, slumped and shuffle-stepping in the heat. These last two weeks the city had felt like an extra layer of clothing depositing itself on your skin in sweat and dust. You'd take a shower, cross the room, and need another shower. A heatwave whipped up from the Sahara and flung across the plains of Europe, broken only by sudden torrential downpours. The worst of both worlds. Geneva looked at her watch but only two minutes had passed since she'd last checked it.

It was supposed to be their third date and she'd begun to think Jim was someone she might want to see, and see often. Some men were only made for one-night stands. But this one.

This one had ravished her so deeply she'd let go all caution in one dizzying tumble.

She'd started going to night classes a couple of months ago, scrutinising poetry again, stuffed into an abandoned classroom in Archway with four or five others and taught by an arthritic professor who claimed she was the only woman Auden had ever slept with. It had begun as a kind of therapy, a suggestion by her counsellor after last year's alley attack that she needed to do an activity entirely unrelated to the job, but it had turned into something else, unexpected and surprising, a part of herself she'd become stranger to.

She'd bumped into Jim at her second class. They'd clashed heads as they both went for the door at the same time, her ears ringing rudely as the pile of books spilled from his hands. She bent down to pick them up, the collision had been her fault, and was stunned to see herself staring up from the cover of an old paperback. It took her a few seconds to realise it was her mother not her, though the same age she was now, and she'd never really thought before how similar they were or about those traits and skin-quirks that had been handed down.

'Do you mind if I have a look?' she'd asked, and Jim had introduced himself, shaking hands, his palm warm and strong and slightly clammy from the heat.

'I'm surprised you've heard of her,' he said.

She stared at the photo, seeing the small differences that had been bestowed by her father, a slight dimple of chin and slant of eye. 'Where did you find it?'

Jim smiled as if a lock had been undone in his jaw. 'This is so weird. I've been searching ages for it and this morning I was a bit early so I popped into Oxfam and there it was!' He mimicked his reaction on finding the book with a wide-eyed cartoon stare. 'I search years for this and the morning I find it I bump into another fan – how strange is that?'

'I'm not a fan,' Geneva said, passing it back to him. 'I'm her daughter.' She loved the crease of surprise on his face and the way his eyes danced between the book and her.

'Are you a poet too?'

She didn't want to spoil the moment by telling him what she did so she asked him out for a drink instead. They'd gone to a funfair on Hampstead Heath and got lost in the sparkled night of candyfloss and rollercoaster screams. They'd sat on a metal scaffold and shared terrible coffee and hot fresh doughnuts and told each other about their lives and it had all come out. Had she said too much? Frightened him off with any of the hundreds of horrible little details she kept stored away in her brain?

It was so hard to know. The relationship was moving far quicker than she was used to but it was her doing as much as his. She saw herself drifting into a life she didn't want – working late, a string of disappointing boyfriends, the confines and comforts of a one-bedroom flat. Time was different in your thirties. Men were harder to find. The good ones were all gone and the bad ones were more desperate. Dating was also different. She wondered how many of the couples entering the cinema had met online and if people in the future would look at the old methods of dating – alcohol and chance – in much the same way as we regard surgery before the use of anaesthetic.

She glanced up to see a couple of girls, painted for the night, cross the road with such abandon and fervour she couldn't help but feel a little diminished and it made her think of Madison, scared out of her mind, unable to trust her own head, scratching away at herself in the tiny interview room. A nurse had finally come and given Madison a shot of Valium. Geneva detailed a uniform to drive her back to the hostel but, at the last moment, had decided to accompany them. Madison didn't speak throughout the entire journey. Geneva left her outside the building, saying she'd be back to reinterview her tomorrow. Madison nodded and Geneva had watched her disappear into the dark hostel grounds but she couldn't get rid of the girl's story quite so easily.

If what Madison said was true then another girl was out there and no one was looking for her. She'd been hoping Carrigan would be hooked by Madison's tale and that he'd pull her off the audit and they would talk it through the way they always did, but he'd seemed strangely absent earlier, as if he'd left a part of himself back at home.

She took out her phone. There were three missed calls from her solicitor. She was suing her husband for her share of their former home. With only a week to go until the case was due in court, this could only be bad news. There were no messages from Jim. She went back and forth between wanting to text him and not wanting to seem too desperate and needy – but what if they'd got their timing mixed up?

Where are you?

Geneva gripped the phone and stared at the screen. The reply came back almost immediately.

You didn't get my email?

What email?

Shit. Sorry. I have to stay back at work. Will call you later.

Queensway was roaring with backpackers and gamblers, pimps and waiters, drunks, pick-up artists and dazed tourists. Hot rain splashed the pavement but provided no relief from the humidity. The Last Good Kiss was located on a side street from the station, one of those interstitial zones of the city, neither Bayswater nor Paddington, yet catering to and determined by both. It occupied a basement next to a souvenir shop full of snow globes, bobby hats and union jacks. But it wasn't the nightclub Geneva was interested in tonight.

She'd thought about going home. She'd thought about seeing the film by herself. She'd almost hidden away in a dark pub behind a wall of White Russians and then she'd remembered the alleyway and how close it was. Something wouldn't let her dismiss Madison's story as readily as Carrigan had done. It was a matter of logic as much as gut instinct. If Madison was telling the truth then the consequences of not acting far outweighed the expenditure and hassle if it turned out to be nothing. So far, she only had what Madison had told her. A girl afloat on a sea of drugs. She needed evidence. Something to convince Carrigan.

Geneva turned the corner and almost collided with two young men in the act of exchanging money. They drew apart, took one look at her and hurried off down the street. It was only after taking a few more steps that she saw they'd dropped something.

A bulging plastic baggie lay on the pavement. The contents

were an intense green. She stared at it for a long moment, surprised by the memories it kindled. Geneva checked both ways down the street then, without knowing exactly why, picked up the baggie and placed it in her inside pocket. A couple of stray dogs watched her, their eyes listless and broken. She continued past a couple of boarded-up phone shops and a Persian grocer and took a left into the alley nestled behind the club.

It hit her the moment she walked in. Ever since the events of last Christmas she'd avoided confined spaces. Alleyways, especially. Her wrists started to itch and her breath caught, the rain warm and sticky on her skin.

It was the perfect place for an abduction. The alley was narrow and neglected, barely wide enough for a car to pass through. It was bordered on three sides by the windowless backs of buildings. Mounds of uncollected rubbish, collapsed cardboard boxes and empty wine bottles littered the ground. A staircase spiralled up from the subterranean bar. Geneva scanned the space above but there were no CCTV cameras. She'd expected that, but a small part of her had hoped there'd be footage to either disprove or verify Madison's story.

The rain stopped and everything glistened and sparkled in the spray of light from her phone torch. She didn't know what she was hoping to find – maybe only the gut feeling that something had happened here – but it was just an ordinary alley, rank and dark.

She walked down one side, taking her time, splashing light over the cobbled ground. Mountain ranges of cigarette butts formed a halo around the bar's staircase. She saw the roach ends of several joints, grease-mottled fast food containers and scattered shards of broken glass. She caught a slight movement out the corner of her eye and swivelled her torch towards it.

A grey cat was lying on its side. It seemed to be moving but, of course, it couldn't be. Its entire belly had been torn open. The cat's skin sagged against its skeleton and Geneva saw that most of its insides had been scooped out. Ants and small beetles scuttled about in the remains. A faint rustling from behind made her turn, her legs tensed against the ground. She scanned the other side of the alley – the boxes, crates, dumpster and bin bags – but saw nothing. She turned back and let all other thoughts fall away, trying to picture the scene.

She saw two girls drinking in their local on a Friday night. They're having fun, relieved the long week is finally over. The perp watches them, perhaps has been watching them for a while. Madison and Anna stand by the bar, making them easy prey. Much simpler to put something in their drinks as you're ordering your own than to do it at a table where the drinks are directly in their sight-line. The perp would then wait until he saw Anna drink from the spiked glass. Geneva forced her eyes shut, took deep breaths. She saw him leave, get his van, parked nearby, and reverse it halfway down the mouth of the alley, effectively sealing it off. It would have been so easy once the drugs kicked in and the girls were disoriented; yet the same incongruity Carrigan had picked up on struck her – why had the perp drugged both girls but only taken Anna?

Fifty yards away people were drinking and having fun. Fifty yards away people were eating, sleeping, living. Geneva ignored the noise and crossed the alley. Her torch snagged on something. A quick fierce glint. She stopped, donned a pair of plastic gloves and studied the object. It looked like a small glass vial, the kind hospitals use. Geneva pulled an evidence bag from her pocket and carefully picked up the vial and placed it inside. She heard a muted thump coming from her left and nearly dropped the bag. She scanned the other side of the alley, the dumpster and pyramid of empty crates, and had almost convinced herself she'd imagined it when she heard it again. It was louder this time and it was definitely coming from inside the dumpster.

She wanted to run, to flee this skanky alley – but what if it was Anna in there? Geneva gripped the torch tightly in her fist and approached the dumpster. Could the entire van routine have been a ruse? Did the perp rape Anna then throw her in the trash?

The dumpster was made of heavy black plastic and was exactly the same height as Geneva. She swapped the phone to her left hand and used her right to lift the cover.

'Anna?'

The smell made Geneva's eyes water and she held her breath as she swept the torch over bin bags, used nappies and old newspapers. She clenched her teeth and gripped the edge of the dumpster with her fingers, leaning in, perched on tiptoes, trying to see deeper inside. The move knocked her a little too far forward. She struggled to regain her balance. The phone slipped from her hands.

It landed on top of one of the black bags. Geneva cursed as she hoisted herself up and balanced her stomach on the edge of the dumpster, letting the momentum of her body swing her down. She stretched out her arm and reached for the phone. Her fingers brushed it, almost lost it, then found it again and finally got a grip. Plastic rustled and shifted. The bags began to move. Geneva heard a low moan as a hand shot out from between the bin bags and grabbed her wrist. She saw broken fingernails and skin crusted with dirt and she threw herself back, kicking her legs against the side of the dumpster, her sleeve tearing in one long silent rip as she fell back, only just managing to regain her balance.

She looked to her left, saw the mouth of the alley, the street outside, and resisted the urge to run. She was turning back towards the dumpster when the lid opened.

She screamed when she saw him.

The man inside the dumpster screamed.

He was completely bald apart from three long white hairs which sprouted from his scalp. His face was matted with dirt and filth. He stared at Geneva, his eyes wide and terrified and then he vaulted over the top of the dumpster with an agility he didn't look capable of. He landed in the alley and ran past her and out into the main street.

6

Carrigan slammed the steering wheel until the pain in his palms drove out the pain in his head. He pushed the accelerator until the city was a flashing streak of colour in his peripheral vision. His temples throbbed and his eyes ached. He was on the way to a crime scene and going in with a head full of problems would only guarantee he'd miss something. He wrapped his fingers tight around the steering wheel, hoping it was an OD or suicide, something he could pass off, yet, at the same time, feeling that guilty rush of pleasure he could only admit to in his most private moments.

The city was still asleep. Everything that was going to happen hadn't happened yet and you could almost pretend it wouldn't, that this one day could be rescued from the chaos but, of course, no day was exempt from the world. An ambulance and several patrol cars, their lights mutely flashing, directed him to the house. He saw bodies moving in the strobed dark, uniforms and techs, a sense of hurry and purpose in their silhouettes telling him this was going to be more than just another OD.

They were on Kingsleigh Avenue, a street parallel to Queensway, populated with tall Georgian townhouses, white and solid in the drizzling rain. Carrigan got out of the car and stretched the morning out of his bones, his knees popping loudly. The building looked like something a child had put together then got bored with and abandoned. The rain and wind had done the rest. The facade was veiled by scaffolding but most of the mesh had been torn away and white fingers of sheeting snapped in the wind. It had become a distressingly familiar sight. Empty houses, boarded-up shops, abandoned construction sites. The crisis had hit like an unexpected wave and left these wrecked reminders in its wake like the ribcages of old ships swirling on the ocean floor.

Two uniforms were standing either side of the front door. They were talking to each other, leaning in, a conversation hushed and intense. They stopped when they saw Carrigan approaching.

'Either of you been inside?' Carrigan asked, the rain coming down hard and heavy and almost obscuring them from each other.

They both shook their heads.

'Good. We don't want any more bodies in there than we absolutely need.' He stopped, seeing the uniforms smirking. 'What's so bloody funny?'

'Good luck with that,' the taller one said.

Carrigan caught something in his tone. 'What's that supposed to mean?'

'You'll see,' the constable replied, still laughing as Carrigan entered the building.

He knew something was wrong the moment he stepped inside. No house, abandoned or not, should smell like this. He trudged his way past drifts of pizza menus, minicab cards and lost dog flyers. The builders had been halfway through stripping the property when they'd abandoned the job. Walls lay partly demolished, covered in plaster dust and brick powder. The smell of excrement was hot and sharp. Flies buzzed and dive-bombed his head. Carrigan could barely see through the gloom and had to put one foot carefully in front of the other, using his hands to steady himself against the walls and ignoring the sticky residue on everything he touched.

It was lying in the dark, twenty feet ahead. There was no mistaking it for anything but what it was. A human being reduced to inanimate flesh. He couldn't believe they'd left it unattended.

The body was sprawled out horizontally across the corridor. Carrigan cautiously took a step forward, crouched down and pulled out his torch. The light revealed a jacket stitched together from yellowed newspapers and grocery cartons. Carrigan leaned in closer and aimed the torch at the corpse's face. Its eyes suddenly blinked open and Carrigan jumped back. A huge snore came from the tramp's mouth. Carrigan glanced towards the room on his right. The mounded humps of more passed-out drunks were curled up on the floor, sleeping off the wine-soaked night. He'd heard rumours that these abandoned properties had become a magnet for the homeless in recent years. The shelters were always full or too expensive and the streets had become a dangerous place. He knew it would make their job that much harder as he turned back into the hallway and found his way to the rear of the house.

He saw the room from halfway down the corridor. The door was open and faint light spilled out. As he got closer he noticed the dark splashes on the wall. A flicker of movement caught in his peripheral vision as a shadow flitted across the doorway, disappearing as quickly as it had appeared.

Carrigan called out but there was no reply. He took a few steps forward and had just reached the door when the figure stepped out.

Karlson jumped when he saw Carrigan, quickly regaining his composure with a shrug of the shoulders.

'Didn't you hear me?' Carrigan kept his voice steady despite the rumble in his chest.

Karlson scanned the corridor, his eyes vacant and skittish. 'Sorry, shit . . . I was totally . . . fuck . . .' He pointed back into the room, the top joints of his fingers still blackened from the frostbite he'd got climbing in the Karakoram last month. 'You mind if I skip this one?'

Carrigan tried to hide his surprise. 'Just make sure Scene of Crime knows who's been in so far – and, Karlson?'

'Yeah?'

'I wanted to say thank you.'

'What for?'

'You didn't talk to Quinn.' Carrigan had scanned the names on the deposition inside the blue file and had been surprised to see Karlson's absent.

'Of course not.' Karlson's easy smile briefly flickered back. 'But don't think it was on your account. I know a cop when I see it, and you, you're just very good at pretending to pass for one.'

It never failed to surprise Carrigan how the people who knew you least could often see you more clearly than your closest friends. 'So, why didn't you?'

'Because you did the right thing for the investigation and

that's more important than bullshit politics or stupid regulations.'

Karlson walked away and Carrigan stepped into the room. The space flickered to life under his torch. Dogs howled in the distant darkness. Wild whispers of wind and rain came in through a large hole in the outside wall. Half a bookcase was still standing, all the books gone. An old sofa with no stuffing or cushions, more an X-ray of a sofa than the actual thing, was pushed up against the wall. Junk and debris were strewn across the floor, plastic bags and fast food cartons, broken bottles, cigarette ends, and the remains of several small fires.

But Carrigan wasn't looking at any of that.

He was looking at the woman laid out on the floor in front of him.

The smell flooded his nostrils and he swallowed it back down before it could overwhelm him. There was so much blood. Blood on the bricks, blood on the sofa, blood on the floor, blood across the ceiling – but barely a drop on her.

She was lying on the floor in the shape of a star, her arms and legs at forty-five degree angles from her body. Her eyes were closed and, midway down her neck, Carrigan could see the tiny red wound through which her life had leaked out.

7

For now, there was only him and the room. Her and him and the blood that covered every available surface as if she'd been hiding a hurricane inside her. Constables were rousing the drunks from their dreams in other parts of the house, strings of foul curses and morning splutters echoing through the corridors. Carrigan shut it out and tried to see the scene as if it were a room without a dead person inside it. To imagine what histories and small painful consolations had occurred within these walls.

The night-dwellers had stripped almost everything that could be sold or burnt. The scenario would be similar to one repeated across the country these past few years. A job had been lost and a family stopped paying the mortgage. They'd fled with their most valuable possessions, leaving everything else behind in a house they could no longer afford. The house had turned into a museum of their lives, depicting a time when everything still made sense and goals were achievable and all that mattered was your wife's smile when she woke you up in the musky morning.

The bank had repossessed the house and sold it, contents included, at auction. The property developer hired a construction company to convert the house into flats. The developer or the construction company went bust. They'd gambled on a boom that would last for ever, a rocket that would never come down. They'd forgotten about gravity and how irresistible its pull is to men. The building lay abandoned but cities abhorred a vacuum. The rough sleepers, junkies and God-touched found these refuges and took shelter in them. The family's possessions had been turned into utilities by the waves of people drifting through – books were worth more for the heat of their fuel than for their ideas. A chair was an hour's warmth, a painting, ten minutes.

Carrigan took out his phone and snapped photos. The SOCOs would thoroughly document the scene with stills and film but he liked to have a set from his own frame of reference. It would help him reconstruct the room in his head later and play out all its different and terrible scenarios.

He avoided her. He could not look at her yet. There was something awful about her positioning, the arms and legs akimbo, her dress neatly laid out. She seemed so vulnerable and exposed, though, of course, she was beyond all worries of that kind now.

Carrigan stepped carefully, avoiding the blood, making sure he didn't disturb anything, though he knew it was futile and that even the breath passing from his lips would rearrange the room in subtle, molecular ways. The SOCOs would be furious but he needed to see the scene like this, before it became con-taminated by presence, as if some trace of the killer might yet linger here.

He crossed to the far end of the room and began searching, his torch dancing across layers of congealed junk in precise, measured sweeps. One corner had been used as a toilet and was spotted with crescents of desiccated faeces. What looked like more excrement was smeared on the walls, randomly, or in indecipherable patterns, pasted over rudimentary graffiti. Plastic bags had fused into cardboard boxes creating sedimentary layers of refuse. Cobwebs bridged high corners and low walls, intricate labyrinths spun out of hunger and need. Cockroaches scuttled through the compacted muck, their shells brown and shiny as miniature violins.

The blood on the floor was smudged in furious brushstrokes of scarlet and black but it was the wall that drew Carrigan. The swerve and smear of blood, archipelagos of drip and spatter. An inexplicable gap. He scrutinised it. He snapped more photos. He looked at the photos then looked at the wall but he could not work it out.

He finally approached the body and tried to understand what it was about her he found so unsettling. Karlson had sensed it too. They'd both seen enough bodies in far worse condition than this for it to be mere shock. The scene by the wall was messy and brutal but here, only a few feet away, everything was carefully laid out – her arms and legs were splayed at equal angles, the dress she was wearing had been freed of any snags or crumplings that must have occurred when he moved her but more than all this, Carrigan thought, it was her eyes, closed as if she were gently sleeping, that gave the scene an eerie and disconcerting serenity.

The techs were dressed in white boiler suits and shook their heads when they saw him inside the room. The Scene of Crime officer swore and cursed but Carrigan could tell his heart wasn't really in it. Carrigan told them to send over their blood spatter expert then left them to it. He called Berman and asked him to set up an incident room then updated Branch on what they'd found. He went out for coffee, the sudden sunshine startling, and came back to find the room transformed.

The interior was lit up by sodium lights and stuttering camera flashes. Techs were silently measuring, taping and sampling. Two video operators filmed the scene. Carrigan looked over at the woman. The illusion of life was gone. Plastic bags were wrapped around her hands and shoes. Her body had been moved so that her head now lay at an awkward angle, making the wound in her neck more prominent, a small dark mouth mirroring her own.

'This is some fucked-up shit, all right.' The blood spatter expert approached Carrigan, breathing in short sharp bursts, his white suit spotted and dark. He was young, clean-shaven and looked like a teenager.

'Shelby.' They were both wearing plastic gloves, there was no reason to shake hands.

'That your first name or last?'

'Neither,' Shelby replied, pointing down at the floor. 'The blood is all hers and the pool on the floor consistent with a severed jugular.' Shelby stroked his chin, his fingers small and delicate as a child's. 'Almost consistent, but we'll get to that.'

Carrigan looked back up at the wall. A checkerboard of blood and brick. That gap. He saw the woman's final moments, freaking on fear and drugs, tied up and helpless as the killer cut her throat, the blood spraying the wall until there was no more left inside her.

Shelby took out a small black tube, pressed a button, and shone a fine blue light at the floor. 'This is all consistent with the victim standing up and having the right side of her throat cut. This is what you would expect. Blood does what blood always does. It has a purpose outside the body just as it does inside it. Blood wants to get out. See how it leaps and arcs and splashes? Those thick streaks over there?'

Carrigan followed the blue light.

'Arterial spray. What you'd expect, as I said, but this . . . this is where it gets interesting.' Shelby swept the light over to his left. 'Smudged sole prints from when he cut her throat. She wasn't wearing her shoes when he did this. He held her up but her feet kept kicking. See the shape of the drops? The way they curve? Now – these?' Shelby pointed to another set of dark whirls. 'He made these moving her into position.'

Carrigan saw the ballet of steps inked out on the floor like an old-fashioned dance pattern. Had the woman been facing the wall when she died? Had she been facing her killer?

'And yet there's not a speck of blood on her clothes?'

Shelby shook his head. 'No, there isn't.'

'What about that?' Carrigan turned and pointed at the wall.

Shelby smiled. 'I was wondering when you'd ask about that. Look carefully and tell me what you see.'

Carrigan didn't need to, he'd already spotted it. 'It's what I don't see that bothers me.'

'Exactly,' Shelby said, and for a dread moment Carrigan thought the tech was going to try and high-five him. 'There's a large gap in the spatter. Something was in the way.'

Carrigan scanned the room. 'The sofa?'

'Too low,' Shelby replied, bending down and imitating blood spraying from a neck with his fingers splayed and thrust into the air.

Carrigan looked at the floor then at the wall. He saw a flicker of presence, a fleeting sense of someone else in the room. 'The killer was standing in the way.'

Shelby nodded. 'Would have taken at least a couple of minutes for her to bleed out. It must have got messier than he'd bargained for. He'd cut her and she was still fighting back so he had to restrain her and most of the blood ended up on him. Stupid mistake to make. People don't realise how messy bleeding to death is.'

Carrigan took a step forward and ran his hand against the grainy brickwork. He felt the shadow's last leavings, these scant clues. He rubbed the dried blood from his gloves. 'What if it wasn't a mistake?'

8

'I killed Diana! It was me!'

The bare-chested man stood atop DC Jennings's desk. His hair was long and white and snarled into thick clumps and his skin deeply tanned by dirt and grime. 'She was cheating on me. She deserved to die,' he told the gathered detectives. 'That was my baby, not Dodi's.'

Karlson and one of the uniforms wrestled the man down from the table and led him away. A chorus of jeers and groans erupted across the room.

Carrigan had never seen anything like it.

Tramps of every variety were being processed and interviewed by members of the team, everyone's chairs a little further back than normal. They'd scoured the abandoned house from top to bottom and found twenty-four people scattered among its many rooms. There were mountain men tramps with beards that seemed carved out of stone. Old Testament types with glowing eyes and seared vision. A woman quilted in intricate layers of litter and a skull-tattooed brute who could have been plucked from the pages of *Moby Dick*. Some looked as if they'd lived their entire life on the streets but there were others whose fall had been more recent, the suits they'd once worn to work now clinging to their diminishing bodies, flesh and cloth slowly fusing together.

Carrigan was fielding questions, issuing directives and trying to corral this unruly mass into a semblance of order. A headache pressed against his skull. The phones kept ringing. Coughs, cackles and cries filled the room as uniforms tried to coax names and memories from people who'd left the world of time long ago. Berman was setting up an incident room but until it was ready they were all squeezed in here, some officers only just coming in, others tired and irritable at the end of their shifts.

Carrigan retreated to his office and noted the latest developments in his policy book. The irony of the timing, that a case should come now, didn't escape him. His forehead creased and he reached for the strip of pills then remembered he'd taken some less than an hour ago. He was putting them back in the drawer when the door swung open. Carrigan looked up to see Geneva standing in his office.

'I need to talk to you.' A small muscle ticked in her left cheek.

Carrigan pointed to the incident room. 'Can we do this later?'

Geneva took in the extra uniforms and assistants, the derelict and homeless being led to desks, a man puking into a bin, then turned back, and he could tell she'd made her decision, her eyes hard and sharp as baby stones.

'I only need a minute.'

He thought briefly of deflecting her, several excuses rapidly springing to mind, but he knew that would only make her more determined. He glanced at the blue file.

'Madison wasn't hallucinating. The alley is there.' Geneva explained about the glass vial she'd found by the dumpster. She'd sent it for analysis first thing that morning. 'It's evidence Madison wasn't making it up.'

Carrigan took a moment to understand what Geneva was saying, his head still focused on the splayed woman in that dark and terrible room. 'Do you really think he'd be so careless as to leave that behind?'

'I don't know, maybe Madison's presence startled him? Maybe he didn't expect two girls?'

'And maybe some junkie dropped it after his fix. It's only a glass vial. Until you can corroborate it with something concrete, it doesn't mean anything.' The phone rang. Carrigan picked it up, listened, mumbled *Yes, fine* and put it back down.

Geneva pulled out her notebook. 'Okay, here's corroborating evidence. Madison's not answering her phone. I also talked to Anna Becker's phone provider.' Geneva paused, noting the flicker in Carrigan's eye. 'They couldn't give me details without a warrant but they were able to confirm there's been no activity on Anna's mobile since 7.24 p.m. on Friday night.' Geneva stopped and slipped a hand inside her pocket. Carrigan saw her bicep flex. 'Madison wasn't imagining it. Someone abducted Anna.'

The phone rang again. Carrigan ignored it. 'You're off the audit.'

Geneva started to say something then stopped, her mouth creasing into a smile. 'Thank you. We should probably start by sending a team to the hostel so we can—'

'That's not why I'm putting you back in rotation. There's something else now.' Carrigan reached over and picked up a slim green file. The phone buzzed again. 'I need you to get up to speed on this. First briefing's in ten minutes.'

Geneva stared at the green file, her mouth pursed tight. 'Did you hear any of what I just said?'

'I'm sorry. You're going to have to pass this off to downstairs. Madison's phone's probably out of battery. Anna might have come back last night. Either way, it's not your concern any more. I need you focused on this. The girl in that file was found dead this morning.'

'This better not be some bullshit.' Geneva frowned and opened the folder, flicking through it, skim-reading the contents, and then she stopped. The file fell from her hands, the papers scattering across the floor.

'Fuck.'

She flipped the photo over so that Carrigan was once again facing the splayed woman.

'I know,' he said. 'I felt the same way when I first saw her.'

Geneva was shaking her head. She took out her phone and swiped and stopped and compared the photo onscreen to the one she was holding. 'You wanted proof? Here's your proof.' She flung the photo onto the table. 'This is Anna Becker.'

9

They were in one of the newly refurbished incident rooms. Gone were the wall-to-wall whiteboards and in their place was a state-of-the-art A/V suite taking up almost the entire wall. The one remaining corkboard stood like a throwback to an earlier civilisation. Carrigan pinned the photograph to it and addressed the team.

'I do this every time. Those of you who've worked with me before know this, but for all of you who've been drafted in, I want you to look at her. Take a good look at Anna Becker.' Her face was curiously serene in death, the angle of the photograph hiding the wound in her neck. 'Burn this picture into your mind. Remember her in every question you ask and every lead you follow.' Carrigan stopped and scanned the room. Even though he knew most of them had heard this talk several times before, he believed it was important to begin with it every single time. You started with the victim – their lives, loves and rages – and only from there did you wind your way back to the killer.

Carrigan studied the control panel for the media suite. He'd uploaded the crime scene photos half an hour ago with Berman's help. He pressed a button and a close-up of Anna's neck appeared on screen. The younger constables were visibly shocked, their good humour quickly turning mute. Carrigan felt a lurch in his stomach as he stared at the glossy image.

However many times he'd done this, whatever things he'd seen, he knew he'd never get used to it and prayed to God it would stay that way. He didn't want to think what became of you when you got inured to it and yet he'd seen it often, in more senior officers, a slow drift away from the world and all it held good.

'Anna Becker was found in the ground-floor bedroom of 12 Kingsleigh Avenue. As I'm sure you'll have noticed, we're interviewing the tramps found sleeping in the property, but the nature of the abduction and the evident staging make it highly unlikely that one of them did it. This was a very organised and controlled scene. Anna was fully clothed but there was barely a trace of blood on those clothes. It's probable the killer made her undress, killed her, then dressed her again. We don't know what this means to him, if indeed it means anything.

'We're hoping the post-mortem will be later today but, initially, cause of death appears to be exsanguination through the wound in her neck. The killer cut her jugular very precisely and then he watched her bleed and flail and struggle to keep her own life inside her.' Carrigan saw constables wiping sweat from their brows or fanning themselves with crime sheets. 'The details of the snatch and the disposal of Anna's body indicate the perpetrator knows the immediate area well.' Carrigan flicked through several more photos – the abandoned house, a succession of ruined rooms, Anna spread-eagled on the floor. He explained what the blood spatter expert had found.

'He did this on purpose?' Jennings said.

'He could have easily avoided the blood but he chose not to,' Carrigan replied. 'Which suggests he was probably naked. There'd be no point to it otherwise.'

'Christ, that's a bit of a stretch.' Karlson's eyes were still jittery from what he'd seen earlier but his voice was back to its usual tart tone.

'It's what the evidence points to,' Carrigan replied. 'There's a man-shaped void in the blood spatter. He stood in front of her. He got extremely close. The blood guy confirmed that to make that particular pattern, the killer would have had to angle the cut directly towards him. The blood on the floor also suggests he spent time positioning her while she was alive and able to kick and it's not as if we haven't come across this kind of thing before. We know this happens. There's plenty of precedence for it. Blood rites were present at all stages of human history and killers and sickos have always been drawn to it, from Caligula to Countess Bathory to the Manson girls.'

'You've got to be kidding?' DC Singh said.

'I can't explain to you the sickness that lies in some men's brains,' Carrigan replied. 'I don't think anyone can, priest or psychiatrist – but that doesn't mean it isn't there. Every act leaves its particular mark on the world, in this case the narrative of blood. That's the only answer we can hope to get and the only answer we need. We do know that for some killers it's all about the sensation of blood – they crave it – the smell, the sticky feel, the pressure at which it leaves the body. It's not the killing but the release of blood that gets them off. He could have let her bleed out on the floor but he didn't. He held her up and positioned her the way you would a shower head.' Carrigan blinked and saw the house on Cielo Drive, the giddy eyes of the Manson girls, their long blonde hair striped with gore, giggling and chanting and baptising each other in Sharon Tate's blood.

'But why do it there?' DC Singh looked up from her notes.

'It's a massive risk. One of the tramps could have interrupted him.'

'We don't know,' Carrigan admitted. 'Could be proximity and ease. The house is only a few doors down from the hostel. Perhaps he thought it'd be empty. But what it does tell us is that he probably can't do it at home – maybe he lives with someone, maybe his place is too small.'

'Or maybe it's symbolic.'

Carrigan looked over at Geneva. She stared back, a wisp of defiance in her eyes.

'If he knows the area, he'd know tramps use the house and she'd be found almost immediately.' Geneva propped her arms on the table. 'Look at the way he staged the scene – how he positioned her, the close attention to detail – he fanned her skirt out, he closed her eyes, he manoeuvred her limbs. He wanted us to find her there. Dumping her where he didn't need to and putting himself at risk by doing so tells us what he really thinks of her. He could have left her body anywhere yet he chose this place specifically.' Geneva paused, a wrinkle disturbing her forehead.

'But?'

She hadn't realised she'd zoned out. Christ. 'But, on another level, it doesn't make sense. The behaviour's contradictory, a mixture of extremely organised and extremely disorganised.' She rifled through her notes. 'The clothes she's wearing are so precise. The cut on her neck is so precise. The angle he must have kept her at while she struggled is precise. But the room? The house? It's the opposite of all that. It's a mess. As Singh pointed out, anyone could have stumbled in and interrupted him, so we have to ask ourselves, was the house merely convenient? Or does it go deeper – does he see her as trash, something to be dumped? Maybe that's how he wants us to see her?'

There was silence as everyone considered this. They knew a random dump site meant the perp had got careless or panicked and that was good for them, but planning would mean something else entirely.

'Do you think he intended to spike both of them?'

Carrigan looked over at Jennings. The constable had been silent and withdrawn this past month, rarely chipping in at briefings, an ever-shrinking presence as if he were subsiding into himself.

'That's a good question.' It was one of the things that bothered Carrigan the most. 'And no, we don't know why both girls were spiked but only one snatched. Once we know that, we'll know much more about his MO. We don't even know if he happened on these women by chance or if it was planned.' Carrigan stopped and waited for the sharp stabbing pain below his left eye to subside. 'We need to put out a request for any sightings of the van. It blocked the alley for at least a few minutes. There's no CCTV coverage on that street but someone might have noticed it. We also need to go back to the hostel and reinterview Madison now she's sober. Hopefully, she'll have remembered something new.' Carrigan scanned the room. 'Anything else?'

'We should forget Madison and focus our victimology on Anna,' Geneva said. 'Anna has to be his primary target. Otherwise, he would have snatched Madison at the same time, when it was easy, when she was incapacitated. And if Anna was the focus of his attentions then he was probably stalking her beforehand, which means there's a chance he may have left a trace, and if he did, that's how we're going to find him.'

63

10

Geneva watched the woman's face sparkle in the neon glare of
the pub. The woman was surrounded by friends, all of them
gathered around a small table stacked with empty bottles, and
it looked as if she was enjoying herself, smiling and laughing
and knocking back several large cocktails.

Gradually, the crowd thinned out, went home to babies and
babysitters, last Tubes and late-night TV. The woman said
goodbye to her friends, her gestures overemphatic and a little
unsteady, her facial expressions turned up a notch by the alcohol. The street cameras pick her up as she attempts to hail a cab,
swaying in the splash of lights and trying to balance on heels
that had seemed a good idea at the start of the night. Geneva
saw the red car pull to a stop beside the woman. It didn't look
like a minicab but it was getting increasingly hard to tell these
days. The door opened and the woman hesitated for a moment
before stepping in. The door closed and the car sped off into
the dark.

'That's how easy it is to disappear.' Detective Sergeant Maria
Lando leaned back in her chair and brushed the top of her
thumb along the crucifix dangling from her neck. 'Someone
found her staggering around Walthamstow sixteen hours later.
No idea how she got there or what happened to her in those
missing hours. They took her to the local station when they
realised the state she was in. The local station called us and a

doctor examined the woman. She'd been gang-raped. The man who picked her up took her to his friends and they had their fun with her then put her back in the car and dropped her off outside the train station.'

Geneva couldn't take her eyes off the screen. The woman wobbled on pause. If she could only have stayed frozen in that one moment she could have arrested the pull of the future, but the second she'd opened the car door, it had snapped shut for good.

'There's more if you're interested.' Lando turned on a sleek chrome espresso machine and popped a capsule in the slot. She was small and slight and bubbled with a fizzy energy as if all her molecules had been more densely compacted within her tiny frame. Her hair exploded from her head in thick black tangles. She wore a tight black polo neck, black jeans and black boots that reached up to her knees. The crucifix was small and silver and her movements were precise and measured. They'd known each other since Hendon, often cruised bars together, but Geneva was here today because Lando worked for Sapphire, the Met's sex crimes unit.

After the briefing, Geneva had taken Carrigan aside and explained that there was something about the abduction she couldn't quite put her finger on, but which felt a little off. She'd expected him to disagree but he'd simply nodded. If she didn't know better she would have thought him drunk.

Geneva turned away from the screen. 'I think I've seen enough. I just wanted to know if it was plausible.'

'Any crime you can think of – someone's already committed it. That's my guiding principle when I'm not sure. I call it *Lando's Law.*'

They shared the kind of smile that allows you not to go mad, not to let the anger and frustration drown your heart when you've just watched a movie of someone's life being stolen in the blink of an eye.

'How often do you get these cases?'

'A lot more than people realise.' Lando sipped her latte, fingers of steam curling through her hair. The wall behind her was entirely covered in photos. Glossy 8 by 10s of both male and female faces.

'People disappear and most of them, despite our best efforts, never come back.' Lando looked over at Geneva. 'Not quite what we signed up for, is it?'

Geneva exhaled slowly, the movement barely registering on her body. 'No, but I couldn't see myself doing anything else.'

'Me neither. Imagine how boring civilian life would be?' Lando took another sip. 'Now, tell me about your case.'

She listened intently as Geneva recounted Madison's story, her thick black eyebrows crossed in concentration, her right hand flicking up to her chest every now and then.

'Does that seem like a typical MO to you?'

Lando put down her cup. 'Yes and no. Everything you've told me sounds like the kind of thing we see every day. Everything apart from that there's two of them. Predators like to pick off strays. This is unusual and suggests someone bolder, more experienced. What connects the girls?'

'They were both staying in the same hostel.'

Lando sighed. 'We see it a lot in those places. It's the perfect victim pool. They're transient, away from home, don't recognise danger because the cultural signifiers are so different and no one reports them missing because no one knows where they're supposed to be at any given time.'

Geneva stared at the wall of faces. 'What happened? Was it always this bad?'

'We stopped believing God was watching our every step. We realised we could get away with anything as long as we weren't caught. That's what happened.'

'Aren't we supposed to be safer nowadays? With CCTV?'

Lando stopped and thought about this. 'Probably. But what technology gives with one hand it takes away with the other – we may think we're safe but how is a camera going to stop a rapist?'

Geneva frowned. 'How many of these cases get closed?'

'Less than three per cent. It's almost impossible to prove anything unless you have physical evidence and most victims don't come directly to us – they're too ashamed and stunned by what's happened. They go home and take a hot shower and scrub themselves clean and there goes all our evidence. With drug-facilitated rape, three in four don't seek help until at least twelve hours later. By then there's not much we can do except take their statements and file them away with all the others.'

'Drug-facilitated rape?' Geneva looked across at the faces staring back at her, wondering whether they were victim or perpetrator.

Lando brushed her crucifix and nodded. 'We don't like to call it date rape any more – that suggests there's a link between the rapist and his vic. DFR is a more neutral term, doesn't skew the jury. But, shit, even if they go down they're out in four or five years and this sort always do it again.'

'We should lock them up for good?' Geneva smiled but Lando didn't seem to get the joke.

'Retributive rape,' Lando replied. 'For every rape the perp commits he gets sentenced to two rapes – only he doesn't know when they'll occur. He might be raped on his way back from the courtroom or in ten years' time when he's forgotten all about it. Let those bastards feel for the rest of their lives the kind of fear they make their victims feel. That's the only true justice there can possibly be.'

Lando stared at her, freaking Geneva out a little. She checked back through her notes. Found question marks and inconsistencies. 'What about the drugs they use?'

Lando shook her curls loose. 'What do you think the most popular date rape drug is?'

'Rohypnol?'

'You've been reading too many trashy newspapers. Rohypnol only accounts for one per cent of cases. Over ninety per cent are alcohol-related. Couldn't be easier – buy the girl a drink then another and another. Or watch and wait.'

'Watch and wait?' Geneva thought of all those nights she'd spent in bars, letting a man buy her drinks until she got bored of him or didn't and took him home.

'There's two types of drug rapist,' Lando said. 'One type spikes the drinks then waits for them to take effect. The second type, much more common, simply lets nature go about its business. Hang around any pub at closing time and you'll see women stagger out who've drunk themselves into a state where anyone can take advantage.'

'It wasn't booze,' Geneva said and explained about the vial she'd found. 'This was planned and highly organised.'

Lando wrote something down on a pad in front of her. 'How did the girl seem to you when you interviewed her?'

Geneva thought back to the hot room, the rasp of fingernails echoing across grey walls. 'She was both spaced out and quite lucid at the same time, which was weird. She'd nod off then snap back into normality. She was paranoid, scratching herself, touching things, the table, the chair. She seemed to have lost all sense of time.' Geneva saw Lando's mouth curl tight. 'What?'

'That doesn't sound good at all.' Lando pulled a large reference book out of a drawer and started flicking through the pages.

'You see this kind of drug often?'

'No. And that bothers me. From what you're describing this is some form of hallucinogen. Rapists nearly always favour drugs that subdue and make their prey pliant.'

'The opposite of an hallucinogen?'

Lando nodded, her eyes small and black. 'An hallucinogen or psychotropic would produce a very different reaction from a sedative like Rohypnol or alcohol. With the latter two you might not even know what was happening until you woke up in agony the next morning. With a psychotropic like you've been describing, you would not only be acutely aware of everything happening to you but it would be magnified a thousand times.'

11

Two bouncers stood either side of the entrance like tuxedoed columns. A sign depicting a pair of stylised lips hung above an unmarked white door. The bouncers didn't say anything when he flashed his warrant card. The door opened onto a set of stairs. Music and heat rushed up to greet Carrigan as he made his way down into The Last Good Kiss.

Lasers and flickering neon reflected off swirling mirror-balls. Fluorescents hissed and blinked. A set of coloured lights pulsed to the beat. To Carrigan's left was a wide horseshoe bar. Four men in suits were draped over it like figures from a painting. A bartender was going about his business, moving with precise calm between the dirty glasses and stacked-up bottles.

On the dancefloor, a girl was swaying alone, slow and drunk, her hair obscuring her face. Booths lined the walls, velvet chairs hiding tables replete with buckets of champagne and gold-ring-encrusted fingers. The soundtrack was early eighties pop, synthesisers and strained falsettos, thin and alien, a music consisting of hiss and sputter only.

Carrigan scanned the walls and ceiling but saw no sign of cameras. The most surveilled city in the world and yet when you needed coverage there wasn't any. CCTV prowled public spaces but the job drew you into darker provinces where neither God nor cameras could penetrate.

He took a seat at the far end of the bar, away from the

slumped drunks and migraining mirror-balls. The double espresso he'd sunk was counteracting the pills, shaking his body with mild electric rushes, but it couldn't make him forget.

If only he'd listened to Geneva then maybe Anna would still be alive. He'd fucked up. His mind had been on other things – the audit, his mother, the blue DPS file – but none of that mattered. The world didn't grant you any dispensations. Geneva had been right and he'd been wrong not to listen to her.

The bartender was tall and so heavily muscled it looked as if his shirt was about to split open. A small name tag said *Alexi*. He finished making an enormous red cocktail, handed it over, then asked Carrigan what he wanted.

'I want to know if you were working here on Friday.' Carrigan moved closer so that the bartender could hear him above the shrieking synths.

'What you care?' The man's accent was old-worldly and heavily vowelled. The muscles on his neck grew taut as he leaned forward, only an inch or two separating him from Carrigan, his fingers strangling the dark rag in his hands. 'I have my visa. I am legal here.'

'I'm sure you are,' Carrigan replied, not moving a millimetre. 'But that's not what I'm interested in.' He took out his warrant card and laid it on the bar, making sure the drinkers opposite could see what he was doing. 'Again. Were you working here Friday?'

The bartender put down the cloth. He cast a quick glance at a red door near the back of the club. 'I'm always working here. Seven days a week. Why?'

71

Carrigan took out the photo of Anna and Madison. He laid it flat on the bar, feeling the sticky residue of spilled drinks cling and suck at the paper. 'Did these two women come in here on Friday night?'

The bartender leaned over and looked at the photo. 'They were here.'

'What state were they in?'

Alexi smiled. 'What do you think? This is a bar. They were drinking. Having fun.'

Carrigan forced himself to unclench his fingers. 'Did they seem drunk at all? Out of it?'

The bartender shrugged. 'Friday night, I don't remember. Too many people. But these two, they come in here often and they like to drink. Why you interested in them? What have they done?'

'They came in together?'

Alexi nodded then changed his mind. 'The blonde came first. The other, maybe ten, fifteen minutes later.'

'Did you notice if the blonde had finished her drink by the time her friend arrived?'

Alexi squinted. 'No idea. But they didn't order the next round for maybe five minutes after the second girl showed up.'

Carrigan wondered if Madison had helped Anna finish off her first drink. It would explain one mystery at least. He looked down, noticing the ridge of bruises on Alexi's left hand. 'Were they doing drugs?'

'I wouldn't know about that.'

'No, of course not.' Carrigan glanced down the bar. The men were staring at their drinks with a remarkable degree of concentration which, if they'd utilised it in life, would surely not have led them here. 'Was there anybody with them on Friday night?'

Alexi laughed. 'Look around you. You think people come for the atmosphere? The music?' The drunk dancer had been joined by an older man, his pot belly protruding from his torso like a shelf. The two were swaying silently to the music.

'Were they that type of girl?' Carrigan knew clubs like this honeycombed the wealthier parts of the city, places where rich men and young women could meet and transact. 'Were they the type to pick up older men?'

'I never seen them do that, no,' Alexi replied, nodding to a customer across the bar. 'But they come here, not go to some other bar, you know, and they're happy to receive a few free drinks on any night, so who knows?'

'Anything unusual take place this Friday night?'

The bartender shook his head and turned to serve the other customers. Carrigan shot his arm across the bar and grabbed Alexi's wrist. He waited until the bartender realised struggle was useless and pointed to the photo on the counter. 'This girl was murdered. We found her body this morning. So, forget your customers for a moment, close your eyes, and think.'

Carrigan let go and saw Alexi take another look at the photo, his eyes squinting deep into memory. A moment of deliberation hung in the bartender's eyes. 'There was someone.' He glanced up at Carrigan, his lips slightly parted. 'Middle Eastern guy, maybe late fifties. He was talking to them and they were making fun of him but I don't think he realised. They argued some. Finally, I guess he'd had enough because he slammed his drink down and walked off. That's how I remember, shit, the fucker left orange juice all over my bar.'

'He wasn't drinking alcohol?'

'No. Just orange juice.'

Carrigan wondered whether this was because the man was Middle Eastern and therefore likely to be Muslim or because he wanted to keep himself sober for later. 'Was he a regular?'

The bartender nodded.

'I don't suppose you have CCTV in here?'

The bartender laughed.

'Did you see him get close to their drinks?'

'Drinks?'

'Someone spiked their drinks then abducted one of the girls from the alley behind your club. We found her body in an abandoned house this morning.'

Alexi leaned forward, the rag squeezed between his fingers. 'Someone messed with my drinks?' He seemed more chagrined by this than by the murder.

'Easiest thing in the world for a bartender to do – mix the drinks and add a little surprise for the pretty ones.'

Carrigan saw Alexi's jaw clench, veins surfacing in his neck. 'This is bullshit. You think if someone was messing with my drinks, I'd not notice? I work hard, okay. I work here all week so my father – no, fuck it. I don't have to explain myself to you.' He glared at Carrigan, his eyes blazing cold pale blue.

Carrigan slid his card along the bar. 'No, you certainly don't,' he replied. 'And a man like you wouldn't let the murder of a young girl go unavenged either, am I correct?'

12

There were over a hundred registered hostels in the Bayswater area and probably twice as many that weren't. Carrigan could see at least ten punctuating the treeless street, some marked with a bouquet of foreign flags, others with nothing more than a small brass plaque or a list of pencilled rates tacked up in the front window.

The Milgram was different. It was one of the oldest buildings in Bayswater, dating back to Victorian times, and had housed one of the most prestigious private schools in London. The school closed down during the eighties recession and lay derelict until the mid-nineties boom when it was converted into a large and sprawling hostel. It occupied its own block on a street midway between Queensway and Paddington and lodged up to two hundred guests. Guidebooks and websites raved and five-starred it, but Carrigan knew it was less for the architecture and history than for the infamous all-night parties that regularly took place there.

The outer building was dark and sprawling, composed of several wings, all in different styles, the upper floors trailing off into sculpted cornices and gothic turrets. A strange not-quite-right sense of perspective gave the appearance that it was leaning towards you regardless of where you stood. The main structure was surrounded by a large gravel drive and a ring of oak trees shielding it from the street. The front yard held a scattering of lawn chairs and rusty picnic tables. At the far end, two young women were engaged in conversation, bowed towards each other, a taut intensity in both gesture and facial expression. Their heads shot up when they heard Carrigan unlatch the gate. They looked from Carrigan to each other then disappeared down a small alley that led to the garden. As Carrigan and Geneva crossed the courtyard they caught the heady smell of weed suspended in the still air, sharp and sweet and slightly caustic.

They climbed a wide set of stairs flanked by enormous armatures, the stonework cracked and crumbling. The front door was open and they stepped into the main hall. A high panelled ceiling arched above, criss-crossed by dark beams, barely visible in the gloom.

'How come you didn't send Singh or Jennings to do this?'

'You know why,' Carrigan said and Geneva nodded as they made their way across the empty hall towards a small reception desk at the far end. 'Any luck getting hold of Madison?'

Geneva shook her head. 'Phone's going straight to voicemail. Let's hope she's sleeping it off upstairs.' She updated him on what she'd learned from Lando. Carrigan told her what the bartender had witnessed.

'An argument? It doesn't feel like this is something done on the spur of the moment. There's too much planning involved.'

Carrigan nodded. It would have to be checked out but he agreed with Geneva.

They reached the reception desk, the counter adorned with glossy tourist brochures, offers for massage treatments and vouchers for all-you-can-eat curry houses. Postcards from around the world – Sydney, Ulan Bator, Bishkek and Brasilia

– hung above the counter. A blue door led to a back office. Faint strains of at least four different types of music collided and meshed in the hallway, the raw detonation of bass trembling the floor at regular intervals.

Carrigan pressed the small greasy buzzer and scanned the ceiling.

Geneva followed his gaze. 'No cameras on the outside, either. I checked.'

'And no security.' He pointed back towards the front door. 'Anyone can just walk in.' He pressed the buzzer again and turned to face Geneva. They were standing only inches apart. 'Thank you.' Carrigan's voice was coated in a slight bleed of reverb as it bounced across the cavernous ceiling.

'For what?' Geneva relaxed her grip on the stress ball and placed it back in her pocket.

'For not mentioning during the briefing that I'd dissuaded you from following up Madison's story.'

'It wouldn't have been appropriate.'

'But you're still pissed off at me?'

Geneva shrugged. 'I am but I'll get over it.'

'For what it's worth, I'm sorry. I should have let you follow your instincts. My head was on other things.'

'You did seem unusually distracted.'

'And there I was thinking I'd managed to hide it.'

'From the others, maybe.' Geneva tilted her head, her mouth slightly open. 'You know, perhaps you should consider finding a job where you don't have to hide so much of yourself away?' She saw the change in his expression. 'What's so funny?'

'It just so happens I might not have a say in the matter.'

'What's that supposed to mean?'

77

'Branch wanted to see me. DPS are looking into the convent investigation.'

'The nuns?'

'Don't worry. It's me Quinn's interested in. This is just a minor technicality. It's all the rest of it.' He saw a scatter of freckles above her left cheekbone he'd not noticed before. 'You ever feel like you've fucked up your entire life?'

'All the time.'

Carrigan laughed. 'I'm glad it's not just me then.' He pressed the buzzer again. 'I've been going over something Branch said. How it's difficult enough living with your own troubles let alone someone else's and I don't know why I'd never thought of it like that before.'

Geneva placed her hand on the back of his elbow. 'For once, maybe Branch has a point. Maybe we're all better off living alone.'

'You too?'

She pursed her lips. 'New boyfriend's starting to be unreliable, Mum's giving me grief, I'm broke, and the divorce hearing is up next week. That's how fun my life is at the moment. My lawyer keeps telling me I should give up, that I've got no chance in court – but, if I don't fight, my mum's going to lose her flat. I can't back down now.'

Carrigan was about to reply when the door to the back office swung open and a man stepped out. He wore a cracked leather jacket over a bare chest and the vestigial mullet of ageing rockers. His fingers were encircled by a collection of chunky silver rings adorned with skulls and tiny silver motorcycles. He reached the desk, used one arm to balance himself, and collapsed into a severe coughing fit. He tried to apologise between coughs but that just made it worse.

'I'm sorry but we only rent to young people.' He coughed again and some of last night's food broke away from his stubble as his eyes tracked Geneva in waves of linger and drift. 'And I'm afraid we don't rent by the hour.'

'I was thinking more along the lines of ten minutes.' Carrigan slapped his warrant card down on the counter.

'I don't care if you're a policeman, we don't cater to that sort of thing,' the manager said as he turned away.

'We're not looking for a room,' Carrigan replied. 'One of your residents was murdered last night.'

The manager turned back as the meaning of the words washed over him, his face transforming in swift stagger-frames. 'Jesus.' He exhaled the word – one long sigh – and used his hands to rub his face awake. 'Who?'

'Anna Becker.' Geneva took out the photo and placed it flat on the counter. 'We need access to her room,' she said, but the manager could have been in another dimension, staring transfixed at the photo, his head rocking slightly from side to side.

'Fuck. We should have listened to her.'

'Listened to whom?'

'Madison,' the manager replied, introducing himself as Max as he unhooked the partition and joined them in the hall. 'Friday night, Madison was running around shouting that Anna had been kidnapped but everyone ignored her. She was off her head, not making any sense, totally in la-la land.'

'What about you? Did you ignore her?' Carrigan asked.

'I told her to go to the police,' he replied, still shaking his head as if he hadn't fully extricated himself from the steely grip of a nightmare. 'I can take you to her dorm.'

'That's okay,' Carrigan said. 'We can find it ourselves.'

The manager smiled and pointed to a stack of hostel maps that could have been designed by Escher. 'Everyone gets lost in here. You'd better follow me.'

He led them past the main hall and into a narrow L-shaped corridor punctuated with heavy wooden doors, a Victorian sternness and rigidity in each joist and dowel. Everything was obscured by dust and in dire need of redecoration. Reminders of the building's past greeted them at every turn – lists of rugby players and star athletes, the embossed names now as brittle as their bones. Paintings fogged with gunk and grime spanned the walls like black windows.

As they ascended, it got darker and colder, entire corridors stretching out into tunnelled blackness. They followed him through a maze of dusty hallways, past mezzanines and split-level walkways. They heard music, laughter, arguments, sex. They saw people shuffling out of rooms and creeping down hallways. Teenagers hugging and screeching on landings. The carpet clung and stuck to the bottom of their shoes, the light fittings high and distant and never quite bright enough.

'How many on your staff?' Geneva asked.

'Me and a night man. We have cleaners come in once a week but they change all the time.'

They continued past shadowy hallways and interminable corridors. They passed the lift several times but Max said it was acting funny and more likely than not would drop you off at the wrong floor. They climbed a last flight of stairs, heading for the residential dorms.

Halfway up, Carrigan stopped. Sweat ran down his face and

stung his eyes. His chest felt tight and prickly. He hadn't expected there to be so many stairs and it made him acutely aware how out of shape he was. When had he started letting himself go? He grabbed the banister and tried to get his breath back.

'You okay?' Geneva called from above.

Carrigan nodded. He hadn't eaten for hours, the pills he'd taken churning and growling in his stomach, his legs trembling like rubber bands.

'Place can do that to you.' Max stood beside a painting of a ruined castle, a golden-haired princess tumbling down to the black rocks below. 'Angles are all off by a couple of degrees – takes some getting used to. Proportions are all wrong too, nothing's quite level or straight, does your head in.'

'Have you seen Madison today?' Geneva asked as Carrigan finally caught up.

'You didn't know?'

'Know what?'

'She checked out last night.'

'Last night? When?'

'About nine.'

'And you didn't try to stop her?'

Max held up his hands. 'I can't force people to stay.'

'Shit.' Geneva looked up. Faint convolutions of dust swirled in the upper reaches of the ceiling. 'Madison say where she was going?'

'*The fuck away from here* is what she said. She didn't really give me a chance to talk. She said she was following your instructions – that you'd told her to check out.'

13

The dorm was not at all what Carrigan had expected. He'd thought it would be crammed with beds, people living in each other's faces, stink and laundry and pressed bodies, but instead it was large and airy with high windows looking out onto a garden. A bunch of daffodils had wilted in their vase and gave off a cloying sour smell. There were three beds, one against each wall of the room. Beside each bed was a small table and next to it a chair, a group of lockers and a chest of drawers. A huge wardrobe stood by the window. A small sofa faced a flatscreen TV and DVD player. Posters of film stars and furry animals covered the walls and celebrity magazines carpeted the floor.

Max pointed to the bed in the far right corner. 'That's Madison's, the one next to it's Anna's.' He looked for a long moment at the wall then gripped the wooden slat of the bed frame and squeezed it.

'What about the third bed?' Geneva gestured to the other side of the room.

'Been empty last few weeks.' Max was holding onto the frame as if it were the only thing keeping him tethered to the ground, a light sheen of sweat prickling his forehead.

'But anyone can get in?'

'There's a lock on the door and only the girls and management have the key, but ...' Max sighed, '... you know what kids're like. Locking a door's just too much hassle and they trust others to behave like they would so, no, it's not always locked.'

'Who was the last person in here?' Carrigan asked.

'Me,' Max said. 'Last night. After Madison checked out.'

Carrigan walked over towards a small standing lamp. The light was off. He snuck his hand in under the shade and touched the bulb. It was still warm. 'You sure you were the last one in here?'

'As far as I know, yes.'

Geneva glanced at Carrigan but couldn't read his expression. She took out her phone and texted Madison, asking her to get in touch as soon as she got the message, then took off her jacket and slung it across the back of a chair. She snapped on her gloves and got on her knees and looked underneath the bed but all she found were tumbleweeds of dust, lost pens, empty drink cartons and stray cigarettes.

Next to her bed, Anna had constructed a makeshift bookshelf by draping a scarlet blanket over a cardboard box. Geneva scanned through the books. Books on acting and actors, drama theory and practice, self-help manuals and several audio CDs on improving your English pronunciation in a week. The CD cases were worn and cracked and it was obvious seven days hadn't been enough. Parallel to the bed, along the thin strip of wall Anna faced every night, were black-and-white photos stuck up with sticky tape. Geneva recognised Joan Fontaine from *Rebecca*, Liz Taylor before the plastic surgery and disastrous marriages, Gloria Grahame, Ida Lupino and Carole Lombard. The photos had a dull lustre as if they'd been stared at so hard it had faded their natural gloss. Below the photos, also taped to the wall, was a square of white paper. In a child's slanted and unruly handwriting, the words: *One Day It Will Happen To Me.*

Geneva tried to imagine living adrift from family and friends, stuffed into a small room in a strange city. How hard it would be. The constant learning curve of each day. The tug of home. But Anna had been determined. She hadn't backed down or crumpled. Madison had said that Anna came to London to study at RADA. She hadn't got in but she hadn't gone back home either.

Geneva checked the wardrobe next. The left side was empty. Madison had taken her clothes with her and that made Geneva feel a little better. She left the bed for forensics and headed for the lockers.

'Do you have a master for these?' Geneva pointed to two identical padlocks affixed to each locker.

Max shook his head but Carrigan had already pulled out his key-ring. He stood beside Anna's locker and selected a small flat Swiss Army knife. Using his fingernail, he teased out a slim silver toothpick. He snapped on his gloves. Anna's locker took him two minutes to open. He had Madison's open in half that time.

'What?' he said when he saw Geneva's expression.

'You sure know how to impress a girl,' she replied in her best gangster moll voice.

Anna's locker held scattered cosmetics, tubes and clasps and powders, a file containing personal documents, a camera and, on a high shelf, a smartphone lying on top of three laptops. Geneva picked up the phone. The screen was spiderwebbed with a fine filigree of cracks. She knew she couldn't turn it on. Computer forensics would be furious if she inadvertently managed to wipe the hard drive. She put the phone to one side and pulled out the laptops. They were of different makes but seemed brand new. Carrigan stopped what he was doing to watch. Max leaned in. Geneva flipped open first one lid then the next, a sharp intake of breath puncturing the silence.

All three laptops had been utterly destroyed. It looked as if they'd been attacked with a hammer. Most of the keys were missing, the screens were lined with cracks and fractals, the plastic casings splintered and shattered.

A gust of wind rattled the windows, causing the door to rebound against its frame with a long hollow thud. They all jumped, exchanging nervous smiles. A commotion of tearing and growling made them snap their heads up and crowd the window, their bodies pressed tight against the glass. They could hear them clearly now, a cacophonous fury of yelps, snarls and barks – one of the many dog packs prowling the city. Too expensive to feed in this current climate, these pets had been dumped and left to fend for themselves and now roamed freely across the capital.

'Fucking dogs,' Max said. 'Couple of residents got attacked last month. I called up the council but haven't heard zilch.'

Geneva watched the pack prowling the alley. They were a motley assortment of retrievers, terriers and beagles but there was a sharpness to them she'd never seen before, a ferocity in the tautness of their hunger and frantic beating of their hearts. Below her was a small courtyard, veiled in shade by the north wing of the building. Max explained it had been damaged in the great storm of '87 and the owners had bricked it off instead of fixing the damage. There were several long sash windows studding the second and third floors but no light escaped.

Geneva looked closely and saw that the windows were boarded up from inside, reflecting black.

She turned back to the locker and took out the solitary file folder. Inside, Anna had kept all her important documents. She flicked through them until she found Anna's passport. They would need it for next of kin details. The passport was warped by heat and well thumbed. Geneva saw stamps for Greece, Peru and Papua New Guinea. The alphabets were curly and mysterious. Tiny multi-coloured worlds within worlds, Anna's handwriting so small and neat it made her chest hurt. Geneva continued flicking, tracing Anna's journey across the remote parts of the globe that previous summer – Laos, Vietnam, Cambodia, Indonesia – and then she reached the last page.

'We need to stop,' Geneva said.

She handed Carrigan the passport. She watched him flick to the last page, his eyes turning narrow as he got to the photo – except there was no photo. Someone had carefully snipped it out leaving only a neat rectangular gap.

14

'We need to seal this room.'

Max started to complain but Carrigan ushered him towards the door. They walked back down the stairs and across the landing.

'What about your partner? What's she doing up there?'

'She's not my partner and I wouldn't worry about her,' Carrigan replied, recalling how Max's eyes had strayed and fixed on Geneva as they stood by the reception desk. 'It's not my concern and it's not yours either.'

Max was about to say something then caught the look on Carrigan's face. He sighed as he unlatched the divider. Carrigan stopped the partition before it clicked shut.

'In there.' Carrigan pointed to the back door.

He followed Max into a self-contained office that held a desk, a row of filing cabinets, a computer and very little else. Halfway across, a curtain divided the office from Max's personal space. Max was taking a seat behind the desk but Carrigan carried on, parting the curtain and stepping into the living room.

'Hey!' Max's protests were immediately drowned out by a blast of bone-shaking rockabilly. He reached for a remote control and turned off the music. 'Sorry about that. Got it rigged to start when I walk through the door. Fuckin' hate being greeted by silence.'

The room was large and filled with books and records and magazines. Framed album sleeves dotted the wall between posters of Miles Davis, Metallica and The Cramps. Photos depicting a younger Max, fronting a three-piece band, were prominently on display. A set of decks and a stack of records lay in one corner. A Fender was propped up against the bed, two of the strings missing. The room smelled sweet and tangy. Max reached for a packet of Rothmans and lit one, his hands shaking slightly as he put flame to cigarette.

'Who owns this building?'

Max shrugged as smoke curled out of his nostrils. 'No idea. Always some corporation, guy in a suit comes and sees me, but as long as they pay my wages I don't care. Far as I'm concerned, the less they interfere the better.'

Carrigan sat down on an armchair with the consistency of a bean bag. 'We're going to need to access your CCTV.'

'There isn't any.' The cigarette disappeared behind Max's fingers as he blew smoke in Carrigan's direction. 'Not good for business. Kids don't want to know they're being watched all the time – it's why they left home in the first place.'

'There's no coverage at all?'

Max shook his head. 'You think the killer took her from here?'

Carrigan was about to reply when something jumped on his lap. He felt a sharp scratch against his thigh and looked down to see a scrawny cat digging its claws into his trousers, white ruffles of fur circling its head like an Elizabethan courtier.

'Lincoln!'

The cat hissed and jumped off Carrigan's knees, coiling itself around Max's feet.

'Where were you on Friday night, between 7 and 9 p.m.?'

Max's head shot up. 'You think . . .? Shit, of course you do. I was here. Friday night I got to be, it's our biggest check-in. You can ask anyone.'

'I will.' Carrigan brushed cat hairs off his trousers and glanced at the photo of Max onstage, guitar slung across his chest. 'How long have you been manager?'

'Five years this November. I was in a band before that. It didn't work out.'

Carrigan could sense the years of frustration and disappointment hanging in that one suspended sentence. It made him think about his own life and how it might have turned out if Africa hadn't intervened. Would his days be like Max's? The eventual realisation that you were never going to make it followed by the slow withdrawal into disappointment and silence? The irony, of course, was that no one lived up to their own expectations of themselves. Everyone came up short. A dream is a dream precisely because it can never come true – yet how did Max feel in the midst of all these young people? What temptations, recriminations and reminders surrounded him every day? You could see the answer in his face, the sagged cheeks and jowls making him look as if he were in a perpetual state of mourning. Carrigan wondered how many of the female residents had ended up in this room.

'What can you tell me about Anna Becker?'

Max put out his cigarette and immediately lit another. 'I liked Anna. Liked her a lot. She was polite. Nice. Not like the rest of them. It's a fucking shame is what it is. You wouldn't have thought she'd be the kind to get herself murdered.'

'No one's immune to murder,' Carrigan replied. 'What kind of person was she?'

'What kind of person was she? I'll tell you what kind of person she was. One day she comes in here to get me to sort out one of the washing machines. I was sitting on the sofa listening to Faust, you know, the Krautrock . . .'

'I know who they are.'

'You do?' Max's eyes lit up in surprise. 'She asked me if I understood what they were singing about and I said no. She then asked me for the album cover and she sat down and took out a pen and a little notebook and translated all the lyrics.'

'Were there any problems? Any complaints?'

Max ground out his cigarette. 'Sometimes she liked to play her music loud and people would tell her to turn it down. She rubbed a few people up the wrong way but nothing serious. Like you, I only really get to know the ones who cause trouble.'

'You said Anna rubbed people up the wrong way?'

'She was very forthright. Not everyone appreciated that. Always said what she thought. Very blunt. Very German that way. Whenever anything broke in the dorm, she'd be the one to hassle me till I got it fixed but she was always so nice about it, I didn't mind.'

'How about money? Any problems there?'

'With these kids there's always problems.' Max ran his fingers through his hair. 'Rent's the last thing they think of. First they spend all their money partying then come and ask me if it's okay to pay next week. Anna was late three or four weeks in a row but she was nice and I let her slide. She must have got a job because a month later she paid back all the rent she owed.'

Carrigan flipped a page in his notebook. 'When was this?'

Max pressed his palm against his forehead as if by doing so

he could physically squeeze the memory into being. 'A couple of months ago.'

'Do you know what kind of job?'

Max shrugged. 'Probably temp cleaning work. They all end up doing it at one time or another. There's several companies that cruise the hostels touting for work.'

'When did she check in?'

'Give me a sec.' Max headed to the semi-office and came back a couple of minutes later, nodding. 'November 29th. She checked in using a voucher.'

'What kind of voucher?'

'You know, pay three weeks and get the fourth free.'

'Where would she have got hold of one of those?'

'Anywhere. We got a bunch on the counter out front. Maybe someone back home gave her one. We also do e-voucher mail-outs, could be she signed on for one of those or had it forwarded to her. It's the only way we get them not to skip between hostels.'

Carrigan wrote it down and flipped the page. 'And there's nothing else you can tell me? No complaints of female residents being harassed? Nothing weird or out of the ordinary?'

Max looked at the magazine on the table. Nick Cave sneered back up at him.

'What is it?'

'Nothing.'

'Everything is important in a murder investigation. The more we know about the victims the more it tells us about the person who killed them.' Carrigan stared at Max until Max looked away.

'Anna complained recently. Told me she had trouble

sleeping, said there were voices in the walls keeping her awake.'

Carrigan felt a tingle run through his fingers. 'Voices?'

'I told you it was bullshit,' Max replied. 'I explained to her these old buildings are like that. Pipes mumble and squeak, the wood contracts and expands, a conversation three floors away can sound like it's coming from next door.'

'And that was it?'

'Pretty much. I went upstairs to check because she insisted and she was nice about it but I couldn't hear anything. I just figured, you know, with all the shit these kids are taking it's not surprising they're hearing voices.'

'Anna took drugs?'

'I'd be amazed if there was anyone here who didn't.'

15

The common room took up most of the second floor and was the gravitational heart of the hostel. A laptop playing Dave Matthews Band tried to compete with the stutter-frenzy of an Italian football commentary. Magazines were strewn across the floor and covered the coffee tables. Glossy scandal sheets and celebrity exposés. A row of unzipped backpacks hung on hooks, gaping like open mouths. People drifted in and out, an impossible number, all quietly alike in their youth and fashion, regional differences erased by a childhood consisting of the same TV shows, the same films and music and computer games. Constables would be here soon to interview them but Geneva didn't want to wait. They would behave differently and give different answers when confronted by uniformed police.

The focal point of the room was a sofa and coffee table around which people had gathered. Wide-eyed spacegirls just back from eight months in India with an expanded consciousness and a stomach virus. Techno hipsters in ridiculous specs and headbands passing around a bottle of cheap wine and staring at an iPad. White Rastas, hip-hop wannabees and tattooed genderless wraiths.

A sweet stinging taste rose in Geneva's throat and she was flung back to her own days of chaos and disorder, inter-railing through the stacked still cities of the Continent as a teenager, the quick spraygun rush of museums and monuments and train stations. Back then she'd felt as if she'd sailed across far and terrifying oceans, the world of her childhood kept safely at bay by the English Channel. There were no mobile phones to call your parents or update your friends, no tablets or laptops to bring up whatever information you needed. It had all been new and unexplored and experienced first-hand and she felt a little sorry for these kids growing up in this strange hurtling world so stripped of surprise.

The phone buzzed her out of daydream. The caller ID flooded her with relief. Madison had texted back:

About to get on a plane. Sorry. Don't feel safe. Thank you for listening to me and keep me informed. Please find Anna.

Geneva put the phone back in her pocket, ignored the body odour reek of microwaved food and tried to get the residents' attention but her voice was drowned out by music and chatter. She walked over to the stereo system and unplugged it. Everyone stopped what they were doing and stared at her.

'You shouldn't listen to that crap. It'll rot your ears.' She smiled but no one got the joke. 'I'm sorry to bother you but I need your attention for a few minutes.' She saw shoulders stiffen and jaws clench when she announced she was from the police. 'A woman staying here was found murdered this morning.' She paused, scanning faces, letting it sink in as phones were put away and conversations died down. 'Some of you may have known her. And if you did, it would help us a great deal if you could tell us anything you remember about her.' Geneva deliberately withheld the name, curiosity forcing their faces into a semblance of concentration.

'Someone died?' one of the boys said. He sported three different haircuts, glasses twice too big for his face and a waxed and tapered beard.

Geneva took her time getting the folder out. No one said anything while she did this nor glanced at their phones. She placed Anna's photo face up on the table.

'Oh fuck,' haircut boy said, blinking rapidly. 'Holy shit . . . you mean all that was real?'

'All what?' Geneva sat down on a couch that sagged so deeply she nearly lost her balance.

'Madison,' he replied. 'She was off her head Friday night, saying Anna had been kidnapped. She was trying to get anyone to listen, asking us if we'd seen Anna. Everyone thought she was just having a bad trip.' The boy stopped and thought about this for a moment. 'You mean . . . shit. You mean she was telling the truth?'

'It's certainly looking that way.' Geneva saw small flashes of guilt ignite behind their eyes. She recounted Madison's story and studied their expressions as they recognised the alley, felt something of the fear Anna must have felt as the man led her to the back of the van. One girl, small and dark and plump, was crying, trying to hide it, and snatching looks at another girl directly across from her. Geneva listened to the multi-accented expressions of shock and grief but all the time she kept her eye on the two girls.

When she was finished, she thanked everyone for their time, gave out her card, told them to call if they remembered anything, then crossed the room and found the two girls conferring at one of the tables.

The girl jumped when Geneva tapped her on the shoulder.

She was drowning in layers of baggy clothing and she was still crying.

'Which one was your friend?'

The two girls looked at each other, came to some unspoken agreement, then both started speaking at the same time, a rapid-fire English flattened of vowels and syllables that Geneva could barely keep up with.

'I knew them both,' the short girl said, wiping tears with her sleeve. 'But I spent much more time with Anna.'

The girls introduced themselves as Sofia and Elisa, they were both from Cordoba and had been living in the hostel since last September. The table was covered in food stains, Geneva made sure to keep her hands well away. 'What can you tell me about them?'

'They were nice girls,' Sofia said.

Geneva frowned and tried to hide her impatience. 'I'm sure they were,' she replied. 'But, you see, when we conduct a murder investigation everyone always tells us the victims were nice. We hear this all the time. Now, they're often just trying to respect the dead and I understand that, but no one is one hundred per cent nice and it's often those very cracks in our personalities which allow the bad shit to creep in. You saying Anna was nice is not going to help me find her killer and that's more important right now than protecting her reputation.'

The girls looked at each other and burst into another round of quick-fire Spanish. Sofia turned to Geneva. 'They like to have fun. Like everyone else, okay? We're here on holiday, most of us know when we go back home it's going to be jobs and the rest of our lives so this is a kind of, how do you say, last chance for us? Say goodbye to being a student, party in London for a few months, then go back and try to work out how to make a living.'

'I understand, believe me, I do. But some people like to get a bit wilder than others, right?'

'Not Anna. Anna was always so serious, one of those girls who always looks like her dog just died. Madison ...' Sofia laughed and looked over at her friend. 'Madison was more of a party girl, loved to be out all night, surrounded by lights, music, alcohol, men. She was fun.' She described the hostel scene, the constant shuffle of bodies, chance encounters and random couplings.

'When did you and Anna first meet?'

'She moved in just before end of last year. There weren't many of us staying here during the holidays so we hung out together.' Sofia stopped and studied her hands, her head performing a slight half-shake. 'She had these big dreams, you know. Most of us are here for a bit of fun but Anna was determined to make it as an actress. So many auditions. God, I could never imagine myself doing that.'

'She didn't have any luck?' Geneva gently prodded.

Sofia shook her head. 'It was her accent. She never got it quite right. She once told me she'd spent her teenage years listening to the BBC and practising. She was very happy with it but, every now and then, you'd hear some German, that crunch at the end of each word, you know? She would sit up nights in her bed and practise saying certain words over and over but I don't think she realised how bad it was. She'd often come back from auditions in a terrible state, mope around her room for a day or two, but she always picked herself straight back up. That was the thing about her. She really wanted to be an actress, that was all she ever wanted, but wanting it badly doesn't guarantee anything, does it?'

Geneva nodded. This was the way it often went. People came to London in search of dreams they'd harboured since childhood and then they got here and the city ate them up and spat them out like so much junk food. There were always more people, more dreams, more disappointments and sad retreats back home. 'Did Anna take drugs?'

'Anna?' Sofia frowned. 'God, no. Never even got that drunk. I always teased her about it, told her it was the German in her that refused to lose control.'

Geneva nodded but she knew no one ever told them the truth about drugs. 'Did she seem at all different recently?'

Sofia and Elisa looked at each other. Two bursts of Spanish passed between them and Geneva could tell they were disagreeing.

'What is it?'

'Tell her,' Elisa said to Sofia in English.

Sofia sighed. 'Something happened to Anna these last couple of months. I think we all sensed it but no one really put it into words or asked her about it. She used to be so assertive and sure of herself. She always had opinions. Three or four opinions on every subject and never shy to voice them but she withdrew into herself recently.'

'In what way?'

'She became a little quieter, less engaged. She didn't want to go out and didn't spend as much time in the common room. Her personal habits changed too – her hair was a mess, there was dirt under her nails, she stopped wearing make-up. She'd become so nervous, jumping every time someone slammed a door, and all this bad shit kept happening to her. She got rejected from RADA. Her father was diagnosed with cancer. She got this terrible rash and she was being stalked online.'

Geneva sat up. 'Stalked?'

Sofia looked over at Elisa but Elisa didn't say a thing. 'It was, I don't know, a month ago? The middle of the night. I couldn't sleep, gave up and came down to the kitchen to make tea. I saw Anna sitting at one of the tables. She had her head in her hands and she was crying, these really big, loud sobs. There was no way I could pretend I didn't hear so I made her some tea and sat down next to her.'

Geneva moved her chair closer to the table as Sofia sniffed, reached for a shredded tissue secreted in her sleeve, and blew her nose. 'It took a few minutes for Anna to cry herself out. I asked her what the problem was. I thought bad boyfriend most likely but it was nothing like that. She told me someone had been targeting her with abusive tweets on Twitter.'

Geneva's pen raced across the notebook's pages as she tried to get it all down.

'I laughed. I mean, who hasn't been trolled, right? And I was surprised, too. I hadn't thought something like that would get to Anna. This wasn't like her at all. I told her to block them and forget about it but she said she'd already done that and new accounts kept appearing. I advised her to stop checking Twitter. I joked it was probably some lonely twelve-year-old loser in his bedroom in South Korea but Anna shook her head. She said *No, he's here.* I asked her how she could possibly know that. She told me he'd called her mobile and left a message.'

'Do you know what it said?'

Sofia nodded. 'He said he was coming to claim her.'

16

Carrigan told Max he'd be back later for further questions and got directions to the common room so he could find Geneva.

He was hopelessly lost within two minutes. A spinning profusion of landings, hallways and identical corridors, all swamped in gloomy funk. The hum in his ears abruptly shifted, a low growl replacing the high-pitched whine he was used to. He took out his phone but, predictably, there was no signal. He continued past an alcove stacked with the broken bones of abandoned ping-pong tables and then he heard noise and chatter and saw light leaking out of an open door to his right.

Dinner time at the hostel. Smoke and steam and spices. Music and laughter and conversations going on in at least five different languages. Carrigan could see residents huddled around a kettle preparing mugs of tea or chatting over bubbling pots of heavily scented stew. Two men were arguing in flustered Ukrainian. A conversation conducted in raised hands and eyebrows as much as words. Three different sources of music clashed and crashed and were ignored. The sweet tang of weed overlay everything.

It was as if the entire world had been compressed into this chaotic kitchen yet they all shared one essential thing – nationality in the country of youth whose borders, Carrigan knew, when they closed, closed for ever. They were lucky they couldn't see the disappointments and setbacks waiting for them. The bump in the road that sent you flying into another life. But he was here because that was exactly what had happened to one of their fellow residents.

Carrigan flashed photos, asked questions, trying to refresh drug-stunted memories, going from group to group, looking for someone who might have known Anna. There were nervous shuffles and sudden losses of English but mainly there was concern and shock that something like this had happened to a girl who'd walked these halls only a few days ago. Most of the residents were new arrivals and didn't recognise her. Others had seen her around but not for several days and didn't know her name let alone anything else. Carrigan could see it in their eyes – this'd be the moment they remembered and would tell stories about when all the other memories of their trip had faded. He was about to call it a day when a young man approached him.

'I knew her,' he told Carrigan. 'I helped her get work.' He introduced himself as Bob. He had long black hair and was so skinny that if he turned sideways he'd probably disappear. He wore a Snoopy T-shirt and sported a pair of glasses with wide rectangular frames, the kind eighties snooker players used to peer over as they lined up a shot. He shook his head several times, as if by doing so he could dislodge the bad news from his brain then reached into his pocket and took out a card and handed it to Carrigan. 'I make a little extra going round the hostels handing them out. That's how I met Anna.'

Carrigan studied the white business card. The words *Sparta Employment Agency* across the top in ersatz Greek lettering, an empty room, spotless and modern, depicted below. 'She was working for you?'

'For the company,' Bob said. 'Fuck. I knew I should have told you earlier.'

'Told me what?' Carrigan glanced across the room. Two girls were sitting at a far table, seemingly deep in conversation. Carrigan recognised one of them – she'd been smoking outside when he and Geneva had entered the courtyard. He could tell she was pretending not to notice him, her rigid refusal to look in his direction giving her away.

'Anna came up to me in the common room one day, wanting to know what the hourly rates were,' Bob explained. 'She wanted to start right away. I think she really needed the money. That first week she must have clocked in like sixty hours at least.'

'Doing what?'

'Whatever was going. Various cleaning jobs. Some of them pretty nasty, hospitals and shit.'

Carrigan stole a look at the two girls. 'And she was still doing this right up till her disappearance?'

'She quit two weeks ago.'

'She say why?'

Bob looked down at the floor. 'She'd had some trouble. She told me that one of the places she was cleaning, the owner had made an inappropriate remark. I said I could talk to my boss and she could file a formal complaint but, I don't know, maybe Anna thought she'd lose the job or maybe she was just the forgiving type. She told me to forget it.' Bob kneaded his hands together. Carrigan could see him battling with the guilt of not having done more at the time but hindsight always pointed the finger. How could you know in advance? How could you tell which small misstep would be the one that derails your life?

'A week later she tells me it's happened again,' Bob said. 'That this time the client had made a pass at her and when she refused, he grabbed her arm and squeezed it and told her that next time she'd better do what he said. She quit right after that.'

Carrigan heard a soft ticking in his skull. 'Do you know if it went any further? If this man tried contacting her again?'

'You'll have to ask my boss,' Bob replied. 'She'd be the one who would have dealt with any complaint.'

'Do you get a lot of this type of complaint?'

Bob nodded. 'Unfortunately, yes, quite a few. It's been getting worse recently. Some clients, they see a foreign girl cleaning their bathroom, they think she's easy prey.'

Carrigan took his details and thanked him. He felt the information buzzing in his notebook and wanted to get back to the station so he could make some calls, but there was one more thing he needed to do here.

Carrigan approached the table with the two girls. He introduced himself and flashed the photo. The girls shared a brief glance, their faces turning pale.

'But ... I only spoke to her last week?' the one from the courtyard said. She gave her name as Barbara and seemed utterly transformed by Carrigan's words. It was all you ever saw in the job – people collapsed by grief and shock, their perfect world crumbling into ashes right in front of you, or people deranged by greed and lust and anger.

'You never think ...'

'Oh God ...'

Death turned everything into cliché. Carrigan took notes

and filtered out the platitudes. Barbara tried to avoid Carrigan's gaze. The other girl, Liv, hid behind the strict curtain of her fringe and nibbled at her cuticles. They spoke of Anna with hushed reverence and muted shock. They recalled drunken nights in scuzzy Camden bars or trawls through the heart of Soho at four in the morning, but they had nothing new for Carrigan.

He studied them for a long moment. Silence was an interrogator's best tool. He counted off the seconds in his head.

'Where do residents get their drugs from?'

The two girls looked at each other.

Carrigan turned towards Barbara. 'I saw you outside. I know what you were smoking. I don't care about that. I'm only interested in finding out who killed Anna. The rest is your business.'

Barbara crossed her legs, her dress snickering in the silence. 'You really mean that?'

'You think I give a damn about weed when I have a murder to investigate?'

Barbara pulled a *how-should-I-know* face and sighed. 'There's no problem getting hold of it. Guys come around most evenings, two or three regular guys, they always have stuff on them.'

'What kind of stuff are we talking about?'

'Mainly weed. Some X, nothing too crazy.'

'What about designer drugs?' Carrigan recalled Geneva's initial suspicions. It was a problem that hadn't existed ten years ago and now they saw it everywhere.

'Wouldn't touch those,' Barbara said. 'Never know what you're going to get from one pill to the next.'

'Isn't that what everyone's taking these days?'

'What do you expect?' she replied. 'Criminalise drugs we

know about and people start taking unknown shit. Everybody becomes the guinea pig, the guy in the cave who gets to see if the shiny red toadstool is good for eating.'

Carrigan laughed. Interviewing teenagers had changed too. A sense of bitter entitlement and anti-authoritarian cant pervaded their every sentence. 'That's all very interesting but I don't really have time for social analysis.' Carrigan gave Barbara his least threatening smile. 'A girl is dead. She was spiked with something and then she was abducted and killed. So drop the crap. You heard about anyone having their drinks spiked at the hostel? Maybe a little touch and feel thrown in for free?'

They both shook their heads. 'There's always too many people here,' Liv said. 'You couldn't get away with it.'

And yet someone had. They'd managed to slip inside Anna's room and carefully snip out her passport photo. This wasn't random. This smelled of obsession and desire. The patience to make these things happen. The cruelty to stretch it out.

'Did Anna take drugs?'

The two girls looked at each other.

'You might as well tell me. She's dead. I can't arrest her.'

Barbara performed a dismissive head-wiggle. Liv parted her fringe and leaned forward. 'I would never have thought so, not Anna, so I don't know, but last week I bumped into her and she seemed pretty fucked up.'

'You're sure it wasn't just booze?'

'I didn't smell anything and no, this was different – she was slurring, jittery, her pupils heavily dilated. I'm not sure she even recognised me. I said *hello* as we passed in the hallway but she just walked right past me as if I didn't exist.'

17

She heard a man scream. An animal howl reverberating through the tiled room. Geneva stood back as a guitar erupted from a speaker on her left, making the instrument tables vibrate and hum. She recognised the song: Hüsker Dü's 'New Day Rising' – two and a half minutes of sheer frontal assault and the joy of noise. She knew it well but she'd never heard it like this. The recording was muffled, saturated with hiss and crackle, the music distant and distorted.

Milan, the chief pathologist, was crouched over a gurney on the other side of the autopsy room. He was peering into a woman's stomach, gently holding up a flap of yellow skin with two fingers. He hadn't noticed Geneva's entrance nor could he hear her shouting his name.

She approached the gurney and placed a hand on his shoulder. He jumped and dropped his scalpel. It clattered against the table and span down to the floor, hitting the front of her shoe. Milan spat out several imprecations in Serbo-Croat then broke into a large garrulous smile when he saw Geneva standing beside him, trying very hard to stop herself from laughing.

'You always have it this loud?'

Milan smiled, his lips disappearing behind his beard. 'It's so I won't be able to hear them.' He pointed to the wall of slabbed bodies and reached for the remote.

'It sounds awful.' Geneva studied the ancient tape deck, already an artefact from the edge of memory. 'I have this on CD. I can make you a better copy.'

Milan muted the music. 'It sounds to you like a shitty old cassette, right?' He snapped off his gloves and draped the dead woman with a sheet. 'To me . . .' He looked up at the buzzing fluorescents as if memory were merely an object that needed illumination like any other. 'It reminds me why I'm here.'

Geneva smiled but Milan shook his head sternly. 'You take me for some sentimental old idiot, right? Listening to crappy cassettes? But that is not why.'

'Are you going to tell me?'

'It's not a nice story.'

'It never is.'

Milan walked over to the sink and washed his hands several times under scalding jets of water. 'During our war, I did some bad things. A lot of bad things. It was not my choice to do these things but that makes no difference to the people I did them to. When I lay in bed in our compound at night, I would close my eyes and curse my parents – every name and disease and misfortune I could think of. I did not curse my enemies, nor my commanders who made me do those bad things, nor even my country which plucked me out of medical school so I could be of use in this camp somewhere in the dark forest – but my parents – because it was they who forced me to become a doctor and if I hadn't been a doctor then I would not be here and they would not ask me to do such things.' He stopped and wiped the back of his hand across his beard. 'Though, of course, I now realise that none of it mattered and that they would have made me do other things instead because war can always find new uses for old skills. The only tape I had with me in the forest was this one. We did not have British and American records in Belgrade those days and when someone met up with a tourist and dubbed one of their tapes it was big news. The tape would be copied all across the city, each copy getting more muffled, more distant from the source. You could always tell who was who in the capital by how many generations their tapes had. And the singer screaming? That was me because music is how we speak to ourselves, no?'

Geneva looked at the gleaming instruments resting on the table. 'Without music, I don't think I could stand this world.'

Milan smiled. 'Yes, indeed. After the war was over, I swore I would never work with live patients again. When I'm alone in this room and I start to wonder how I got here, this tape reminds me.'

Sudden confidences always unsettled her, the way they wove themselves into your life and demanded things of you. 'After all that, this is going to sound pretty banal. But my boss sent me and . . .'

Milan waved her off. 'No need to apologise. Your boss is the one with the beard, yes? I deal with him often. Can't be an easy man to work with?'

Geneva shrugged. Milan winked conspiratorially and walked over to the freezer. He wheeled out a slab from the middle row. The runners hadn't been oiled in a while and the gurney screeched and rattled as it slid out.

Geneva looked down and saw Anna staring back up at her. Beseeching her. Blaming her. Because even the dead carry grudges. Anna's hair lay limp across her shoulders and her mouth was almost closed but not quite, one tooth showing.

'First of all,' Milan said, 'there was no sign of sexual assault. This is the good news. But it's also strange because the killing otherwise bears the hallmarks of a sexually motivated slaying.'

Geneva studied Anna's neck. It was long, slender and shapely – until your eyes came to rest on the small black mouth gaping midway down the right side. She looked away. 'Why do you say that?'

Milan took a deep draught of air. Small black hairs twitched in his nostrils as if he'd inhaled a spider. 'She is a woman,' he said flatly. 'When a woman is murdered, you always have to ask is there a sexual motive to this? It is not how it should be but it is how it is. That's number one. Number two, there's something very personal and, yes – don't take this the wrong way – sensual about putting a knife to a woman's throat, holding her body with your other hand, slowly pressing the blade, feeling the skin part to let you in, and then the hot gush of blood flowing over your fingers and across your chest.' Milan looked up and his eyes were small and hard. 'Don't you agree, this is something?'

Geneva nodded, wondering what that first soft scratch had felt like and how much of what was about to happen Anna had understood. 'What can you tell me about the incision?'

'It's very precise. Almost a work of art, if you'll excuse the expression. Just the right length and depth to make it fatal.'

'Someone with a knowledge of anatomy?'

'Twenty years ago I would have said yes. These days? Anyone can learn how to do it off the web in fifteen minutes – but there's no hesitation marks and it was done very cleanly, so who knows?' Milan pointed to Anna's collarbone. 'He held her up as she bled to death. There are bruises on her shoulder and underneath her chest.'

Geneva saw what Milan was referring to, a curving constellation either side of Anna's ribcage, the unmistakable span of human hands. It confirmed Carrigan's theory about the killer angling Anna's body so that her escaping blood would drench him. Milan lifted Anna's right arm and turned the wrist towards Geneva. Small red bands criss-crossed the skin.

'Restraint marks. From a leather ligature. We took a sample. Leather's unique so it might provide a match at a later date. It tells us he held her captive. I also found two small puncture marks that could be from a hypodermic.'

'Two?'

'Yes. Why? Were you expecting more?'

'We know from Madison's account that he injected Anna with something before he abducted her, this was on top of whatever he'd put in her drink. Why would he need to inject her again? To keep her docile?'

'He had her tied up. He wouldn't need it for that. I think once you know what combination of drugs he used, you'll know a lot more about why he does this, why he needs to do this. There's a period of roughly forty-eight hours between her disappearance and the probable time of death. What happened to her in these hours? Where did he take her? What did he do to her?'

Geneva nodded. She knew they had to start asking these questions but she also knew that the answers would only ever come, if they did at all, when they'd apprehended the killer.

'I also found tiny bits of wood splinter stuck to the back of her legs. Trace are examining them but if I had to guess I'd say the killer strapped her to some kind of tortureboard.'

'Tortureboard?'

'The majority of serial killers use some kind of restraining device to incapacitate their victim – you see it especially in the sadistic variety. They need the torture to go on for as long as possible and they need to keep the victim in place to do this. So they modify existing furniture or make their own. Dean Arnold Corll created an elaborate contraption to keep young boys immobile – while they were strapped to it he could do anything he wanted to them, and did. Fred West made one out of metal at his job then took it home and tried it on his daughter.'

Geneva shook her head but the words wouldn't leave so easily. She thought of generations of women locked in cells and basements across the centuries. Fingernails breaking against brick walls. Screams that no one hears. Berlin, Smyrna, Ravensbrück. Richard Ramirez singing along to AC/DC as he stalks the LA streets, Wayne Clifford Boden, the vampire rapist of Montreal, gorging on blood. The planning and persistence. The savagery of men when they know no one's watching. 'So, let me get the sequence straight,' Geneva said. 'He drugs her once with the spiked drink, then again as he's taking her to the van. He injects her at least once more and keeps her strapped to a tortureboard for an indeterminate period of time. Then he takes her to the abandoned house, strips her, cuts her neck just so, holds her in place so he can shower in her blood, then dresses her back up and positions her on the floor with arms and legs at forty-five degree angles. Finally, he closes her eyes.'

Milan nodded.

'Carrigan suspects it's all about the blood.'

'Undoubtedly, that's a large part of it,' Milan said. 'But if it was just that he'd have no reason to keep her captive and yet he did. He closed her eyes after she was dead. Why undress her? There's something else that's making him tick and we're not seeing it yet. It is unfortunate that for a pattern to be discernible there needs to be several bodies for comparison. It may, of course, also be a misdirection.'

Geneva shook her head. 'It's too precise and controlled for it to be him trying to trick us.'

Milan smiled. 'The misdirection comes from our own minds, not the killer's intention. The way we see a thing and think it is the primary thing because it seems so. But what seems so is not necessarily what is.'

Geneva took one last look at Anna. She wanted to whisper a promise to her the way she'd often seen Carrigan do but thought better of it. 'Did you clean her when she first came in?'

Milan turned, surprised by Geneva's question. 'No, of course not. Why?'

'She should have been covered in blood.'

'There was barely a trace of it on her skin. A few drops and smears on the neck and collarbone, but that's all.'

'That doesn't make any sense.' Geneva studied the white cold flesh. 'We know he took her clothes off – they were spotless. Could he have scrubbed her after she died?'

'Not in that place. Not without leaving a trace.'

'But even if he angled all the blood towards him, surely more than a few drops would have landed on her skin?'

'I agree. But the evidence doesn't.'

Geneva thought about this. 'You sent her clothes to forensics yet?'

'All packed and sealed and ready for them to pick it up.'

Milan pointed to a steel shelving unit.

Geneva scanned the shelves. Everything was bagged and tagged, all these clothes no one would ever wear again. She found Anna's on the third shelf down. They were individually sealed in separate evidence bags. Geneva pulled them off the shelf and laid them out on a nearby table. She peered through the clear plastic and shifted the contents and examined what she could of the material.

The dress was white and looked like a rare leaf, pressed inside the plastic. The shoes were in a separate bag, as was Anna's blouse and underwear. She'd seen these clothes in the death scene photos but she'd been focusing primarily on the wound in the girl's neck at the time. She thought back to the clothes in Anna's wardrobe as she scrutinised the long old-fashioned dress. Anna wore skin-tight jeans and a Pixies T-shirt in the photo with Madison. Geneva remembered seeing more of the same in Anna's wardrobe. She didn't remember seeing anything like this.

The clothes were drab and curiously child-like, but without a hint of sexualisation, almost the opposite in fact, chaste and grey – a high-necked T-shirt, a dowdy dress and headmistress shoes.

Geneva jiggled the clothes within the plastic, wasn't supposed to, but she had to know. She glanced at Anna's body but there was no way to tell from here.

'Do you know her measurements?'

Milan looked momentarily confused as he shuffled over to the desk. He pulled up a file and read out the numbers.

Geneva double-checked her notes and asked Milan to read them out again. She picked up the bags and squeezed and manipulated the clothes within until she found what she was looking for.

She read the sizes off the small printed label.

She went back to the slab and studied Anna, a slow eye-crawl and silent reckoning, then pointed to the bagged clothes. 'Are you sure this is what she was wearing when she came in?'

Milan walked over to the table and examined the bags. 'Yes. I cut them off her myself. Why?'

'They're two sizes too big. These are not her clothes.'

18

The incident room, 6.30 p.m. Rain crashing against the windows. Distant thunder on the motorway.

The case was gaining momentum. Clues and leads rolling in, a faint glimpse of the man they were chasing in the things he'd done and the things he'd left behind. Anna being harassed at her job was their first strong lead. It felt good. It felt right. A forensics team was currently searching the alley behind The Last Good Kiss. Uniforms were rechecking the alibis of Max and the other hostel staff. CCTV footage from neighbouring streets was being scrutinised by video techs. Geneva would soon be back from the pathologist.

Carrigan tried to update his notes but the facts were coming in too fast to properly process. He needed to control the flow of data. The brass called it *creating slow time* – the eternal dichotomy between fast-track actions necessary to secure ephemeral evidence versus the danger of too much information causing them to miss a vital clue. Sharp hooks wriggled under his eyes. He slid open his drawer and looked at the pills. He promised himself he'd quit tomorrow and quickly swallowed two. He called the doctor and was told there were no new developments. He avoided the one call he knew he had to make. He drew graphs and made lists of people to interview, people to rule out. He was in the middle of writing a summary for Branch when the door to his office burst open. He looked up and saw two men he didn't recognise. They both wore suits and bored, blank expressions.

The taller of the two men took a step forward. 'My name is DI Patterson and this is DI Larkin. DPS.' The internal affairs detective was smiling, expecting Carrigan to be surprised, dismayed, give himself away, but Branch had prepared him for this.

'We'd like to see you tomorrow afternoon.' Patterson's accent was pure boarding school and Sunday cricket matches and his cheeks red and smooth.

'That's impossible.' Carrigan pointed to a stack of files on his desk. Two of the phones started ringing in syncopated time. 'We've just launched a murder inquiry and as I'm sure you understand – you were once policemen too – the first forty-eight hours—'

'You feeling okay, Carrigan? You're looking a little peaky, if you don't mind me saying. We can always get someone to replace you if you think it's too much for you.' Patterson's eyes were small and expressionless.

'And waste a day getting them up to speed?'

Patterson leaned over Carrigan's desk. 'These are grave charges. We're not talking about dismissal or a slap on the wrist here. You illegally hacked into a private church database. I don't think you're taking this seriously enough.'

Carrigan dropped the file he was holding. 'I've got a dead woman and her killer still out there. I apologise if I'm taking that a little more seriously.'

Patterson's nostrils wrinkled and Carrigan knew he was trying to detect the presence of alcohol. 'You need to hurry up and decide what's more important, Carrigan – your career or this case?'

'You came all the way down here to ask me that?'

'An email seemed a tad impersonal.'

'And, of course, this would be personal.'

Patterson smiled. 'Touché, Carrigan. But your facility for language won't help you here. Did you really think no one would find out? That what you did wouldn't leave a trace? You can only blame yourself. You chose to do something. You knew it was wrong. You could have chosen any of a multitude of other options but you chose this. A man makes a choice, he has to prepare himself for how that action will unravel across the remaining days of his life.'

'I did what I had to do to solve a case. If you were a real police officer, you'd know that.'

'That's exactly the kind of attitude that's caused so much trouble and lost us so many cases over the years. Wake up, Carrigan. The days of policemen like you are over.'

Carrigan stared at the blue file as the door to his office closed. He'd almost managed to forget about it in the spin and rush of the last twelve hours. He'd known they were coming and yet the visit had rattled him far more than he'd expected. He called Branch and said he needed to see him then put the phone down. His hands were trembling – with rage or shock, he didn't know. Dark thoughts swooped, black-winged birds cawing at his ear. At eighteen, a cop was the last thing he could have imagined himself as and yet here he was. He knew what the others in the station thought of him, how he wasn't a proper copper, how he'd arrested his own best friend but, staring at the blue file, he was surprised at how keenly he would miss it if it were gone. The hooks in his eyes returned. The phone rang and he knocked it off the table. Everything always came at once. The moment you thought your life was running smoothly you hit the bump.

He had one more thing to do before the briefing, aware he'd been putting it off all day. Normally he would have delegated it to Geneva or Jennings, but Anna's parents deserved to hear from the head of the investigation. It was the least he owed her.

Anna's passport had been scanned and indexed by forensics. Carrigan pulled out the relevant print-outs and examined the neat empty rectangle where her photo should have been. For some reason, this small act disturbed him more than anything else. Murder was often comprehensible, most killings came down to money, sex or a sudden loss of control, but occasionally they strayed into murkier places where men did things that only made sense to their secret selves and, though on one level you could understand their motivations and compulsions, on another level you couldn't understand them at all.

Carrigan flicked through the print-outs until he got to the last page. Next to where the photo should have been was what he was looking for. Anna's handwriting was small and precise, her parents' names and contact details rendered in a careful block print to make sure no one would make a mistake. Carrigan picked the phone up from the floor and dialled, his fingers hesitating for a split second before punching in each digit.

'*Ja?*'

The woman who picked up sounded impossibly old, or maybe it was the crackle and hum of static rushing through undersea cables and bouncing across the atmosphere over high satellites that made it so. It took Carrigan three attempts before the woman understood who he was. A part of him had been hoping no one would be in. '*Sprechen Sie Englisch?*' Carrigan asked, one of the only things he knew how to say in German.

'*Ja, ja*. Who is this?'

Carrigan took a deep breath. 'My name is Detective Inspector Carrigan. I'm calling from London. I'm afraid I have some bad news for you.' He waited for an acknowledgement but there was only the soft rush of static. 'Your daughter ...' He stopped, rubbed his head and cleared his throat. 'There's no easy way to say this. We found your daughter's body this morning. We believe she was murdered.'

At first there was no reply. Then a soft '*Nein*' crackled through the earpiece, followed by the same word repeated over and over again. Carrigan was about to say something when the woman started wailing. He heard the phone drop to the floor, a series of shuffles and muffled words, then a man's voice, deep and gravelly, prickled against Carrigan's ear.

'Who is this?'

Carrigan had to go through it again, the words sticking to his tongue.

'No. That is not possible,' the man replied. 'We only spoke to her a few days ago. She is starting in her play tomorrow.'

'Her play?'

'*Ja*, she had a role in the National's production of *Othello*. She was so excited about it. She called us to say the director had come to her school – she is in RADA, you know?'

'Yes, we're aware of that,' Carrigan said, the lie coming easily.

'This director, he picked her out during an audition. He

asked her to be in the production, not a big role but still good. We were so happy for her.'

Carrigan didn't say anything. He waited for the man to catch up to what would become the rest of his life. He felt a deep ache within his own chest as he heard the man's breath stutter and stop.

'I don't understand?'

He never would. Death was always a puzzle even when the answer was staring you right in the face. 'I'm so sorry.'

The rain slashed the windows and obscured the outer world. A car alarm sang in the street below. Carrigan put the phone down feeling as if he'd left a part of himself behind.

*

'*You* made the decision, Carrigan.' Branch took the unlit pipe out of his mouth and examined it. He carefully selected a metal spike from his drawer and used it to stir and loosen the tobacco. 'What's worse is you encouraged a member of your team to break the law.'

'I ordered him to. He didn't have a choice.'

Branch tapped the pipe against the table.

'What's going to happen to Berman?'

'They're pressing charges against him too.'

'He had nothing to do with it. It was my order.' Carrigan stopped, sat back and caught his breath. 'Tell Quinn if he leaves Berman alone, I'll do whatever he wants.'

Branch paused and a faint smile crept across his lips. 'All very noble, Carrigan, but Quinn doesn't give a shit about Berman – he's using him to get at you and now it's dragged the entire department into it.' Branch seemed to be considering something, his fingers pinching the bridge of his nose.

'Hypocritical fuck.'

Branch's eyes flicked up. 'I hope you weren't addressing that at me?'

'Quinn pretends he's the model of new policing and integrity but when it suits him he does exactly what he wants.'

Branch's nose wrinkled as if he'd caught an unpleasant odour. 'You know something I don't?'

'Quinn was giving a significant amount of money to those nuns. He had to know what they were using it for.'

'Is there any way you can prove that?'

Carrigan thought back to last Christmas and shook his head.

'I thought not. All you've got is that he donated money to a convent.' Branch emptied the pipe into a small ceramic saucer splashed with Chinese ideograms. 'When they interview you, make sure you don't lie. Assume Quinn knows your every secret and it's written down in their files. It would also be very much in your interest to have the case closed by then.'

'It would be in Anna's interest too.'

'Don't get smart with me. You know exactly what I meant.'

'That's not going to happen.'

Branch's jaw clamped shut as Carrigan ran through the investigation from Madison's appearance in the police station to the latest set of leads.

'You do have a way of picking them.'

'It was Miller this time.'

'Christ. I should never have put the two of you together.' Branch wrote something down in his pad. 'The press are starting to get irritating and upstairs are calling me every five fucking minutes. Have you considered bringing in a profiler?'

'No.'

'No, you haven't considered, or no you're not bringing one in?'

'I don't need some psychiatrist cluttering up my team's brains.' Carrigan knew employing a profiler was more about looking as if all avenues had been exhausted than for its operational value, a PR move to silence second-guessing in the press and pub. 'They have more than enough data to deal with. Whatever a profiler comes up with, it's not going to be specific enough to warrant all that extra focus.'

Branch scraped the inside of the bowl. 'Well, like it or not you're going to have one seconded to the case as of today.'

'You're kidding me?'

'Not my doing. Sorry. Quinn's order. He's trying to cover his back with the press if this goes tits-up.'

'And relishing the chance to fuck with my command, no doubt.'

'No doubt. But we don't have a choice in this. He's already allocated someone.'

'This is bullshit and you know it. We don't need a profiler. We've done well enough without one for a long time. We certainly can't afford the expense.'

Branch waved his hand across the table. 'This isn't a choice.'

'Is this all a prelude to being told I'm off the case?'

Branch put the pipe down. 'Nothing so dramatic, Carrigan. But you have more important things to be focusing on – safeguarding your future, for instance. Would you really rather pursue this case than sort that out?'

'If it means catching the man who killed Anna, then yes.'

19

'Anna Becker checked her emails at 8.25 a.m. on Friday morning then spent twenty-three minutes browsing two acting employment agencies. Ten minutes later, Anna used her Deutsche Bank debit card to buy a skinny latte and a Diet Coke at Costa on Praed Street.'

DC Singh was pointing to the A/V screen and the timeline she'd constructed for Anna's last day. The team watched in silence. 'Ten minutes after that, Anna swiped her Oyster and got on the Tube. There's footage of her reading *The Seagull* while waiting for the train. She swiped out fourteen minutes later at Piccadilly Circus.' Singh stared at her notebook, trying to unravel the mystery of her own handwriting. On the screen behind her, a mixture of grainy and hi-def CCTV captures witnessed Anna's final hours.

'Anna ate a chicken curry and drank another Diet Coke at Itsu on Shaftesbury Avenue then bought a copy of *Variety*, *Screen International* and the *Guardian* at WH Smith's on Oxford Street. She went to a matinee of *Vertigo* at the Renoir, purchasing an extra large popcorn and a super-sized full-sugar Coke. She caught the Central Line to Lancaster Gate and reached Paddington at 6.12 p.m.' Singh glanced up, saw everyone's eyes fixed on her and looked away. 'Anna bought a single margarita in The Last Good Kiss at 7.45 p.m. on Friday night. Twenty minutes later she bought two more margaritas and that's it. She leaves no electronic trace after that and her phone isn't used again.'

Everyone was a little subdued by the end of Singh's rundown. There was something unsettling in watching CCTV grabs of Anna blithely walking through London, unaware that her every move was being tracked and stored. But this was the new frontier of policing. Technology had not only changed the nature of crime, it had also fundamentally changed the nature of policework, screen gazing replacing shoe leather, data crunching instead of hunches.

Carrigan thanked Singh and scanned his notes. 'We have a lead now. Anna was working for a temp agency, Sparta Employment. One of the houses they sent her to, the owner tried it on with her and became violent when she refused. The kind of men who react like that are exactly the kind of men who will nurse their slights, brood and plan and never forget. Miller? I want you handling this – get a list of Anna's clients from Sparta and see if there've been similar complaints from other girls – if there are, you can cross-check the addresses against Anna's list.'

Geneva nodded as she wrote down the details.

Carrigan turned to Karlson. 'The alley yield anything?'

The sergeant tapped his fingers on the table, black crescents of frostbitten skin covering the tips. 'Nothing we can use. We're still waiting to hear back from forensics on the vial. We did find two more eviscerated cats inside the dumpster as well as leftovers from the one Miller discovered in the alley. There were signs the vagrant was living in there, at least temporarily, and we can assume this was his dinner.'

Karlson smiled as everybody groaned. 'Forensics have also cleared the tramps who were dossing down in the abandoned house. They found no traces of fresh blood on them and he'd definitely have blood on him.'

'What about the hostel?' Carrigan asked.

Karlson flicked through his notes. 'Nothing much, what you'd expect – drugs and drunken fights, nothing that seems to connect to our guy.'

'Did you look at the manager?'

Karlson nodded. 'Max Duchowsky. Born London, 1958. No criminal record. His alibi checks out. Four residents said he was at the desk all evening.'

'The abduction couldn't have taken more than five minutes.'

'You think he looks good for this?'

Carrigan shrugged. 'He knows the hostel and had contact with both Anna and Madison.'

'How did he come across when you interviewed him?'

'He was forthcoming.'

'But?' Karlson had sensed something underlying Carrigan's words.

'But I can't tell whether he's shifty by nature or because he was hiding something.'

'I'll speak to some people and see what I can find,' Karlson said.

'Good.' Carrigan ticked off several items in his notebook. 'Branch has released a holding statement to the press that should keep them off our backs for a while. Some joker managed to film the body being taken out of the abandoned house and posted it on YouTube.' Carrigan waited until the groans and catcalls had subsided. 'We can't keep this stuff hidden any more. That's the way it is. Demons tend not to like going back into their bottles so we better get used to it. I don't want you talking to anyone. By tomorrow, something else will snag the press's attention and no one will care about this but us.' He looked over towards Geneva. 'Miller? I want you and Singh doing background on the hostel. See if anything raises flags, any complaints from women, you know the drill.' He waited till she'd finished writing it down. 'How did you get on with our ever-cheery pathologist?'

'He sends his regards too.' Geneva scanned her notes. 'Cause of death was the incision on her neck. She'd been strapped down to something made of wood prior to her death. No indications of sexual assault.' Geneva paused a beat. 'But that may be misleading.'

'You think this is sexual?'

'There was no blood on her skin.'

'That's impossible.' Carrigan remembered the tumult of blood arrayed across the room.

'That's what I first thought too. And it didn't make any sense until I looked at her clothes. The clothes she was found in weren't hers. They were two sizes too big.'

'Maybe she just liked them loose?' Karlson said.

'You obviously don't know much about women.' A faint scatter of giggles. 'It's also entirely unlike anything else in Anna's wardrobe. I think he killed her while she was wearing her own clothes then stripped her body and dressed her in these.'

'That makes him sound like a serial killer,' Singh said.

Carrigan frowned. That dreaded phrase again. Whatever clinical meaning it had once held was long gone in the obliterative rush of media. 'A serial killer is minimum three victims, so let's not start spreading that kind of language around. It's far more likely someone she knew or came into contact with killed her – statistics bear this out. And we should be thankful for that. If he's appeared in her life before then he's left some trace and we *will* find it.'

'I disagree.'

Carrigan looked up, startled by the unfamiliar voice.

He was sitting in the back row, by the door. He must have come in during the briefing. It only took Carrigan a brief moment but the recognition was there. He tried to control his expression but knew his eyes would give him away. He turned to face the monitor.

'I think you're wrong,' the man at the back of the room said. He got up from the chair and introduced himself. 'Ed Hoffmann. I'm a clinical psychologist. I was sent here to offer you my help.' He had a slight stutter but spoke fast, overriding the defect, sometimes cutting off words or running them together as if he couldn't get his thoughts out fast enough.

'We weren't looking for help,' Carrigan said. Geneva glanced over at him, unsettled by his tone. Carrigan tried to process what was happening. Why was Hoffmann here? Did the profiler recognise him?

Hoffmann laughed, an easy garrulous chuckle that spilled out the side of his mouth. It was easy to see why he was such a hit on the lecture circuit despite his appearance. He was short and round and almost completely bald, with a monk's tongue of hair circumnavigating his skull. His arms seemed too small for his body and his clothes were mismatched and frayed as if a blind man had picked them out at random from a charity shop. When he smiled, his teeth glinted an unnatural white. He was one of three or four profilers the Met used on big cases – his day job was lecturing on behavioural aberration at UCL. 'That's as may be, Mr Carrigan, but both you and I answer to those above us and this is the decision they've made.' Hoffmann took short, fast strides, nodding at the gathered detectives as he made his way to the front. 'I understand how you may feel. I know bringing in someone from outside presumes a lack on your part – but that's the wrong way to think about it.' He was addressing the entire room now, standing only a few feet away from Carrigan. 'I'm more like a computer application you download to help you with one particular task.'

'It's nice to know you think so highly of your talents,' Carrigan said and, as soon as he'd said it, he wished he could take it back but it was too late. 'We're doing perfectly fine as it is.'

Hoffmann placed both hands in his jacket pockets. 'With all due respect, I very much doubt that. What you've just told your team proves it. We *are* looking at a serial killer, regardless of how many he's killed so far. It's not about quantity – it's about pathology and the pathology fits. I've had a quick look through the case files and nothing in there makes me doubt that conclusion.'

'What makes you think this is a serial crime?' Carrigan forced himself to make eye contact with the profiler. They were standing just two feet apart. He tried to read Hoffmann's expression. Did Hoffmann know? Did he know that Carrigan knew?

'Everything I've read makes me think that. The way he positioned her body, the blood shower, the drugs. It's a ritual, a set of steps he needs to take to make this fulfilling for him.' Hoffmann paused. 'You're expecting me to tell you he's white, intelligent, a loner, working a manual job he resents, but you know all that already. Of course he is. You can pretend you're normal for a few hours but not for a lifetime.' Hoffmann rubbed his knuckles across his forehead. 'What we do know about him is that he's extremely organised. The abduction, the snipping of the passport photo, the fact he hasn't left behind any forensics. It's done with an almost military precision. Which, to me, suggests you've got a hunter on your hands.'

'Aren't they all?' Singh said, trying to make her tone light, but nobody laughed.

Hoffmann turned towards her. 'This is a special designation of serial killer. They get their kicks as much from stalking their prey as from the actual kill. Like a lion on the Serengeti they pick off the weak and strays, sometimes spending weeks tracking them, savouring each moment of the hunt. They tend to be males in their late thirties to fifties, older than usual for serial killers and, like this guy, are very organised. He enjoys the hunt. That's what's getting him off. He's also displayed quite pronounced sadistic tendencies. Anna was strapped to a tortureboard. We know he didn't rape her but we don't know what he did do to her. She went missing on Friday night but, according to the autopsy, wasn't killed till Sunday. That means he needed that time to do something to her – but what? The answer will be as much a part of his signature as his MO.'

'What's the difference?' Jennings asked.

Carrigan was about to reply but Hoffmann cut him off. 'His MO is how he commits the crime. His signature is what he needs to do to satisfy his urges. The MO adapts as he becomes better at evading us. The signature never changes. The blood shower is certainly part of it – it's a very intimate act, someone's life emptying out over your body. He could have cut her neck all the way across – it would have been quicker – but he didn't. He made the smallest puncture he could. He closed her eyes, tidied up her dress. I agree that he must have swapped her clothes afterwards but I don't know why, only that it's important to him.' Hoffmann paused. 'He won't be sitting around gloating. He almost definitely has the next one in his sights now he's claimed Anna.'

'How do you know that?'

Hoffmann gave Jennings the briefest of glances. 'Because there's always a next one.'

20

'You need a favour?'

Geneva was halfway to Berman's desk when his head shot up. He'd been burrowed in front of his computer and she hadn't realised he'd heard her coming. 'Now, why would you think that?'

Berman swivelled his chair away from the desk. She always forgot how tall he was, most of the time she only ever saw him sitting. He stretched out his legs and rubbed his left knee. His black trainers were large and square and looked exactly like the hard drives on his desk.

'You're smiling,' he said. 'And you're smiling in that way I've seen you smiling at suspects. Not the way you smile when you think no one's looking and you're lost in your headphones.'

She pulled out a chair and sat down. 'And there I was thinking you were just another autistic geek with no interpersonal skills.'

He laughed and she'd rarely heard him laughing and was surprised by how carefree he sounded. The briefing had ended twenty minutes ago and Geneva had snuck out for a cigarette and gone through her lists of things to do. She would start on the hostel tomorrow. It was too late to go to Anna's cleaning agency tonight and that too would have to be done tomorrow. She needed to borrow money from her mother to pay this month's rent – it would mean a visit rather than a phone call and she should have done that right after the briefing but there was something she needed to check first.

'So, this favour?' Berman tapped his pen against the table, the frayed tassels of his prayer shawl peeking out from beneath his shirt like a petticoat.

Geneva zoomed back to the present. 'Anna was trolled on Twitter. Bad enough to make her cry, apparently, and often enough to make her delete her account.' She watched as Berman's body snapped into focus. 'You find that interesting too?'

'Very much so.' Berman swung back into place, his legs completely disappearing under the table. 'And you were wondering if I could get into deleted Twitter accounts?'

Geneva held up her hands in mock surrender.

'An eight-year-old can do that. What I can get you is that . . .' He started to type, a series of fast and rhythmic strokes. '. . . and a record of everyone who ever interacted with her on Twitter, both publicly and by direct messaging.'

Geneva tried to conceal her smile.

'That's more like it,' Berman said. 'That's the kind of smile I was talking about. Your little private smile.' He turned back to the computer, one hand pounding keys, the other rotating the shawl's tassels between the tips of his fingers. The computer pinged. He scanned it and a broad grin cracked his face. 'Here we go.' He tilted the screen towards Geneva and moved his chair out of the way. 'It's all yours. I also ran a check on other sites – Facebook, Pinterest, etc. – but she wasn't active on those. Need any help, just text me; I'm off to get a burger.'

Anna Becker hadn't tweeted much. In the last six months she'd posted only 613 tweets. Her account name was her own name and she'd used the photo of her and Madison as an avatar. She had 89 followers and followed 321 people. Geneva cut and pasted and printed out a list of both, then scrolled back to Anna's first tweet and began reading.

Anna had only started tweeting on her arrival in the UK. The tweets were in English and most consisted of terse exclamations of delight and wonder. Geneva read of Anna's excitement at seeing the Globe for the first time, the lights smearing the river outside the National, burrowing through markets filled with strange smells and even stranger languages. Anna spoke of the bustling life of a city after the dry cow fields of home. Of how much she hated the grey drizzle but loved the bookshops, couldn't stand the Tube but spent entire afternoons riding the top decks of buses.

The day grew dark, long skinny fingers of shadow spreading across the table and freckling Geneva's face. Phones rang in empty rooms. Thunder rattled the window frames. She drank Coke, made lists, charted repeat conversations and constructed a timeline.

Anna interacted with a small circle of friends, Madison most of all, and Geneva winced as she read through their dialogues, revealing their every step – where they were going to meet up and when, planning their evenings on Twitter rather than by phone or email. They made it so easy. Orwell had been wrong in thinking governments would need to install apparatus to spy on the daily lives of their citizens – we'd already done it on our own, gladly and willingly and without a thought to consequence.

The girls discussed bars and clubs and which cinemas were the cheapest. They talked about how much they hated the weather, the rude people and astounding prices, but Geneva saw nothing which might have focused a stalker's interest. Not that you needed much – a casual glance in a crowded cafe, a chance encounter on the Tube, your avatar reminding him of the one that got away. If someone was determined enough they could find out everything about you from the web, every hidden fold of your personality and taste so that when you met them in a crowded bar they'd say all the things you'd always dreamed a man would say before they took your hand and led you out of this world.

A door banged shut in the corridor. Geneva heard the lift doors opening but no one got on or off. Lightning forked the sky. She drained her Coke and continued reading. The world telescoped down to 140 characters and the parameters of her computer screen.

Anna went to see a production of *Ghosts* in February and it provoked her most sustained burst of tweeting, complaining that the director had completely misunderstood Ibsen's play, the actors delivering their lines as if they had no idea what they meant. Anna tweeted considerably less in March and wasn't interacting much with her friends. Geneva looked up their separate accounts and saw they'd still been going out and carrying on as usual in her absence.

The first abusive tweet came at 9.37 p.m. on Monday, 5 April.

It was just one word.

FAILURE.

It was cruel and simple and effective.

The tweet was sent from a 'Paul Smith', the avatar was the default Twitter egg. The profile was blank. Paul Smith had only tweeted this one tweet. Anna had immediately blocked his account. She probably thought it was a mistake or one of the many spiders and sex bots that crawled across cyberspace.

The next tweet came two days later. The account belonged to a 'Doug Mantle' and said: *TRY HARDER NEXT TIME.* It coincided with the one veiled reference Anna had made to a part she didn't get. There could be no pretending it was a mistake or random spam now.

She hadn't replied, and Geneva respected her for that, for not rising to the bait, knowing what trolls wanted most was to goad others into the kind of shrivelling they felt in their own souls. But Anna had simply blocked the account and made no reference to it in subsequent tweets.

Three days later, she received the next one: *YOU WILL NEVER BE GOOD ENOUGH.*

A pigeon collided against the window, the sound huge and sudden. Geneva jumped almost straight out of her chair. She looked over and saw flapping wings and blood zigzagging the glass. She shook her head and stared at the words onscreen. There was something decidedly sadistic about the timing of the tweets. The gaps just long enough to lull Anna into thinking it was over before the next one appeared. The pattern repeated for the next two weeks. The tweets were becoming increasingly more personal and vicious. Every time Anna blocked one account, a new one would appear. Then everything changed.

On the morning of 24 April, Anna Becker received 436 abusive tweets from 67 different accounts in the space of two hours. It continued the next day and the day after and the one after that. Then it stopped and for a week there were no more tweets.

The photos came next.

The captions accompanying the photos were saccharine endearments: *THINKING OF YOU – WITH YOU IN MIND – THIS REMINDED ME OF YOU.* The images below the words were of diseased penises. Colour and hi-res and pretty much the most disgusting thing Geneva had ever seen. Graphic close-ups of pus-bubbled membrane, cracked skin, mushrooming growths and pulsating red wounds. The photos were sent every hour for the next two days, all from different accounts.

There was only one more tweet after that. It contained no words, just a photo of a tropical beach at sunset. Geneva stared at it. It was an odd coda to this sustained campaign of harassment. There had been no activity on Anna's Twitter since the photo. A couple of days later, Anna deleted her account. 9 May. Seven days before she disappeared.

21

He'd spent an hour sitting in the dark room, thinking about Hoffmann's surprise appearance and watching his mother lost so deep within herself she could never find her way out again. He'd talked to her, told her about Louise and the kids and what they'd got up to on the weekend. He drank hospital coffee and read two chapters of *The Great Gatsby*. The appalling sense of squander and decay struck him hard. Despite having exactly the same text, it was an entirely different book from the one he'd first read when he was fifteen.

It had arrived yesterday, in his letterbox like all the others, anonymous missives posted once a month for the last year and a half. A couple of weeks ago he'd finally worked out who his mysterious benefactor was but he liked it this way, a secret conversation conducted through the printed words of strangers.

He stopped at a late-night coffee shop and picked up a quad espresso and two croissants. He parked opposite the hostel and sat in the car, sipping the hot syrupy drink, sprinkling crumbs over his jacket and rereading the case files. The killer had probably sat out here and surveilled the hostel for several days, getting to know its rhythms, when staff shifts changed and the desk was left unoccupied. Carrigan watched as a steady stream of backpackers trickled in and out, some checking in after long flights, others with crates of beer under their arms, heading out for the endless night. A building site occupied the opposite corner. It promised luxury apartments and a platinum lifestyle. He'd already forgotten what had previously stood there, the city continually remaking itself and obscuring its own past. London had changed so much since his childhood, it was almost unrecognisable. These shifts were not only topographical. As the city grew and became more unruly, it split into discrete fragments, a Balkanisation in miniature community against community, religion against religion, the rich against the poor, man against woman. Carrigan looked up and saw the ghosts of V2s raining down on Moorgate and Morley, Limehouse and Lancaster Gate, the wobbly descent and unearthly hiss, the stunned wreckage and cold tea served in the dazed communal dawn.

The sight of Max exiting the hostel snapped him out of reverie. There was an urgency in the manager's manner that had been totally absent earlier. Max had a spring in his step and a look in his eyes Carrigan knew well.

Max's car, a yellow Cortina, emerged from the hostel driveway two minutes later, turning left and heading north. Carrigan waited a beat, then started the engine. He kept several car lengths between them. It was chucking-out time and the roads were clogged with taxis and buses and it was easy to follow Max without being spotted. Max took a right down Chepstow Road and drove past the elegant Georgian terraces and pet boutiques then turned the corner into another world.

The Westbourne Park estate stood dark and eerie, a deserted Crusader castle buttressed by high walls and shuttered windows. Rough sleepers squatted in bus stops and doorways, hugging a bottle, a dog or a cardboard blanket. Carrigan watched as three vagrants pulled apart a black rubbish bag, ripping into it and emerging with a chicken leg and two slices of pizza. Packs of dogs roamed freely in empty lots, fighting with the winos and each other over scraps of food.

Carrigan smelled Golborne Road before he reached it – a unique and delicious mix of smoky fish, doughnuts and skunk. He eased the accelerator and slowed to a crawl as Max swung into a narrow cul-de-sac. Carrigan cruised down Golborne Road until he spotted Max's Cortina near the entrance to one of the estates. He parked his car and waited. The long grey shadow of Trellick Tower occluded half the street. Young men stood on corners and whispered into phones or kept their eyes peeled on the road ahead. Carrigan knew they'd already spotted him but he wasn't here for that.

Max emerged from the estate eighteen minutes later. He looked as if all his bones had been replaced with rubber substitutes. He staggered out of the gate in a slow-motion stumble, a large beatific smile on his face. He tried to light a cigarette but couldn't find the tip with his lighter. His jaw hung slackly and his eyes were slitted and puffy. He made it back to the car, managed to get inside, and sat there with the unlit cigarette dangling from his lips.

Carrigan waited. Ten minutes later, Max snapped awake with a big sloppy grin on his face. He dropped the cigarette, picked it up and lit it, then rolled down the window, The Ramones leaking out, chanting nursery-school mayhem into the night. Max pulled out and headed towards the hostel. But instead of turning down Queensway, Max continued south. At first, Carrigan thought he'd become confused, understandable given the state he was in, but Max's driving was steady and his direction purposeful.

*

Max stopped the car outside a house on a quiet residential street in Knightsbridge. Not the kind of area Carrigan expected to see him in but Max seemed to know exactly where he was going. The house was a semi-detached Victorian, set off from the street with its own private garage and driveway. Large oak trees protected it from the prying eyes of passers-by. Carrigan stayed in the car. If Max was here to do what Carrigan thought, he'd be out in five minutes.

Forty-seven minutes later, Carrigan's curiosity got the better of him.

He stepped out of the car into the warm drizzle and looked both ways down the street. There were no CCTV cameras and that was good. Carrigan put on his raincoat and crossed the road. He unlatched the gate and entered the driveway. Thick curtains covered the windows. There was a video intercom yet no security camera above the door. But it wasn't just that.

There was something too neat about the house, too careful. A car went past and Carrigan flattened himself against a tree and waited for it to disappear then walked up to the front door and pressed the buzzer.

Less than a minute later, a middle-aged woman drowning in an Aran jumper opened the door.

'What do you want?' Her voice was harsh with years of smoke and booze, her eyes raking up and down, appraising Carrigan with a professional efficiency.

'Where is he?' Carrigan said.

The woman tried to shut the door. 'I don't know what you're talking about and if you don't leave right now, I'll call the police.'

Carrigan smiled and pulled out his warrant card. 'I am the police,' he said and brushed her aside as he entered the house.

He walked down a long corridor, studded with solid wooden doors. He should have radioed it in, gone back to the station and followed protocol. But he knew what Max had in his pocket and that Max could not complain without admitting his own wrong-doing.

He heard Max's cries coming from the second door on the left. He waited just in case it was his mind playing tricks on him but then he heard it again and opened the door and stepped into the room.

He blinked because what he saw made no sense at all.

Max was lying in a large double bed, fully clothed and in the arms of a middle-aged woman, also clothed. A duvet covered their legs. The woman was cuddling Max as he wept in her arms. Candles flickered the room into shadow. Mahler was playing at a discreet volume. Max cried as the woman hugged him tighter to her and then she looked up and noticed Carrigan in the doorway.

'What you want from me? Why're you following me? What've I done to you?' Max's words came out in a torrent of crushed syllables and compacted consonants as he sat in Carrigan's car. He wailed and pleaded and begged as they drove up Knightsbridge. 'Why me? Am I so important you have to follow me everywhere?' He braced his arms against the windshield. 'Why not someone else? A man is allowed to do what he wants in privacy. You had no right to go in there. None at all.'

'You're correct.' Carrigan stopped at a set of lights. 'I didn't.

I'm sorry. I heard you crying and I thought someone was hurting you.'

'My fucking hero.' Max glanced out the window at a homeless man puking in someone's front garden. 'That was private shit, man. It's not about sex or anything weird like that. There's nothing illegal about it.'

'I'm not saying there is.'

'Plenty of people do it.'

'You don't need to justify yourself to me.'

'I never wanted anyone to see me like that. It fucking kills me that's what's in your head right now.' Max looked away. 'Fuck it. I bet you have nowhere that makes you feel as good? You don't, do you? And, besides, I'm not hurting anyone, there's far worse places than this.'

Carrigan turned down Kensington High Street. 'Like what? *Extreme* cuddling? You're telling me there's more of these?'

'Everywhere, man. Whatever you want, whenever you want it. You like licking women's armpits? There's a private club in Purley specialises in that. You like having your chest shaved by a beautiful woman? Places in Mayfair, Edmonton and Fulham. Like dressing in baby clothes? Perivale and Ealing. Or maybe you get off on having your balls kicked? Norwood and Earslfield. There's an exclusive club in Haymarket where you can dress up as a concentration camp inmate while the girls strut past you in SS uniforms. In Walthamstow there's one set up to be an exact replica of the Central Line so you can grope the women as if you were on the 5.15 back from work.'

Carrigan shook his head and parked by the south entrance to Holland Park. The street was deserted apart from the occasional bus and stray cab.

Max looked at the swaying trees outside. He'd put his T-shirt on back to front and his hair was matted down where he'd been lying. 'You bastard,' he hissed at Carrigan's reflection in the window. 'You can't do this to me. What went on in there, it wasn't illegal.'

'No,' Carrigan replied. 'It probably wasn't, but what you have in your pocket from Golborne Road is.'

Max slumped in his seat and Carrigan knew he was finished. 'Now, you can come with me to the station and we can process the heroin, or you can tell what you didn't tell me earlier.'

'I told you everything I know. I swear.'

Carrigan leaned across the seat. 'No, Max, you didn't. You were far too nervous and evasive. At first I thought it was because your place reeked of weed but it wasn't that, was it?'

'I'm a nervous guy.'

'Enough bullshit.' Carrigan slammed his palm into the dashboard. 'What didn't you tell me?'

Max took several deep breaths, the smell of stale cigarettes filling the car, and Carrigan waited to hear how Anna had really loved him and he'd loved her and how age didn't matter when two people find each other and so it took him a moment to realise what Max had just said and when he did it changed everything.

II

22

There was another girl. Anna wasn't the first to disappear from the hostel.

Max's late-night confession rattled through Carrigan's head as he shut the door and pulled the blinds. Jennings switched on the fluorescents and everything turned buzzy and bright. They were in one of the smaller rooms off the main incident room. It was supposed to be for interviews but Carrigan liked to keep it empty – the one room in the station where you were guaranteed not to be disturbed because it was too far down the corridor for most people to bother.

Carrigan had a double espresso by his side and a raging headache. He couldn't stop thinking about the mistakes he'd made. He'd ignored the obvious. They should have been looking for patterns, not anomalies. The abduction had been too slick for it to have been the killer's first time. An investigation had its own momentum and the minute you let up, it slipped away and you could never get it back. This was the most delicate point in a case – the choices he made now would determine the investigation's success or failure. He popped two codeines from their silvery jacket, dry-swallowed them and went back to the files.

Max's revelation had been like a concrete block thrown into the investigation pool. It was something they'd all considered and weighed and hoped wasn't true but now they knew it to be so it only brought forth deeper and darker questions. They would need to go through everything again. To look at it in the light of this and see what new connections presented themselves.

Max had protested and pleaded when Carrigan asked him to explain but he'd eventually come out with it. Katrina Eliot had disappeared in November of last year. Max apologised for not telling Carrigan earlier. He sweated and shook his head and said a lawyer from the management company had visited him a few days after Katrina's disappearance and explained that if he wanted to keep his job, it would be wise to keep his mouth shut. Things like that weren't good for business.

Carrigan had ordered up the case files on Katrina Eliot as soon as he got into work. Her last known address – the Milgram. They hadn't made the link because Katrina had only been reported missing – without a body, the case had stalled. Carrigan had the files laid out in front of him but he found it hard to tear himself away from Katrina's photo. She was almost identical to Anna – the same blue eyes, long hair and forlorn expression. They could have been sisters.

Katrina Eliot had last been seen at a bowling alley in Bayswater. She'd complained of not feeling well about an hour after arriving and had gone outside to get some fresh air. When she didn't reappear, her friends assumed she'd gone home. That was the last time anyone had seen her.

She was twenty-one, originally from Leeds, and had just graduated from the University of Lancaster. She'd spent the summer travelling then relocated to London to start her own band. She was staying at the hostel to save money and performing weekly to tiny audiences in the upstairs rooms of decrepit pubs. She liked Eminem and Cath Kidston shoes. She'd moved into the hostel in late August and had gone missing on 15 November. Anna had checked in two weeks later. Their paths hadn't crossed. It made Hoffman's theory of a stranger killing more plausible. The drinks. The dizziness. The fact they'd slept in the same room.

Carrigan ignored the phones, went online, and checked out Katrina's band. They weren't bad. There was definitely something there between the crackle snap of drums and ringing guitars and Carrigan felt a distinct buzz as the chords tumbled through him. It had been a long time since he'd properly listened to music and, until now, he hadn't realised quite how much of himself, or the world, he'd shut out. The band had been halfway through recording a demo when Katrina disappeared. There were messages of hope and condolence from friends and fans in the comments section. A tribute site to her life. More ripples.

Carrigan stretched, yawned and popped his shoulders. Lightning illuminated the city as if God were photographing his creation. Jennings was reading and shaking his head simultaneously. The phones kept baying, the rain tattooing the windowsills. Katrina's parents had travelled down from Leeds and filled out a missing persons report after not hearing from their daughter for two weeks. By then it would have been too late. Every detective knew the initial twenty-four hours of a case were far more likely to yield results, that ninety per cent of abducted women are killed in the first ten hours. Carrigan glanced out at the rain and considered choices and paths taken, his own African odyssey and how it had shunted his life onto an entirely different track, managing to wipe out his youth with one swift flourish. He often wondered if the two tracks – his life as it was now and his life if Africa hadn't intervened – would meet up at the end or remain for ever separate, disappearing into different horizons.

He made notes and kept reading. It was only the dogged persistence of Katrina's parents – who turned up on the steps of the station every morning demanding an update from the officer in charge, who bombarded the phones with voicemail messages and flooded cyberspace with pleas and petitions – only this that had turned the case into something more than one of a thousand forgotten reports hiding in the darkness of a computer database. Her parents had been unusually persuasive. Carrigan could see that DI Tony Forsyth of the Mis/Pers unit had marshalled all his resources in trying to find Katrina – he'd interviewed the hostel staff, her friends and bandmates, and constructed a solid timeline for her last day – but he'd never been able to find out what had happened to her after she left the bowling alley.

These kinds of cases were always the hardest. Carrigan thought of them as *pure* cases. There was no relevant backstory, history or simmering resentments coming to the boil. There was only the killer and how much he'd left of himself. There was CCTV footage of Katrina going up the stairs. Carrigan and Jennings watched it several times, mesmerised by the knowledge of what came after, the small unrecorded moments lost to history.

'It's the bloody same.' Jennings's voice was dry and uncharacteristically bitter. He took the file from Carrigan and scanned it. 'Not to mention the hostel.'

'Look at the photos.'

The similarity between the two girls registered on Jennings's face, the corners of his mouth turning pale. 'If there's two, what's to say there isn't more? What's to say he hasn't been getting away with this for years?'

'We don't know that,' Carrigan replied, though he'd been thinking exactly the same thing. 'We might be lucky. We might have discovered him early.'

A car alarm went off in the street below followed by a staggered chorus of canine howls. Jennings was staring off into space instead of going through his stack of files. Carrigan called out his name but there was no reply.

'Jesus, at least tell me to mind my own business or shut up,' Carrigan said. 'But, either way, you need to pull yourself together.'

Jennings continued staring at the rain, transfixed and oblivious as a moviegoer.

'Look,' Carrigan continued. 'I know I'm pretty crap at this side of it but if you need someone to talk to . . .'

'What's the point in talking?' Jennings turned so quickly he knocked a stack of files to the floor. 'Not going to make anything better, is it? Not going to change anything. After we found the body, I went home and sat on the sofa and cried.' Jennings stared at the rain-smudged city and seemed to be speaking to his own reflection. 'And when Rose asked me what was wrong, I started going off on her. I've never done that before.' He looked up. 'What's the point? It never ends, does it?'

Carrigan moved his chair a little closer. 'And, what? You're going to stop cutting your hair because it'll only grow back? You think we don't make a difference?' It was something every good detective struggled with. It was what kept Carrigan up at night, lost in folders and data, inputting facts into a machine that didn't care. 'I don't have to remind you what happened when we took our eye off the ball a few summers ago – the riots?'

Jennings nodded mutely.

'You want me to justify the job? I can't do that but I do know that without us the cities will descend into blood and chaos that much sooner. Every time we turn on the news we see what happens if we're not there to stop it. We have to do what we do and we have to keep doing it in the face of diminishing returns.' It was as close to a mission statement as Carrigan had. 'Everything is sliding towards chaos. Given enough time, everything falls apart. That's a fundamental law of the universe. That's physics. We can't change it and there's no use moaning about it. It's like your desk.' Carrigan pointed towards the outer office. 'Are you going to let things pile up on your desk until you can't find anything? Or do you try and keep a balance, tidying up regularly even though you know it's only going to get messy again?'

'I know you're right,' Jennings replied, the soles of his shoes pressing against the floor. 'I know it's logical and rational but that doesn't stop me thinking about it all the time, fucking dreaming about it. I've had to move into the spare room so I don't wake Rose up with my screams.'

'I don't know what to tell you.' Carrigan understood he had to tread carefully. Jennings had been bottling this up for a long time and was close to snapping. It wasn't the first time Carrigan had had this conversation in his role as DI and he knew it wouldn't be the last. 'This job takes away much more than it gives. You'll lose family, friends, lovers, children – if you stay, you have to accept you're no longer like everyone else, that there's a different weight on your shoulders. You need to decide if this is something you want to keep doing.'

Jennings didn't reply, his eyes vacant and soft as he stared out into the rain.

Carrigan placed a hand on his shoulder, aware that no one ever listened to advice. Everyone had to come to their own unique and slippery accommodation with the world. 'Whatever you decide, you've got my support, you know that. But there's nothing else you can do about it today so go and watch a movie, eat a nice meal and try to remember it's not always like this.'

Carrigan waited until Jennings was gone then reached across to Katrina Eliot's file and dialled the number for DI Tony Forsyth.

He introduced himself but the only reply was Forsyth shouting at one of his officers.

'I wanted to talk about a case of yours.'

There was nothing but static on the other end of the line and Carrigan thought Forsyth had hung up when the man's deep burr came bouncing through the handset. 'I've got a lot on at the moment. This isn't a good time.'

'I was just about to have lunch,' Carrigan continued as if he hadn't heard. 'I thought Chinese food might be nice, what with this weather, some hot soup maybe? You need to eat too, right?'

The DI didn't reply.

'And while we enjoy our food you can tell me about Katrina Eliot.'

'Katrina Eliot?'

Carrigan waited. He counted off the seconds.

'Where do you want to meet?'

23

Sparta Employment Agency was located on Queensway above an old sign for a Vietnamese restaurant. Geneva remembered dark drunken nights in its cloistered interior with Lee, her ex-boyfriend, slow strong cocktails and the endless rounds of bizarre and delicious dishes – but the restaurant had closed down and in its place was a charity shop totally devoid of stock.

She felt that familiar prickle at the back of her neck as she finished her cigarette and waited for Singh. Anna had worked part-time as a cleaner. One of her clients had become abusive and she'd had to quit. But those kind of men never quit. Geneva hadn't been that surprised when Carrigan told them about Katrina Eliot at the morning briefing. The nature of Anna's abduction, the Twitter trolling – everything they'd learned about their killer suggested he'd had plenty of practice to hone his skills. She flashed back to the abusive tweets. Her hunter was proving to be as adept at virtual stalking as he was at the real thing. The Twitter trolling and Anna's murder were too close together to be unrelated. The abuse was too well orchestrated, too detailed, personal and persistent for him to have stopped when Anna deleted her account. Ironically, it could have been that very action which had caused him to escalate.

Geneva checked her watch, took out her phone and called Madison. She hadn't heard back from her and feared the worst but when she punched in the number it began to ring, the languid stutter of foreign interchanges immediately making Geneva feel a lot better. She tried to do the maths in her head, a twenty-four-hour flight to Australia, time spent in security lines and layovers, and realised Madison was probably somewhere over the vast Pacific right now.

Singh's fingernails clicked against her BlackBerry as they made their way upstairs and entered a small waiting room crowded with young men and women, standing, sitting, texting or chatting among themselves. A receptionist sat behind a table at the far end, head bobbing to unheard music, eyes fixed on the screen in front of her. Geneva headed for the desk and was about to snag the receptionist's attention when someone grabbed her arm. She turned around to see a tiny woman, not an inch over four feet, her hair the bright orange of cheap fizzy drink.

'What the fuck d'you think you're doing?' The woman sneered to reveal pink gums and three tongue piercings. 'Some of us have been waiting hours.'

Geneva shook her off. 'Do I look like I need a job?'

The woman backed away, her eyes small and narrow. 'You bitch,' she said. 'You think I dreamed of cleaning English toilets?'

'Please. Can you all just settle down?' The receptionist had taken off her headphones and was staring at them like a stern and unforgiving headmistress.

Geneva pulled her arm free. 'We need to talk to your boss.'

The receptionist studied Geneva, a private assessment and pursing of lips. 'I'm afraid that would be impossible.'

'Really?' Geneva gestured to the room. 'All these people? They're not waiting to see him?'

The receptionist smiled. 'You'd probably be better off coming back tomorrow.'

'Thank you,' Geneva said, walking straight past her and into the main office.

A woman was sitting behind a large, oval table. She was tapping something on the screen in front of her. A young man with a ponytail was leaning over and staring at the screen. The woman's eyes shot up the moment Geneva and Singh entered.

'What on earth do you think you're doing?' Her accent was sharp and crisp as broken glass.

'I'm sorry for bursting in like this,' Geneva explained, surprised to find herself cowed by the woman's unwavering stare. 'But your secretary was less than helpful.'

'I should hope so. That's what I pay her for.' The woman ran an elegantly manicured finger down the right column of a large appointments book. 'You're certainly not making the best impression if you've come for a job.'

Geneva bit down the insult and took a couple of steps forward. 'That's lucky, because I'm not here for a job.' She took out her warrant card and flicked it open. The woman's expression didn't change as she stood up, took the wallet and examined it. Finally satisfied, she handed it back and sat down. She turned to the ponytailed young man. 'Come back in ten minutes.' The boy nodded and left.

'Sorry about that,' the woman said. 'Eleanor Harper. How can I help you?'

'We need information about someone who worked for you.'

'We're a brokerage for temporary cleaning staff. People work for us on a freelance basis. We don't directly employ anyone.'

Geneva sat down. The room was tasteful, elegant and soulless. There were no family portraits, knick-knacks or personal items. Framed prints of Mediterranean scenes lined the walls; small rocky bays, dismal towns, the rushing urgency of the sea.

'We're investigating the disappearance of Anna Becker, a woman who might have got work through you.' Geneva took out Anna's photo and placed it on the table. 'Please have a look and tell us if you remember her.'

Eleanor examined the photo with the same scrutiny she had given to Geneva's warrant card, then shook her head. 'Afraid not.' She pushed the photo away. 'I see about three hundred people a week. Even if she came through here, I very much doubt I'd remember.'

'We'd like to take a look at your appointments book,' Singh said, her forceful tone a surprise to Geneva. 'See where she was in the weeks leading up to her disappearance. We heard there was some trouble.'

Eleanor nodded almost imperceptibly. She pivoted towards the screen and keyed in a string of commands. 'Becker, you said?'

'Yes.'

Eleanor scanned the screen. 'She worked nineteen jobs for us, starting just over eight weeks ago. She handed in her notice two weeks ago. There's no reason stated.'

'One of the clients made a pass at her. When Anna said no, he took it further. That's why she quit.'

'She should have reported it.'

'Perhaps she didn't think you'd take it seriously enough?' Singh suggested.

'I take it very seriously. This kind of thing should never be allowed to happen.' She tapped her nails against the table as if to underline the point. 'I've reported many clients over the years to your lot but you're the ones not taking it seriously. You go and speak to the client but how long do you think that lasts?'

'Things are different now,' Geneva said, knowing Eleanor was partly right.

'Good. I'm glad to hear it. Women have suffered in silence long enough. We encourage the girls to report even the tiniest infraction.' She reached into her drawer and took out a folded leaflet. 'We produce a guide so they know what's not acceptable in this country. It tells them their rights and how to deal with any given situation.'

She handed over the leaflet and Geneva flicked through it, impressed.

'Which client was it?'

'We don't know,' Geneva admitted. 'We need a list of all the residences she worked at.'

'Of course.' Eleanor slid her mouse across the trackpad and clicked. The printer roared to life and ejected a single page. She took the page from the tray and handed it to Geneva.

'Can you also check for a Katrina Eliot?'

Eleanor's black-painted fingernails tapped the keyboard. It was her only affectation. Otherwise, she was one of those women, like Geneva's mum, who'd abrogated their futile battle against the onslaughts of time. She'd let herself grow old, not bothering to dye her hair or hide her blemishes, and she looked all the better for it. 'I have no one by that name registered here.'

'How does it work?' Geneva skimmed the report. Anna had done shifts at St Mary's Hospital, local schools and several private residences. They would need to interview and eliminate them one by one. 'Do they come here every morning to see what's available?'

Eleanor clicked her fingernails. 'Of course not. That would simply be a mess. After the initial interview, it's all done by phone. Once we've found them work, they're in our system. They get a text in the morning and they have fifteen minutes to accept or decline the job.'

Geneva flicked through her notes. 'Do you tend to get a lot of backpackers?'

'About a third of our clients. They've run out of money and don't want to go home yet. London's a very expensive city if you're young and like the nightlife, but backpackers are terribly unreliable. One day they're clamouring for work and the next day they're in Sydney or Lima.' She studied her nails and shook her head. 'They haven't yet realised how quickly the world falls away.'

Geneva noted the undertow of sadness to Eleanor's words, her outward poise arrayed like a shield around her. 'You said a third of your clients? Who are the others?'

'As you'd expect we have a lot of Poles and other new EU member states, all of them hideously overqualified but, often, this is the only work they can get in the UK. We also have a lot of students who do a few shifts here and there to pay off loans or save for a holiday. Recently, we've had quite a number of housewives supplementing the family income with part-time work. There's not the stigma to cleaning there was a few years back.'

Geneva thought about her own mother who'd worked as a cleaner when she first came to this country and how ashamed she'd been, almost as if she were selling her body, not her time. 'How much do they earn?'

'It's minimum wage, I'm afraid. But they can work whatever hours they want, as little or as much as they like.' Eleanor looked up. 'You ever need any spare income, you know where to come.' She smiled and stood, announcing the interview was over. She led them to the door and was already ushering in the next interviewee before Geneva and Singh had left the room.

24

Carrigan arrived five minutes early, but the restaurant had closed down. He tried to remember the last time he'd been here. No more than a week ago. There'd been no sign of any imminent change. The waiter had been his usual rude self, the food good as it always was. But this was London. Rain dripped and smudged the notice of administration posted by Westminster Council. Carrigan was halfway through reading it when he noticed a man's reflection coming towards him, one hand slowly emerging from a jacket pocket. Carrigan spun around, legs tensed, quickly realising he was trapped, his back up against the door.

'He's done it again, hasn't he?'

Carrigan blinked the rain from his brow. 'What did you say?'

'He's taken someone again. The man who took Katrina Eliot.' This time it wasn't a question.

'Why do you think that?'

The repeated click of DI Forsyth's lighter sizzled against the rain. 'Because it was only a matter of time.'

'Before he killed again?'

The cigarette sparked and Forsyth let out a small strangled chuckle. 'No.' He took three hard pulls on the already damp cigarette, the end briefly flowering into life then sputtering out. 'Before we stumbled on him again.'

They turned away from the restaurant and crossed the street, their bodies braced against the rain. There weren't many options. Half the shops on Queensway had closed down and the other half sold things you could never afford.

Carrigan led Forsyth to a small cafe snuggled between a bank and a currency exchange. The manager, an overweight, middle-aged Greek named Nikos, greeted Carrigan effusively the moment he stepped in, pumping his palm and clapping him on the shoulder. He greeted Forsyth in the same manner and Carrigan saw the DI stiffen as Nikos shook his hand.

'Please. Take a seat, anywhere you like.'

The place was empty. Carrigan followed Forsyth to a square marble-topped table in the back. The chairs were modern, cheap and uncomfortable. The marble was cracked and dull. The menus were white and uninspiring – paninis, pizzas or variations on an English breakfast. The unpainted walls held ripped and curled tourist posters for a Greek island named Palassos.

'I assume it's the food and not the ambience we're here for.' Forsyth shook his head as he went to the toilet.

'Katrina Eliot.'

He hadn't heard Forsyth come back but there he was, shaking his hands dry, his face animated and slightly red as if he'd just had a swig of some raw and ready booze. 'Haven't heard that name for ages.'

'But you've thought about her, haven't you?' Carrigan saw something narrow in Forsyth's eyes and knew he'd been right.

'Why are you interested in Katrina?' Forsyth spread his forearms across the table, a fierce grey moustache hiding his top lip. The owner reappeared with the food they'd ordered.

'I have a case that's similar,' Carrigan said when they were alone again.

'Similar how?'

'Same type of victim. Same hostel. Same MO.'

Forsyth pushed his plate away. 'When?'

'Couple of days ago,' Carrigan said. 'She was abducted from a local bar and dumped in a derelict house.' He told Forsyth what they knew about Anna. Forsyth didn't take notes and he didn't take his eyes off Carrigan.

'Any leads?'

'Nothing from either the abduction scene or the dump site. He's very good at counter-forensic measures.' Carrigan paused. 'We found her passport . . .'

'Photo carefully snipped out, right?'

Carrigan nodded. He'd hoped that the two cases, despite appearances, would prove to be unconnected. If Anna was the only victim then the motive and killer would be found in the unravelling of her life, but another victim from the same location suggested a territorial serial killer.

'We didn't get anything either,' Forsyth said. 'I worked that case four months. Found out everything there was to know about Katrina Eliot. Spoke to everyone. Went through the files three or four times, even brought in a review board to check I hadn't missed anything, and in all that time I learned absolutely nothing about him.'

'You kept at it, though? Even with so little to go on. Four months is a lot for a missing persons case. Was it the parents?'

Forsyth examined his plate. 'At first, yes. That's why I looked into it, and as I did, you know how it is – you start to feel there's something there, you can't name it or place it but you know something's not right and the more I looked into it, the more certain I was he'd do it again.' Forsyth pulled out a cigarette and rolled it between his fingers. 'We interviewed everyone. The hostel staff, residents, members of her band, people she met only once.'

As the food got cold, Forsyth told Carrigan about the Eliot investigation, the hours and days and hundreds of dead ends and played-out leads. 'It's like she vanished the minute she walked up those stairs. There's been no trace of her since. What happened to her? I'd like to think she met a man and they ran away together and she's on a beach somewhere enjoying her life but when I close my eyes I see cellars, basements and shallow graves. Unlike Anna, we never found Katrina. And that keeps bugging me. Is she still alive? Is he keeping her captive somewhere?'

Carrigan had been asking himself the same questions. 'Her parents still come to see you?'

Forsyth looked up sharply. 'You didn't know?'

'Know what?'

'Shit. They both died in a car crash, middle of January.'

Carrigan looked down at his plate. 'Our killer?'

'Don't think so. At least not directly. Her father had been drinking steadily since her disappearance. That day he came into the station pissed out of his mind, causing a scene, shouting and assaulting the duty sergeant. Security had to escort him out.' Forsyth clenched his fist and ground it into the table. 'I had no fucking idea he had his car and wife waiting for him outside. Or that he would drive straight into a bus on Lancaster Gate.'

'Suicide?'

Forsyth shrugged. 'Or bad luck, or booze, or all three. Take your pick.'

Carrigan flicked through his notes. Geneva had told them about the Twitter trolling at the morning briefing. 'Do you know if Katrina was being harassed on social media?'

Forsyth's eyes dropped to the table. 'We didn't even think about it at the time. We only checked for updates, any recent activity. We were short-staffed. It didn't seem ... fuck.' He clenched his right fist again and Carrigan knew he would now have a new reckoning on which to assign his failure.

'It's impossible for you to have known its significance with so little context. You can't blame yourself,' Carrigan said, knowing Forsyth would, just as he knew he would were he in the same position. 'I was wondering if there was anything else? Anything you didn't put in the report? You know – you feel something, are almost sure of it, but don't want to put it on paper so it doesn't come back to bite you?'

Forsyth avoided Carrigan's eyes. 'I talked to her friends quite a bit,' he replied. 'There was no evidence to back this up so it never went into the file but there was one thing – it seemed so ridiculous I never wrote it up but, as I mentioned, I spoke to the other members of her band and they said she'd been getting increasingly weird during rehearsals.'

Carrigan gripped his pencil a little tighter. 'Weird, how?'

'The bass player was an old friend of hers from Leeds. He said she'd grown withdrawn and sullen recently. She'd stopped taking care of herself. Rehearsals fell apart. They couldn't even get one song recorded the whole way through.'

'He say what happened?'

'She would just lose it, he said. She'd be in the middle of a song and suddenly she'd be screaming and ripping off her headphones. She told them she heard voices whispering to her inside the music. Telling her to do things. They tried different headphones, changing frequencies in case they were picking up mobile signals, but it kept happening until Katrina was such a wreck they had to abandon the sessions.'

'He ask her what the voices said?'

'He did. Some rubbish about coming to claim her. I didn't put it in because it didn't seem relevant. I just assumed she'd flipped from too much skunk.'

Carrigan scraped his chair forward. 'She said those exact words? *Claim her*?'

Forsyth nodded.

'That's him. That's his phrase.' Carrigan looked down at his plate. 'I think he's done it again.'

Forsyth let out a dry snort. 'It's not whether he's done it again you should be asking yourself. It's how many times he's done it between Katrina and Anna.'

25

'This is a complete waste of time.'

Brown files covered the only table in the room. Carrigan had come back from lunch buzzing with the Katrina information. He'd tried to find Geneva but Geneva was out. He got stuck with Hoffmann instead. Now he wished he hadn't told the profiler about Forsyth's suspicion that there were more victims.

'I wasn't asking for your opinion.' Hoffmann took a long unhurried swallow of cappuccino, the foam flecking his top lip, setting off the dandruff in his eyebrows. 'The more data we can amass, the easier it will be to discern a pattern. You and I both know he's done this before, and I don't mean Katrina.'

Carrigan surveyed the table. Too much information could be as bad as too little. An investigation got weighed under by the profusion of leads as much as by their lack. Hoffmann had requested every female missing persons file from the Queensway area in the last five years. Carrigan had been staggered by the amount of paperwork they'd received – 4,268 files.

'I'm not arguing with that. I agree. It's highly likely he's done this before. And I know what you're looking for. But I don't think digging up the past is going to help us catch him. We already have several strong leads. We need to focus on Anna – she was his most recent and we're more likely to pick up a trace, electronic or otherwise, from his interactions with her.'

'This is just as important.' Hoffmann pointed to the files on the table. 'Don't you see? – Katrina changes everything. Previously we only had Anna to go by and we couldn't tell if she was chosen at random or not. Katrina answers that question. It means he's territorial. The hostel is the connection. There's no point looking into these girls' lives. It won't tell us anything about him. Only the bodies of his victims can do that. He's a hunter and they've strayed onto his territory. We need to widen the investigation.'

'No, we need to narrow it down.'

'How about we compromise and start by narrowing these down?' Hoffmann picked up a file at random and opened it. The first page held a photo, clipped to the original missing persons report. The rest of the file contained additional information on the subsequent investigation. Most of the time there was no investigation, no leads, no hope.

'We should begin by excluding all women that don't conform to his type.' Hoffmann skimmed pages. 'They always have a type and Anna and Katrina give us plenty to go on.'

With each assumption they made, the probability of it being accurate diminished and yet without making assumptions they would be stalled and stranded in the forest of data. It was the central paradox on which any investigation hinged. Carrigan looked at the stacked mounds of missing lives, took a file, and began.

They scanned photos. They flicked open folders and came face to face with a legion of lost women. They weeded out brunettes and redheads. They excluded non-Caucasians. They looked for facial similarities. Things the killer might have picked up on. After forty-five minutes they had 568 files left from the original 4,268. Still way too much. Carrigan checked the time and popped pills. As he put the foil back in his pocket, he caught Hoffmann watching him. The profiler quickly looked away without saying a word.

'It's still far too many,' Carrigan said, overwhelmed by the stories and testimonies he'd read. So many holes in so many people's lives. 'Besides, whatever we discover here isn't going to help us find him.'

'The more victims we can unearth and the more data sets we gather, the better chance we have of understanding him.'

'I don't need to understand him. I just need to catch him. God can do the rest.'

Hoffman crossed his arms and shook his head. 'I don't see how an intelligent man like you, with all you've seen, can still believe in God?'

'Most of the time, I don't understand it either.'

Hoffmann wrinkled his brow. 'What did your God do for them? What kind of God would allow this and this and this . . .' He pointed to each file in turn. 'And this to happen? Religion's just another coping mechanism. There's nothing beyond our world. It's ludicrous to suppose any different.'

'How can you live believing this is all there is?'

Hoffmann snorted. 'How can *you* live believing God would allow such a world to happen? History disproves God. The senselessness and suffering and violence and hatred. There is only now and I intend to enjoy every moment of it expressly because it's all there is.'

Carrigan wondered if there was another meaning behind the words. He examined the profiler, looking for any signs or tells, but you could read anything into almost any gesture or the lack thereof – yet, whenever Carrigan looked at him, he couldn't help but assess him as a man, as *she* would have done, and though he realised this was getting in the way of the investigation, he couldn't stop himself, not after so many years of wondering.

'Take this case,' Hoffmann continued. 'What kind of God allows a man like this to prey on women? Is that the kind of God you really want to worship? Perhaps you believe justice will be served when you catch him and lock him up for good, but that's not justice. The only justice would be the ability to bring the dead back to life and God hasn't been in that business for nearly two thousand years.'

Carrigan stared at the files, fighting the urge to get side-tracked into the argument. He wasn't sure if Hoffmann was goading him or if the profiler was always like this. He picked up a file, remembering Madison's account of the abduction. 'He spiked their drinks.' Carrigan started opening folders. 'And the two abductions we know of happened at night.'

They had to dig deeper this time, checking and corroborating timelines. They read until their eyeballs ached and the words swam off the page and across their hands, but after another hour and a half they had it down to forty-eight files. They split the files and began rereading them, a slow painstaking trawl through every badly typed sentence and scrawled note. Each spent an hour going through their own set then swapped to make sure they hadn't missed anything.

'How many do you think he's killed?'

Hoffmann tapped the file against the back of his hand. 'If I was guessing, I'd say four or five before Katrina. He would need roughly that level of practice to get this good at it.'

'And he's got away with it. That's only going to make him more confident.'

'It also means he's going to take more risks.'

'He's enjoying this, isn't he?'

'Yes. Yes, he is. But not in the way you think. He's not evil, he's simply programmed to feel like this. We demand explanations for evil and, sadly, all too often people in my profession and yours provide them, the abusive histories and substance-abuse cycles, but we forget that for some people killing is like sex or swimming. It's fun.'

'Everybody has a choice.'

Hoffmann shook his head. 'That's your easy way out, believing that. Yet all the latest research suggests evil may be no more than a chemical reaction inside our brains, a misfiring synapse. One we have no hope of controlling. How does your God fit into that? A faulty bit of wiring in your skull and you're Joseph Stalin or Jeffrey Dahmer.'

Was that all it really came down to? Carrigan wondered. A few defective neurons?

'You look for clues in the world,' Hoffmann said. 'But you forget that the greatest mystery is our own lives and yet it's the one mystery we can never hope to solve.'

Was that an admission?

Hoffmann couldn't possibly know because Louise never knew. Carrigan never had the chance to confront her. It was all over so quickly. He felt a muscle twitch in his cheek as he saw the profiler's manicured nails brush the top of a file and imagined those fingers . . . No. He had to stop thinking like that.

*

He'd discovered it by accident. Louise had been using his laptop that summer while waiting for hers to be repaired. He'd logged on to his email one morning but it wasn't his email. Louise had forgotten to log out. There were only two things in his life he regretted – that was a lie; there were many, but only two which stood out – taking the short cut in Uganda that lost him his two best friends and opening Louise's email.

It was wrong in every conceivable way. He'd known it at the time and he knew it now. But he'd been a cop too long to be able to resist, almost as if the job had snuck into his DNA and he resented it a little for changing him in this way.

They were lying in her inbox. There were so many of them. He would never have looked otherwise but Louise's inbox consisted primarily of emails from Ed Hoffmann.

He'd spent the next couple of hours reading through Hoffmann's emails and Louise's subsequent replies, a love affair conducted through electronic signals, though they'd also used it to arrange meetings and assignations, Carrigan's long hours on the job proving handy for once.

Louise's aching declarations of love utterly undid him – yet, at the same time, he was surprised to find that they also moved him in a way he could not explain nor control. He loved Louise more than he remembered loving anyone and to see the un-trammelled joy in her words made it impossible for him to hate her. Instead, he'd decided to leave. He made plans and ar-rangements. A few days later she came back from her doctor's appointment and that was that.

Carrigan snapped out of the past to see Hoffmann scrutin-ising him, a thin smile playing on the profiler's lips.

'You bastard.' Carrigan slammed the files down onto the

table at the same time the door to the incident room flew open and Geneva burst in, breathless and dishevelled. She stopped suddenly, her eyes darting from Carrigan to the profiler and back.

'Whatever it is I've disturbed, you boys can go back to it later.' She had a file clamped under her arm. 'You both need to see this.'

26

'The lab were able to fast track the trace evidence from the vial we found in the alley.' Geneva opened the file and tucked a stray hair behind her ear. She read out the list of chemicals the lab had isolated, evil and suffering reduced to precise medical notation. She saw Carrigan's face stiffen. It was obvious he and Hoffmann were avoiding each other, standing as far apart as they possibly could, stacks of files delineating a strict border between them. 'The liquid in the vial was a cocktail of several drugs. The main ingredients were DMT and LSD with trace amounts of ketamine, crystal meth and mephedrone, as well as several unknown compounds.'

'Jesus, that's bad.' Hoffmann scratched at the few hairs left on his skull and, for a brief moment, the air of indifferent authority surrounding him disappeared. 'These drugs are all hallucinogens to a greater or lesser degree. They're also known to cause severe time distortion. That's when they're ingested alone. God knows what combining them would do.' Hoffmann paused. 'You found this in the alley, right?'

Geneva nodded.

'He wouldn't have been that clumsy unless he wanted you to find it.'

'Why would he want that?'

'So we know how much Anna suffered before she died. Damn it.' Hoffmann closed his eyes. 'We've been looking at

174

this the wrong way around. He's not using the drugs to subdue them. He's using the drugs to torture them.'

Geneva remembered Madison scratching at herself in the interview room, the girl's eyes restless and flat, the sudden startling whimpers that had escaped her throat. 'How? What effects would they produce?'

'The DMT is particularly nasty. It was popular in the late sixties as a kind of beefed-up acid, a couple of hundred times more powerful. More importantly, of all the drugs we know about, DMT causes the greatest time distortion effects.'

'Time distortion?' Carrigan asked.

'You smoke or pop some DMT and you go on an incredibly intense trip, colours streaking by you, everything speeding up and slowing down simultaneously, everything happening all at once. Total sensory overload. It's like being trapped inside a kaleidoscope. You spend ten hours in this whirling chaos, unable to move, terrified out of your mind, holding on like you're on a rollercoaster ride from hell, and then the drugs wear off and you come back down to reality and look at your watch and only five minutes have passed.'

It took Carrigan a few seconds to fully comprehend this. 'People do it for fun?'

Hoffmann nodded. 'I'm guessing you've worked out the implications for our victims? He might have held Anna for only forty-eight hours but in her mind, under the influence of this, it would have felt like twenty years.'

'Twenty years? But he only had her for two days?' Geneva found the idea of it almost too vertiginous to accept.

'Not in her mind. In her mind, she lived through twenty years inside those forty-eight hours. Remember – time is relative. Time doesn't actually exist at all. It's the same as watching a film – if it's boring ninety minutes can seem like an eternity, but if it's great it'll go by in a flash. We know so little about time perception it's embarrassing. But we know certain drugs exacerbate its ebb and flow and that a person can go mad inside their own head in five minutes.'

'What about the other drugs?' Geneva made sure she was getting this down, the words clear and solid and logical, unlike the feeling in her gut.

'The LSD would enhance the visual side of the trip, maybe add some bad vibes to it. Ketamine's another nasty one. Used to be a horse tranquiliser. Gives people out-of-body experiences. Don't know if it worked like that for the horses but take enough K and you observe yourself from the other side of the room. The meth and mephedrone will induce feelings of dread, fear and terror. He might only have her for a few days but with these drugs he can torment her for years.'

There was silence as they made notes and stared into a sky cancelled by rain. Carrigan thought of his mother trapped inside her own skull – was she going through this kind of suffering? Like most things, it was better not to think about it. As you got older the unexamined life became the only one worth living.

Hoffmann gave the list of drugs back to Geneva. 'This is great. It tells us a lot more about why he does what he does.'

'It tells us nothing we didn't already know,' Carrigan snapped. 'Yes, he's a sick fuck. Yes, he's researched this and thought it through. We already know he's bright enough to mix these drugs and apply them without killing his victim. That's not what's important here. What we should be asking is why we found Anna but not Katrina. We've checked all unidentified dead females in London from the last six months but none of them are a match – so, where is she?'

'Maybe he's keeping her alive?' Geneva suggested. It had been the one possibility she hadn't wanted to consider but could avoid no longer. 'Perhaps in a house or a basement. Feeding her drugs and enjoying her prolonged suffering.'

'Keeping her is a lot more difficult than disposing of her body,' Hoffmann replied. 'It requires a totally different mindset. It would be too hard, logistically, to hold her captive somewhere like London.'

'I'm aware of that,' Geneva said. 'And yet Ariel Castro managed to keep three women for ten years in his cellar in downtown Cleveland. John Jamelske kept an entire stable of girls in his bunker in Syracuse.'

'Yes, but that's different. They were—'

'Look,' Carrigan interrupted. 'This may sound crazy, but are we even talking about the same killer? I know the MO is similar and both victims were staying at the hostel but is it possible we have two different killers? That we've been seduced into seeing him as one because of this similarity rather than the obvious dissimilarities?'

Hoffmann closed his eyes and thought about it. 'It would be too much of a coincidence,' he said. 'The MO is too specific. It's much more likely he's escalating. We know all serial killers do this. They continually refine their fantasies. They get better at knowing what they like. They get cleverer at evading us. Maybe killing Katrina and burying her in an unmarked grave wasn't enough. Maybe he felt an overwhelming emptiness when she was gone. So, this time, he leaves Anna in plain sight.

She may be dead but now he's watching the news, watching us, keeping track and keeping score. The kill lasts much longer this way but he'll also be profiling his next victim. I wouldn't be at all surprised if he was already trolling her on Twitter, laying out the bait, getting her softened up and broken down.'

'Profiling her?' Geneva opened a can of Coke.

'Serial killers profile their victims just the same as we do. You see it especially in hunter types like this one. They can smell loneliness and vulnerability. They can look across a crowded room and know immediately which of the women to go for – but what makes your killer much more interesting is that both victims were described by their friends as being assertive and strong.'

'And predators always go for the weak and strays?' Carrigan said.

'Exactly. That's what makes this one so unusual. He searches specifically for assertive women, probably through their social media presence, and he does this expressly so he can break them down. He starts with the tweets, then escalates to photos and threats. It's a challenge for him – what's the point in targeting someone who's already frail? Much more sport in going after the lion than the gazelle. Social media allows him to pick out women with those characteristics. It allows him to learn a great deal about them and to track their movements and their inter-actions with others.'

'Sometimes I think it's almost as if the Internet was designed expressly with stalkers and sex fiends in mind,' Geneva said.

Hoffmann laughed softly. 'It may seem so, but humans have been very good at adapting technology to their own secret needs for thousands of years. No, what's new is the profile.

We're seeing a type of killer we haven't come across before. The Internet has transformed their pathology as well as their MO. Doesn't matter if the cause is world jihad, white supremacy or a schoolyard grudge that ends with a class full of dead kids – the profile's the same. Our killer will be very smart, mendacious and obviously computer savvy. He'll pretend to be older, have an obsessive need to tinker, and above all, he'll be convinced he's right, which means he'll have no moral limits, everything he does will be rationalised as necessary.

'But you know all this. This hasn't changed. There have always been unfulfilled men hiding in small rooms, disenchanted with the promise of their lives, harbouring feelings of inadequacy and filled with a yearning to solve history through one grand act. But now, they sit seething behind their screens, planning intricate and terrible atrocities, and no matter how extreme their views, they can instantly find thousands of like-minded followers – and then the echo chamber goes into effect and they become even more radicalised, until one day they turn off the computer and hit the streets. We'll be seeing more and more of this – in bus stations and festivals, beaches, parks and schools – Breiviks of the world, unite, you have nothing to lose but your modems.'

Hoffmann smiled and Carrigan was annoyed to find himself agreeing with the profiler. Luckily, his phone rang before he could reply. He listened to what Berman had to say then flipped open his laptop.

'We just got an email from Anna's account.' Carrigan looked up and saw Geneva and Hoffmann had moved closer. 'There's nothing in the email apart from a link.' Carrigan hovered over the long string of meaningless consonants and random numbers and clicked.

The screen refreshed and an embedded video player appeared on an otherwise blank page. Carrigan pressed PLAY.

They saw a room. An old woman on the phone. Ancient Christmas decorations and a grandfather clock ticking in the background. The speakers burst into life and the woman's voice cracked like a whip.

'*Ja!*'

Carrigan watched Anna's mother nodding and assimilating the information he was giving her over the phone. He knew what was coming next and he gripped the edge of the chair as it came. Anna's mother dropped the handset mid-sentence and collapsed to her knees. A man hurried across the room and helped her up. He asked her something in German. The woman shook her head. The man picked up the phone. 'Who is this?'

Hoffmann leaned forward, propping his elbows on his knees. 'Jesus. He filmed them receiving the death notice.'

They continued watching as Anna's father listened to Carrigan's message, the old man nodding, mute and rock-faced, the tears streaming down his cheeks. He put down the phone and knelt by his wife. She opened her arms and he folded himself into her. The two held each other and sobbed and shook their heads as the minutes quietly slipped from the grandfather clock.

27

The incident room. A late afternoon lull. Departing bodies and unanswered phones. Geneva sat at her table, cocooned by lights. She tried to focus on her research into the hostel's history but all she could think about was the sight of Anna's parents curled up on the floor of their living room.

They'd watched the clip several times, Carrigan repeatedly stealing glances at Hoffmann, the air between them thick with unspoken history. Hoffmann speculated that targeting the families was something important they'd missed but Geneva suspected it was more than that. The clip had set something clicking inside her brain. She tried to focus on her task. She printed off web pages and bookmarked sites. She ran searches and checked links. A decade ago, this kind of work would have taken a week – visits to the library, the town hall, the newspaper morgue – but now it was available at the click of a button. Doors slammed outside, banter and laughter and the wheeze of the coffee machine. She shut it out, pumped the stress ball and focused on the material in front of her. Her phone pinged before she'd got to the end of the first page. Her gut clamped shut as she stared at the caller ID, the contained anxiety of the last few months rising inside her.

'Miller.'

Her lawyer sounded distracted as if he had more important things to do while talking to her, which he undoubtedly did. 'I have some good news for you.'

'That would be a first.'

The ensuing silence was threaded with crackle. 'There's no need for that. In fact, the reason I was calling was to inform you that as of today we're no longer going to be representing you.'

Geneva took a deep breath. 'You're dropping the case?'

The lawyer laughed softly. She imagined him sitting behind a curving mahogany desk, so buffed you could see your reflection in it, drinks and briefs spread out in front of him, a secretary simpering in the wings.

'Quite the opposite, actually,' he replied. 'It's your ex-husband who's dropped the case. Remarkable, frankly, when it was obvious to everyone involved he was going to win, but then, I suppose one can never underestimate the vagaries of the heart.'

The line went dead. Geneva stared at the phone as if it were an hallucination conjured up out of hope and need. She was suing her ex-husband, Oliver, over the proceeds from the sale of the house they'd called home for five years. Had the solicitor really said Oliver was dropping the case after three years of aggressively defending it? It didn't make sense and Oliver never did anything that didn't make sense.

The rain lashed the windowpanes in soft smacking kisses. She pushed Oliver to the back of her mind and dialled Carrigan's extension.

'I need to check something at the Milgram,' she said.

'You're calling for my approval?'

'No. I'm calling because I thought you might like to come. The clip of Anna's parents reminded me of something.'

'Are you going to tell me what it is?'

'No. I'm going to show you.'

Carrigan got out of the car and waited for Geneva to finish her cigarette. He studied the tall dark upthrust of the Milgram as it towered above the neighbouring houses. From out here, the hostel seemed contained and knowable, but once you were inside, it was a different matter.

'See what I mean?' There was no one on the front desk. Geneva craned her neck and scanned the ceiling. 'Anyone can just walk in.' She stopped to scrutinise a small black speck in the far right corner. She took out her phone, snapped several shots then examined them, zooming in and flicking back and forth until she was satisfied. She put the phone back in her pocket and they made their way upstairs.

'Look. I was going to find some subtle, clever way to bring this up but there's too much going on and I haven't got the time, so please, tell me – what the fuck is up with you and Hoffmann?'

Carrigan stopped. The stairs receded into the far distance. 'This is our case and we can handle it perfectly well by ourselves.'

Geneva crossed her arms, blocking his passage. 'Bullshit. I saw your face when he first came in. You recognised him. And I've noticed the way he acts whenever he's near you. He gets uncomfortable, his voice drops and he overcompensates.'

'Are you profiling him now?'

'No. I'm trying to understand what history the two of you share and how it's going to affect the case.'

'I met him for the first time yesterday.'

'Fine, if that's how you want it – but whatever it is, you two need to work it out. It's having an impact on the investigation.'

'My personal problems are not important right now.'

Geneva uncrossed her arms and took a step back. 'You know you can talk to me?'

Carrigan smiled. 'I know and I appreciate that. But right now I'd rather you tell me what you found out about the hostel.'

Geneva started back up the stairs knowing that, for now, this was all she was going to get. 'There was nothing useful or relevant. The usual ODs, suicides and accidental deaths you'd expect in a place like this.' She turned into another dust-speckled corridor. It was only now that she realised how tense she'd been since the solicitor's phone call. She should have been relieved by the news but she wasn't. What the fuck was Oliver up to?

They ascended the last set of stairs and emerged on the fifth-floor landing. They ducked under the crime-scene tape. The door to Anna and Madison's dorm was unlocked. The drop in temperature was instant. Geneva checked the windows to see if the SOCOs had wrenched them open but they were still tightly sealed. Light from another dorm spilled across the courtyard and through the windows. Anna and Madison's beds, snug and neatly made, waited patiently for their former occupants.

Carrigan surveyed the room. It was exactly as it had been the day before. He looked up at the ceiling, the walls and window frames, thinking back to what Geneva had told him in the car. 'You really think he was watching Anna?'

'You seriously reckon he wasn't?' Geneva said. 'There's got to be cameras in here. It's what the evidence points to – you saw the tape of her parents.'

Carrigan nodded, thinking how quaint that we still called it a tape, as if we were too terrified of the onrushing future we had to cling to recondite names in the vain hope of holding it back.

'It's the only thing which makes sense,' Geneva continued. 'He has to watch. To see the effect of his actions. He wouldn't be able to resist. It's what he needs to do for this to be meaningful to him. More so, it's a natural progression from the Twitter trolling. Someone who has the patience to do that, who feeds them exactly the right cocktail of drugs to exacerbate their fear – someone like that wouldn't be content without seeing the results of his actions. If he went to the trouble of filming Anna's parents receiving the news of her death, you really think he wouldn't keep her dorm under surveillance?'

'He went all the way to Germany to plant those cameras?'

'From everything we've so far gathered about him, I'd say yes. He's patient and methodical and he enjoys watching. In his mind it would be worth the trouble and expense. He can watch this feed over and over again until their grief wears out.'

'It never does.'

Geneva stopped, noticing the crease in Carrigan's forehead. 'You still miss Louise that much?'

'It gets worse every year. That thing they tell you about time healing all wounds, it's bullshit – only the cessation of time can do that.'

They began searching from the back of the room. Geneva aimed her torch into corners and behind dado rails. They searched every wall and joint. Every stain or mark was scrutinised until they were satisfied it was nothing more than stain or mark. They checked bookshelves and books, light fittings and doorframes. Under the bed and behind the posters. They studied the TV set and ran their fingers along the sides of mirrors and across skirting boards. They looked between the dark accordioned spines of radiators and along the burnished edges of wardrobes. They scoured windowsills and electrical sockets but found nothing to substantiate Geneva's theory.

'Maybe he removed the cameras when he came for the passport photo?'

Carrigan shook his head. 'We'd have found traces.'

A door banged downstairs. A conversation in Urdu floated into hearing then just as quickly receded. The lights flickered on and off. Geneva felt her skin tingle and goosebumps burst out along her arms. She quickly turned her head, certain that someone was watching her from the corner of the room, but it was only the curtains flapping, throwing shadows against the wall.

'The sooner we're out of here the better.' Geneva watched the shadows flicker, keeping an eye on them. 'Maybe we can grab a coffee?'

Carrigan looked out the window at the storm-tossed trees, the branches rattling like arthritic limbs. 'I'd love to but I need to get back to the station.'

'Branch?'

Carrigan shook his head. 'DPS.'

'They asked you to go to them? You told me this wasn't serious?'

'It's not.' It was a lie but it felt good to say it, a necessary distancing, even if only for himself.

'That's crap. I can see it in your face. Whatever it is, I can help.'

Carrigan smiled. 'I appreciate it, but for the moment you're off Quinn's radar and that's how I want to keep it.'

Geneva looked at him for a long moment. A fly buzzed close to her ear, the sudden rush of noise like a drill starting up. They resumed their search in silence, pulling up rugs and peering behind curling wallpaper. Geneva stood on a chair and aimed her torch at the ceiling. There were specks of random dirt, dead insects, brown stains, but no cameras.

28

Carrigan sat on the hard metal chair and thought about all the times this scene had been reversed. It was supposed to be an informal chat but Patterson had taken him straight to this room deep in the heart of the DPS. Even though the recording equipment was off, Patterson and his partner, Larkin, were making their intentions very clear.

Carrigan checked his watch. He thought about the case. He thought about his mother languishing between worlds. 'Look. I know what this is about and why you—'

'DI Carrigan. Please speak only when you're answering a question. I'm sure we both want this to be as brief as possible.'

'You told me this was meant to be an informal chat.' Carrigan studied Patterson. He was young and smoothly shaven and wore a suit that stuck to his body like cling film. Larkin was playing bad cop, skulking in his chair, seemingly bored by the proceedings, but Carrigan could see flashes of intelligence behind his eyes and knew he was the one to watch.

Patterson chuckled, revealing perfect white teeth. 'Oh, I assure you, this is exactly that. You haven't been cautioned yet, have you? Haven't been told to bring in your rep?'

Carrigan bit his lip and kept his mouth shut.

Patterson pulled out a file and from it, several sheets of paper. He pretended to be reading from one of them but his eyes didn't move. 'Did you order a member of your team to illegally gain access to the diocese of Westminster's electronic database on 18 December 2013?'

Carrigan had thought long and hard about how to answer but in the end there was only one answer he could truthfully give. 'It was the most efficient way to pursue the investigation.'

'I didn't ask why you did it.'

'But that's the point.'

'No, it isn't,' Patterson said. 'And you should know better than that. Have you had your head in the sand these past few years? Good men, better policemen than you, are in prison over exactly this.'

'This isn't the same.'

Patterson let out a weary sigh. 'Take a moment and listen to yourself, Carrigan. You sound like any scrote suspect down-stairs.'

'The diocese lied,' Carrigan said. 'They impeded a murder investigation, a multiple murder of their own nuns.'

'So you and DC Berman thought that justified breaking the law, did you?'

'Berman had nothing to do with this.'

Patterson smiled. 'You're familiar with code? You can hack into a secure system all by yourself?'

'I ordered him to. He had no choice.'

'He had a choice. He could have said no and reported back to us. But we're not here to talk about him. He'll get what he deserves, no more, no less.' Patterson cleared some papers from his desk. 'Were you aware at the time that unauthorised access into a private server constitutes a crime?'

'Oh, come on . . .'

'Just answer the question. Were you?'

'Yes. I was.'

Patterson's lips twitched as he looked down at his sheet of questions. 'Did your intrusion into the database directly result in the apprehension of a subject?'

'That's not how it works and you know it. Each piece adds to the puzzle.'

'Yes or no?'

'No.'

'How long have you been a policeman?'

'Is that a serious question?'

'It was a rhetorical one, Carrigan, meant to indicate you should have known better. This is a different world from the one you and I came up in. The things we used to get away with, the corners we used to cut – you simply can't do that any more. Every single action you take is recorded and stored for later analysis. Anyone who doesn't understand this has no place in today's Met.'

Ironically, Carrigan thought, Berman hadn't left any traces – the leak had come from someone in the room. The weakest link was always the person standing right next to you.

'You do understand why these rules were put in place?'

'I'm not an idiot.'

'Then why behave like one?'

Carrigan sighed. 'If you were a proper cop you'd understand – you have to make snap decisions. All this data's hurtling around your head – facts, speculations, divergent theories, disagreements. You have to do whatever's necessary to push the investigation forward, to make sure it doesn't lose momentum and stall.'

Patterson nodded. 'Other DIs manage to solve their cases

without resorting to breaking the law. Perhaps you should consider whether you're really cut out to be a policeman?'

Carrigan laughed.

'What's so funny?'

'I think about it all the time.'

'I'm glad you can find some absurdity in this situation.'

'This entire thing is absurd.' Carrigan shook his head, got up and slammed the door behind him.

29

As soon as she got back to the station, Geneva sought out Berman. The discrepancy between what she knew and what they'd found, or rather not found in the hostel, was bothering her. It didn't make sense.

Berman was at his desk, spooning yoghurt into his mouth, his eyes glued to a waterfall of numbers cascading down the screen.

'That some kind of geek Sudoku?'

Berman blinked twice. 'Actually, you're not that far off.' He laughed, spinning his chair towards her. 'It's the seventy-two names of God.'

Geneva craned her neck and scanned the screen. 'He has that many?'

Berman smiled. 'None of them are His real name but, somewhere in this text, exists an intersection of letters that reveal the true name and therefore nature of God.'

'What? God is a computer program?'

Berman shrugged. 'Why not? Take us, for example, our DNA – what is it? Just a string of coded commands that allows the program to run for an indefinite period. It's like that old joke about boffins spending decades building the perfect computer and when they finally manage it, they realise it's us – human beings.'

Geneva stared at the screen, seduced by the calm precision of numbers. 'Well, I'm sorry to drag you away from theology and back down to earth, but I was wondering what kind of spy cameras people would use these days. What do I need to be on the lookout for?'

Berman seemed to find this funny. 'No one uses cams any more. That's so last century.'

Geneva sat down. She explained her theory about the women being watched and how they'd searched every part of the dorm but hadn't found any corroborating evidence. 'What do they use instead of cameras?'

'Your own computer.' Berman pointed to the top of his screen, the almost invisible convex camera eye. 'They turn your own laptop against you. Same principle as a police state. Why bother with elaborate spy devices when you can get the next-door neighbours to listen and inform? Much easier and more effective than installing cameras. Besides, a camera just gives you images – this lets you into every corner of someone else's life.' Berman clicked open several windows simultaneously and began typing.

'But they'd still need to get into her room, right? To modify the laptop?' She was thinking of the weak security and lack of CCTV in the hostel, how easy it would be, but Berman was once more shaking his head.

'You can do it from anywhere. It's called Ratting.'

'Ratting? Jesus. As in rats?' A shudder went through the back of her legs.

'It stands for Remote Access Technology or Remote Administration Tools, whichever you prefer. Same as when you've got a problem with your computer, call the helpline, and the tech at the other end takes control of your screen to fix it. Except, of course, this is non-consensual.'

Geneva nodded and made notes. A new world was being mapped out, invisibly and everywhere at all times. Pundits claimed the Internet had freed us but all she could see was a place where people argued and fought and hated. The world was splitting into discrete blocks of enmity. That was nothing new. The ability to do it twenty-four hours a day was. 'Explain to me how this Ratting thing's done.'

Berman spun away from the screen. 'You have your laptop?'

She went over to her desk and got it.

'Just start it up and do your usual thing.'

Geneva opened her inbox and immediately knew it had been a mistake. Her entire avoided and saved-for-later life was lying in wait. The list of unopened emails scrolled below the visible screen. The most recent message was from Jim. She was about to open it when a new email landed in her spam folder. It promised her untold Central African wealth in a fortnight. She deleted it without opening and switched back to the inbox.

It was gone.

All her emails had disappeared. The page was empty. She refreshed it several times but nothing changed. She clicked the SENT folder but it too was empty.

'That's how easy it is,' Berman said, a wide grin cracking his face.

'Easy for you, maybe.' Geneva balanced the laptop on her knees. 'How much tech knowledge would someone need to do this?'

'Not very much. Everything's on the web in step-by-step guides. From smallpox to IEDs to this. You can download RAT programs off the dark web for free.'

'Lovely.' Geneva glanced down at her laptop and saw, with a

slight slump of disappointment, that her emails had returned. She'd briefly considered using this as an excuse for not getting back to people, but miracles, she found, rarely lasted very long. 'Be a good way to steal someone's financial details, right?'

Berman shook his head. 'The point of identity theft is the victim doesn't know it's happened. The longer they don't realise, the more can be milked from their accounts. Ratting is the opposite. Ratting is all about intrusion.'

She stared at the screen, wondering whether for every benefit technology bestowed there was a corresponding evil? Or was it simply that human hearts had the gift of turning everything to their own dark slidings?

'This fits in with the trolling,' Berman explained. 'Same kind of tech skills, same kind of pathology – Ratting would be the next logical step.'

'Was thinking that myself,' Geneva replied. 'I know I probably don't want to hear this but what do people use Ratting for?'

'Spying on chicks,' Berman said, a sardonic twist to each word. 'The hacking community is predominantly male so victims of Ratting are, predictably, almost exclusively female. The Ratter finds his chosen one's email address. Easy to do with Facebook, Twitter, all the stuff we pour onto the net every day. It's a fitting name because that's exactly what it is – a net – to catch all our secrets and wishes and sell them to the highest bidder. He then sends her an obviously spam email like the one I sent you. She instantly deletes it just as you did. That sets off a worm that lets him take control of the computer remotely.'

'What do they do once they're inside?' Even the terminology was making Geneva acutely uncomfortable.

'The most popular use of Ratting is switching on someone's

webcam and filming them. As long as the computer's on, they can see and record anything occurring within the camera's frame. Plus, if he's inside your system, he'll know everything about you – it gives him untold power and control.'

'Wouldn't you notice the webcam light?'

'The RAT programs disable it. The Ratters also like to mess with you. They delete emails like I did, or disable programs, change the screensaver, the colour of your desktop. You'll be on your favourite website and suddenly twenty windows of Lassie porn will pop open.'

Geneva thought about this and how it slotted in to what they already knew about their killer. 'And they film the reaction?'

'Exactly. They post the clips on specialised Ratting forums as trophies.'

Geneva could only shake her head. This was the face of twenty-first-century voyeurism. Technology had made it exponentially worse. The whole world was now witness to your humiliation. 'We need to have a look at these forums. We need to see if Anna is—'

Berman was smiling.

'What?'

'Way beyond my capabilities. One mistake and they'd shut everything down and burn the data. You need to talk to someone in computer crime – they deal with these things and might already have an in to Ratting forums.' He wrote down a number and passed it over. 'DS Neilson's a friend. Talk to her. But you should ask yourself whether you really want to do this. I worked in computer crime three months. I saw things I never thought I'd see. That's why I transferred here. A dead body is easier to assimilate than someone alive in hell.'

30

The Last Good Kiss was packed, a heavy pulsating throb of
bodies and bass notes trembling the dancefloor. He'd received
the bartender's text ten minutes ago: *He's here.* Carrigan approached the bar. Alexi gestured towards a booth up against
the far wall occupied by a porcine middle-aged man and a pale
young girl.

Carrigan tried to shut out the screechy music and swirling
bodies as he made his way to the booth.

The girl was even younger than he'd initially thought, eighteen or nineteen, awkward, pimply and puppy fat. Her big blue
eyes were captivated by the man sitting opposite her. He had a
straggly comb-over, as if someone had painted three horizon-
tal stripes across his skull, a neatly clipped grey moustache and
piercing green eyes. He was wearing a double-breasted cream
suit which bulged at the middle, revealing a perfectly spherical
and enormous belly. Coarse black hair sprouted from his cuffs
and spidered his knuckles. Neither he nor the girl noticed Carrigan standing beside them.

'You should find someone your own age to hang out with.'
Carrigan bent down so they could both hear him. 'They'll be a
whole lot more fun, I guarantee it.'

The girl looked over at the man. Something passed
between them and the man began to rise. Carrigan placed
a hand on his shoulder and gently pressed him back down.

'Not you. You're staying here.'

The girl shot Carrigan a glare then picked up her handbag and left. The man's eyes tracked the sway of her behind as she slalomed across the dancefloor and found a seat at the bar.

He turned to face Carrigan. 'What the hell do you think you're doing?'

'I was just going to ask you the same question.' Carrigan slid into the seat the girl had vacated. It reeked of cheap perfume. He moved a lipsticked champagne glass out of the way. The man sitting opposite him was drinking orange juice. He tried to slide out of the booth but Carrigan shook his head and flicked open his warrant card.

'What's your name?'

'Farouk.'

Carrigan took out the photo of Anna and Madison and placed it next to the orange juice. The man looked down then quickly looked back up.

'Do you recognise them?'

Farouk's gaze drifted towards the bar, searching for the girl, trying to comprehend how life could so quickly go from that to this.

Carrigan slammed his fist on the table. The glasses jumped. 'Stop looking at the girls and look at this.' He pushed the photo across.

Farouk glanced down. 'I don't know them.'

'Never seen them before, huh?'

Farouk smiled and shrugged, mock innocence a strange fit on his face.

'That's funny, because I have someone who saw you trying to chat them up on Friday night.'

Farouk pushed himself into the booth's soft leather as far back as he could go. 'I don't know what you're talking about.'

'Of course not.' Carrigan pulled the morgue shot of Anna from his pocket. He laid it next to the other photo.

The man blinked twice and turned the photo over, his hands trembling. 'What . . . what is this?'

'I think you know exactly what this is.'

Farouk scooped up a handful of pistachio nuts from a bowl to his right. 'I know nothing about this.'

Carrigan took a deep breath. 'Anna Becker was murdered. She was abducted from the alley behind this bar on Friday night and I have someone who remembers you trying to chat her up that evening. Who remembers her laughing at you and you cursing her as you walked away. All of which doesn't look too good for you.'

Farouk took this in, his eyes shrinking further into their sockets, and when Carrigan was finished he put his head in his hands and exhaled slowly.

'Do you still maintain you've never seen them?'

It took a good few seconds for Farouk to shake his head.

'You come here often to pick up girls?'

'There's no law against it.'

Carrigan looked towards the bar. The girl who'd been sitting with Farouk was now laughing at something another man said. 'What does a girl like that see in someone like you?'

Farouk's laughter surprised him. 'You really have no idea, do you?' He clicked open a pistachio shell with long curved fingernails. 'You think we force these girls to come here? There's a hundred other places they can go, cheaper drinks, better music, but still they come here and they come here for the same reason we do.' He popped the stripped nut into his mouth. 'These girls are the ones who understand the world better than their friends. What can a man their age give them? A night in the pub, a film and a takeaway? I can take them to the finest restaurants, restaurants so good they're not even listed. Or take them shopping, say buy yourself a small gift, whatever pleases you . . . a weekend in Marrakech, a month in Dubai. You think men their age can offer them that?'

Carrigan looked around the room and saw the same demographic repeated everywhere. 'And in return they have to sleep with you?'

'It's their choice what they do.' Farouk clicked open another shell. 'Women in this country are free to do what they please, are they not?'

Carrigan let that pass. 'It must have made you furious then, when these two brushed you off? After all, if that's not what they were after, what were they doing here in the first place, right?'

'That's not what happened.'

Carrigan leant forward until he was breathing into Farouk's face. 'Either you tell me what happened now or you tell me tomorrow morning after a night in the cells.'

Farouk dropped the remainder of the nuts onto the table. 'I saw them come in,' he said. 'They looked so young and happy, I thought, why not? I offered to buy them a drink but they said no.'

'And a man like you . . . you didn't like that, did you?'

A small vein ticked under Farouk's right eyebrow.

'They laughed at you in front of everyone. Humiliated you.'

Farouk shook his head violently but Carrigan continued. 'It

made you feel like doing something to them. Something to make them feel the way they made you feel. Like dirt. Like garbage. Like shit.'

Farouk's grip on the armrest tightened. 'That's not the way it was. It has nothing to do with that. We had a small disagreement. That's all.'

'A disagreement about what?'

'Nothing. It doesn't matter.'

'It matters to me.'

Farouk looked down at the empty shells. 'I thought I recognised one of the girls.'

'What?' It wasn't what Carrigan had been expecting to hear.

'I was asking them if they wanted to come over to my booth. It was pretty obvious they weren't interested and that's okay, there's plenty more girls, so I'm telling them one last joke and about to say my goodbyes when I recognised one of them.'

The music and lights and dancing stopped. 'Which one?'

'Her.'

Farouk pointed to Anna.

'We were talking and I kept looking at her. She seemed so familiar but I couldn't tell if I'd seen her on TV, met her here, or if she just resembled some girl I once knew. I said something like *Haven't we met before?* but, of course, she thought it was a chat-up line. I kept insisting I knew her from somewhere and that's when she went crazy. Telling me to back off. Knocking over my drink. Calling me a liar. That girl was not right in the head. A troubled girl. Even her friend was shocked by her outburst, told her to forget it. So yes, I said some words, perhaps not so kind, as I walked off. She didn't need to be that rude.'

Carrigan tried to keep his handwriting steady as he noted it down. 'Did you eventually remember where you recognised her from?'

Farouk looked at the constellation of shells starring the table.

'Where was it?'

Farouk wiped his nose with his sleeve. There was a yellow stain where he'd performed the same action countless times before. 'The Internet.'

'That's a big place. Stop fucking around and tell me.'

'Sites . . .'

'Sites? What kind of sites?'

'Sites with women on them.'

31

She had to try the key three times before the lock agreed to co-operate. Her flat felt damp and musty. The living room was silent and strangely comforting and for a moment Geneva simply stood, letting the chatter and spark of the last few hours dissolve into the thick darkness, but she couldn't stop thinking about the solicitor's phone call. Oliver never gave up. It made him a brilliant lawyer and a terrible husband. Dropping the case meant he'd have to pay back her share of the house sale. Why would he do that?

She flung open windows and felt the air rush across her skin. There were no messages from Jim and several from her mother. She deleted them all. She knew what her mum was going to say, these things never changed, the way parents still saw you in shorts and smudged face even when you were approaching your forties. She would have to call her mother back but not tonight. She heated up a supermarket pizza and ate it while flicking through the news – Snowden in Moscow, Assange cowering in a broom cupboard in London, chemical rain on Raqqa and tanks on the Steppe, torture, execution, corruption and economic failure. All over the world, millions of little lights were going out.

There was nothing new in all this. Men had always found fresh and devious ways to kill other men, children were always dying and women were always being exploited. What had changed was that everyone now owned a camera and every possible evil, every gang rape and supermarket bomb, disease and natural disaster was on film, endlessly repeated to an audience who could do nothing but watch and seethe.

She switched it off and lay in bed, unable to sleep, staring at the ceiling and trying not to think about what was lying in her desk drawer.

After an hour of telling herself she wouldn't, she got up, headed to her desk and took the small baggie of weed from the drawer. She opened the seal and a rich, ripe smell rushed up to greet her, setting off a thousand memorysnaps. She knew it was wrong, against the law, worse for her than for other people, but the alternative was spending the entire night staring at the ceiling then coming into work tired and grouchy, missing something important and getting the next girl killed.

She didn't have any papers so she unpacked one of her cigarettes, crumbled the sticky weed and mixed it in with the tobacco then carefully funnelled it back into the cigarette. She put on some Pavement, loud swervy grooves and fucked-up rhythms that suited her mood perfectly. She smoked the joint down to the filter, her body feeling weightless, went to bed and fell asleep instantly.

In the dream she was traversing endless corridors and a bell was ringing. A loud, insistent pulse that followed her through the black hallways until she found the room that held her father. But the door wouldn't open and the ringing wouldn't stop. She snapped awake and sat up in bed but the ringing still didn't stop. It was coming from somewhere inside her flat. Her heartbeat snickered up her throat as she reached under the bed for her spare baton.

Trying to make as little noise as possible, Geneva shook off the sheets and crossed the room. Slowly, she turned the handle and nudged the door open. The ringing was instantly louder. She waited for some errant shape or figure to rush the bedroom but there was nothing. She flicked the baton so that it extended to its full length and entered the hallway.

She looked left towards the living room. The corridor was empty and seemed undisturbed. The alarm was making it hard for her to isolate any untoward sounds. She slowly made her way to the living room and kicked the door open with the point of her foot. She stood back and surveyed the room but nothing looked out of place.

She checked the kitchen last. The ringing doubled in volume when she opened the door. She shook her head and dropped the baton when she saw what was making the noise.

She crossed the tiny room and turned off the oven. The alarm stopped but a faint ghostly echo continued in her ear. Had she forgotten to switch it off after taking out her pizza? It was possible but why was the alarm ringing? She hadn't set the timer. In fact, she couldn't remember ever having used the timer in the three years she'd lived here. She stared at the oven's dark mouth for several minutes then went back to bed, keeping the baton pressed to her body throughout the night like a wayward lover's arm.

32

Carrigan spent an hour uploading files onto his computer when he got home. It was his usual routine, a way to unravel from the day's adrenaline, but tonight it wasn't working. The mountain of photocopied reports beside his desk never got smaller no matter how much work he put in. There were always more cases, more people lost to the world and never coming back. He tagged body types. Weapons. Locations. Timeframes. Wounds. The more data you inputted, the more connections showed up. Everything was linked, if not in one way then in another.

A strange, lopsided melody began to play inside his head, slashing guitars and a woman singing about dead oceans. He had no idea where he'd heard it before but it kept him company as he opened a new document and began writing up a report of his interview with Farouk. After a little encouragement, Farouk had provided more detail. Carrigan had assumed Farouk meant porn sites but he hadn't meant that at all.

Farouk apologised for not remembering which site he'd seen Anna on. He said he flicked through so many every day, viewed so many different girls, that it was impossible to tell where a particular one came from. But he remembered the clip. With the honed eye of a stalker or novelist he recalled details most people wouldn't have even noticed. He said the quality wasn't very good, grainy and dark with no close-ups. He said he only remembered it because there was something strange about the clip, something he couldn't quite put his finger on but which had made him uneasy enough to turn it off. Farouk swore there was no sex in the clip, that he didn't use the Internet for sex, that it was reserved for rarer pleasures.

Carrigan completed the report, emailed it to Branch and scanned his inbox. Hoffmann had sent his preliminary profile through. The sight of the profiler's name at the head of the email pulled Carrigan back through five years as if they'd been nothing but a momentary dream. He thought he'd come to terms with everything that had happened but, of course, he hadn't. Hoffmann's surprise appearance was yet another bump he'd not seen coming. He couldn't tell if it was coincidence or a cruel joke played on him by Quinn.

The song kept repeating in his head, frustratingly familiar yet just out of reach, and he caught himself humming the melody as he made his way to the kitchen. There was nothing in the fridge, but in one of the cupboards sat a bottle of Wild Turkey he couldn't remember buying. The first drink burned his throat. The second was much better. He had several more, skimming the profiler's report, but all he could think about was that day five years ago.

It had been a while since he'd got this drunk and he'd forgotten how the past could swerve and spin and surprise you with such impossible clarity. He saw Louise's face in stunning detail, the erasures of time supplanted; memory, as always, failing the very thing it strives to protect. He remembered her on that first day, in the slicing wind off the East River and as she was in those final weeks, curled up into the bareness of herself. He saw the sofa she used to sit on, the dog they loved and raised and lost, the daughter they never had – she'd be eighteen now, tall, arch and geeky, a girl of her generation, shopping together for an iPad to take to college, and it made him think of Anna and Katrina, both trying to make their way in the city, enflamed by art and life but, in the end, finding only suffering and death.

And suddenly he knew exactly where he'd heard the song before.

He went to Katrina's website, found the page containing sound files and clicked the second track down. The music was strangely intimate, the dead girl's voice filling the yawning emptiness of his flat. He played it twice and, as he did so, he scanned the band's Bio and Blog pages. In the past, you very rarely got to know the victims – all you had were the tainted testimonies of those close to them, but now you could read their actual words, hear them speak and see how they inter-acted with the world, their little jokes and snaps of rage. In one way, it made the investigation easier, but it also made it that much harder.

Carrigan put the song on repeat and flicked through the site, seeing the tributes fans and friends had put up, reading through the band's gigography and staring at photos of Katrina screaming into a microphone at various concerts throughout the capital.

Below the pictures was a set of links. One for each member of the band. Next to Katrina's name was the Twitter symbol, followed by Facebook and Flickr. Carrigan clicked on the first link but Katrina's Twitter account had been deleted. He wondered whether the killer had also targeted her through so-cial media. Her Facebook page had been inactive since she'd disappeared. He made a note to get Berman to look into it first thing tomorrow then clicked on the Flickr link.

Katrina had posted 1,345 photos in the previous two years and she had a good eye for composition; most looked professional, whether of a sunset over Silvertown or the band rehearsing at a rain-soaked festival in Frankfurt. It was the vast number of photos that surprised him. Carrigan had only ten or twenty from his own youth, cameras being expensive and clunky back then, and he wondered how having your life detailed so minutely would change the way you saw yourself and those around you.

He drained the bottle, the table swerving away from him as he browsed through the rest of the photos. They were mainly from Katrina's backpacking trip. Carrigan liked these the best – the exotic locations and goofy holiday grins. Katrina on the steps of Angkor Wat; Katrina half-hidden down a VC tunnel; Katrina on the beach with other girls – guitars, bottles of beer and thin straggles of smoke swirling into a postcard sky. Others were of local colour – men without teeth peddling single cigarettes, mummified women squatting in the main street; a distant shipwreck; a beached fish . . .

He thought it was the booze or maybe the pills. He rubbed his eyes and scrolled back but it was the same. He opened the photo in a new window and enlarged it, his eyes widening as he studied the group of girls.

They had their arms around each other and smiles on their sunburnt faces. Behind them was the beach, the sun setting somewhere over to their left. There were six girls in the photo. Katrina stood on the far right of the group. Carrigan zoomed in on the girl standing on the far left until the magnification turned her into pixelated chaos.

He pressed a button and waited as the printer chugged and wheezed. He snatched the photo out of the tray before it was finished and stared at it, finally believing his eyes now that it was there on paper.

Katrina was standing on a beach next to five other girls. It was the perfect snapshot of a summer evening. A group of friends surrounded by palm trees and glary light. Carrigan had enlarged the photo to show only their faces. He scanned the girls again but his eyes kept sliding to the one on the far left. Standing at the opposite end from Katrina, in a red bikini and holding a large red cocktail, was Anna Becker.

III

33

It was chaos. Noise and movement, a hall full of geeks. Carrigan scanned the room. The high arched roof rose above him and made it feel as if he were trapped in the belly of a whale. People ducked and staggered between stalls. Bloggers sashayed on free booze and donned insect-like devices. Hawkers jostled and cried and pestered passers-by with leaflets extolling their latest software. Sirens whooped and beeped and echoed across the cavernous Art Deco interior.

How they were supposed to find DS Neilson, Carrigan had no idea.

Neilson was a friend of Berman's but also a sergeant in the computer crime division. She'd called Carrigan back and suggested they meet here, opening day at the Earls Court surveillance tech trade fair. Stretching in every direction were rows of walled-off cubicles, poster-splashed sales points and wired-up demo spaces.

'The photo means we have to look at everything again,' Geneva said as they traversed an aisle full of mechanical dogs doing parlour tricks. 'How the fuck could we have missed this?'

'We didn't have enough data,' Carrigan replied while texting Neilson. Earlier, over coffee, he'd updated Geneva on Farouk's info, then shown her the beach photo. He'd loved the way her eyebrows had shot up when she recognised first Katrina, then Anna. He sent the text then glanced at a booth to his right, seeing Geneva displayed on their 80-inch TV screen. She was saying something, her lips moving, while underneath, subtitles scrolled:

The photo means we have to look at everything again.

A grinning salesman beckoned them over. The sign above his head said: *Read My Lips – Lip-Reading Algorithms at the Touch of a Button.*

Geneva saw herself and cringed. She felt dull, hungover and ashamed of her own weakness in succumbing to the weed last night. 'Why couldn't we have met Neilson back at the station?'

Carrigan glanced at his phone, memorising the directions Neilson had just texted back. 'Computer crime are giving one of the keynotes tonight. She said she couldn't leave and, be-sides, we're the ones asking for a favour,' Carrigan explained as they navigated alleyways of blinking screens and trailing wires, the noise unbelievable, a symphony of competing and counter-pointing shrieks.

'Okay, so Anna and Katrina knew each other,' Geneva said. 'Let's think about this a moment. It doesn't change the profile. We're still looking for the same man.'

'Yes, we are,' Carrigan replied. 'But we need to rethink our suppositions. Obviously, we also need to find out where that photo was taken and when.'

'The last tweet he sent Anna was of a beach.' Geneva took out her phone and scrolled until she found it. She tilted the screen towards Carrigan. It could have been any beach. There was no way to tell.

'The photo *does* change the profile,' Carrigan said. 'Hoffmann thought the hostel was the killer's hunting ground and that the girls had drifted into his orbit but it's the other way around. The girls are the connection – not the hostel. We've been focusing too much on the Milgram. We should have been looking for links between the girls.'

'You're right, we should have been, but that's all beside the point now. We're getting close to him. If he posted any clips of Anna to a forum then we can trace him. That's our most viable lead. All you have is a photo of two girls on a beach somewhere. By itself, it doesn't mean anything. We don't even know what country it was taken in.'

'I know a way to find out.' They finally reached the Met's booth but there was no sign of Neilson.

'How?'

Before Carrigan could answer, a woman approached him. He was about to tell her he wasn't in the market for gadgets when he saw the stern crease of her eyebrows. She held out her hand.

'You'd thought with a name like mine I'd be some snow-white Nordic see-through type? Sorry to disappoint you.' Neilson was small and slight with a steadiness that impressed Carrigan as they shook hands.

'I know it's a bit much to take in.' She brushed back her short dreads, her eyes scanning the room even as she was speaking to them. 'But I thought you might find this a bit of an eye-opener. David told me about your problem.'

'David?' For a moment, Carrigan had no idea what she was talking about. He'd popped a couple of pills earlier and had to force himself to focus.

'David Berman? He told me what you're looking for. But you

should know – I'll listen to what you have to say then make a decision if this case is right for my team. Most cases that people think are right for us are not. We're a very specialised unit and we have very narrow parameters as to what we do.'

Neilson walked fast, as if in training or pursuit, her entire body telescoped down to this one activity. She pointed to a booth studded with cameras, hundreds of tiny screens, each displaying a different part of the fair. 'Real-time surveillance,' she explained as they strolled past the bulging glass. 'We'll never have to leave the station again.'

Carrigan couldn't tell if this was something she was happy about or not. Looking around him he suspected she was right and he wondered how much room there'd be for cops like him in the new electronic policing.

'We have to keep up,' Neilson said, and for a moment, Carrigan thought she meant physically and that this was why they were setting such a fast pace.

'Otherwise, we're fucked,' she added. 'We're fucked anyway. The tech's too sophisticated and unruly, but this way, maybe we'll be a little less fucked. The future came too fast. We weren't prepared for it.' Neilson stopped every now and then to chat with people manning the booths, swapping tips and gossip and making notes in a small red notebook she kept in her back pocket.

As they traversed the aisles, Geneva ran through the basics of the case, Neilson stopping her occasionally and asking seemingly random questions. Geneva told her about the abduction, the drugs and the Twitter trolling. Neilson perked up at the mention of the latter as she led them past the last booth and into a separate, roped-off enclosure.

'You should see this,' Neilson said as she approached the table. Geneva and Carrigan looked at each other, equal parts frustration and puzzlement on their faces. They were standing in front of a desk. The word INFOCATCHER stood in stark relief on the wall.

Unlike most of the other booths, which were crammed with high-tech boxes and trailing wires, this one contained only a large oak table and a single wireless computer terminal. Neilson nodded to the woman behind the screen and she got up and vacated her seat. 'Plug your name into this,' Neilson said to Geneva and Geneva sat down and entered her name into a blinking grey box.

The screen flashed once, then twice, and words began to fill it. Geneva leaned in closer. She saw her name at the top. Below it was her home and mobile numbers, the names and addresses of her next of kin, her NI details and sergeant's number. There was a list of the last hundred shops and cafes she'd visited and every single item she'd bought there. Her complete Internet search history. Her email and banking passwords. She looked away, her face drained of colour.

'Don't you just love it?' Neilson beamed. 'You get a suspect's name and plug it into InfoCatcher – within seconds you know almost everything you need to know about them.'

Geneva looked at the screen, her entire life rendered in blocky green letters. 'That scares me a little.'

'Scares the judges too,' Neilson replied. 'But soon it won't matter. The crims will have so much technology in their hands that only something like this will give us the slightest chance of catching them.'

'Stalin would have loved this.'

'He managed pretty well without it,' Neilson snapped back. 'It's here. Nothing's going to change that. The only thing we can do is learn how to use it to our advantage. Criminal intrusion, government intrusion – it's all going to get a lot worse in the coming years. The technology is still in its infancy – imagine what it'll be capable of in five, ten, fifteen years?'

'We're always being told criminals have some new unbeatable technology that's going to destroy the world. What's so different about this?'

'It's totally different. A quantum leap. Extremism, for example, was never that big a problem for us – some nutter on a soapbox, how many people is he going to reach? Maybe a few hundred at most. Now, on the net, they can reach millions of like-minded idiots, form a critical mass and cause major grief. We saw it with the English Defence League, we see it with jihadis, and it's no different with common criminals – gangs getting together to perpetrate transnational smuggling and trafficking – as the web brings them into contact we're going to experience an exponential rise in crime. It's the future, Carrigan, whether we like it or not. We're throwbacks. They'll look back at our methods of detection with pity and wonder.' Neilson pointed to the computer. 'Try it, if you don't believe me.'

He sat down behind the computer and stared at the blinking cursor. He was genuinely interested in what it would say about him. Sure, it would have his details and habits but would it have Africa? The third song on his debut album? The last thing he'd told Louise? He typed in his name. The screen flickered rapidly. Carrigan looked up at Neilson. Neilson looked over at the saleswoman. The computer beeped again – a series of high-pitched notes, the intervals between them steadily decreasing, and then the screen blinked once more and turned blue. The saleswoman ran over, frowned at Carrigan and ushered him from the chair. She began frantically punching different combinations of keys and muttering under her breath. She looked up at him. 'You've broken it.'

Carrigan shrugged. The woman continued staring at the screen in utter bewilderment as Neilson tugged at Carrigan's sleeve and led him away.

'Hackers have access to that?' Geneva asked, rattled by what she'd seen – the key to so many lives nestled in undersea cables and the veiny tangle of fibre-optics. So many interconnection points and so many vulnerabilities.

'They're often the ones who developed it in the first place. We're always late to the party.' Neilson allowed a smile. 'But we catch up pretty fast. Soon every member of the force will be fitted with body cams. Ninety-five per cent of all Scotland Yard cases last year used CCTV as evidence. At the moment we're not sure if technology is better for them or for us. It's always a double-edged sword but pretty soon we'll be able to see everything that goes on at the click of a button.'

'And that doesn't scare you?' Geneva had grown up with her mother's fear of a police state. It was one of the main reasons she'd taken this job.

'Not as much as not being able to see what's going on.'

'Look,' Carrigan interrupted. 'This is all very interesting but we're in the middle of a case. We came here because we were told you had an in to these forums and all we're doing is wasting time looking at bloody gadgets.'

Neilson turned to face him. Her voice was calm and even

and totally uncowed by Carrigan's stern expression. 'I'm not wasting your time. I took you around here because you need to understand what we're up against. The kind of resources these crims can draw upon. You have to realise this isn't like any other investigation you've pursued before. And the reason I don't want to hear more about your case is because I've decided we'll take it and I'd rather read everything myself in the right order.'

Carrigan nodded, muted by her logic and by having got what he wanted. 'I take it that means you think it's possible Anna's image ended up on one of these forums?'

'More than possible,' Neilson replied. 'It's like the tree in the forest. A hack doesn't exist until other people have seen and commented on it.'

34

The first thing Carrigan did when he got back to the office was pull up the Anna file. He flicked through the first few pages – lab reports, forensic results, autopsy findings – until he reached her passport. They'd copied the entire document once the SOCOs had analysed it for fingerprints and other trace evidence. But the missing photo wasn't what interested Carrigan now. He looked at the print-out of the beach photo. The image of the two girls, existing in the same frame, unsettled him and made him realise how wrong he'd been. Where were they? What were they doing there? Did they know each other or had they simply stumbled into the same photo?

After returning from the trade fair, Carrigan had gone to see Branch and received authorisation to second DS Neilson to the hostel case. He'd explained to the super that the killer's computer skills far outweighed their own and that they needed a much deeper immersion into the dark waters of the net than Berman could give them. Branch had only understood half of what Carrigan was saying but he'd grudgingly signed off on it. They both knew they were peering into a future where Murder Investigation Teams would have more geeks than gumshoes and that the next generation would see them as hapless idiots, no better than men in white sheets trying to understand the future from the spilled entrails of a goat.

Carrigan put down the beach photo as the door to his office opened and Karlson came in, the smell of aftershave instantly swamping the room.

'We've been through the list of clients Anna cleaned for.'

'And?'

'And nothing so far. She worked at nineteen different addresses. Twelve of these were hospitals, two were schools and two were offices. The remaining three residences were all private and belong to single men. Out of those, two had Anna visit more than once. None of them admitted making a pass at her, which of course they wouldn't but, and I hate to say it, I believed them. Their alibis have so far checked out but we're going to have to look at those a bit more carefully.'

'Good. The more we can eliminate from the investigation the better.' Carrigan looked down at the beach photo. 'Anything else?'

Karlson rubbed his stubble with a blackened thumb. Carrigan winced, thinking of the pain the sergeant must have endured as his fingers swelled up like baby bananas then blistered and popped – five days lost in a blizzard high up on K2, two of his fellow climbers dead, an avalanche that severed their guide ropes, scrambling down in the terrifying dark.

'We have managed to verify Max's alibi,' Karlson said. 'That place you told us about in Knightsbridge? Turns out they film their clients, cameras embedded in the walls, all conveniently time-stamped too.'

'I thought they might. Why give up a good opportunity to make money?'

'Max came in for a cuddling session Friday night after leaving the hostel. Before that, we have several residents who saw him manning the desk all evening.' Karlson noticed the photo beside Carrigan's laptop.

'What the fuck?' Karlson picked up the photo. His eyebrows shot up and his mouth went slack as he recognised Anna and Katrina. 'Were you even going to show me this?'

'I wanted to hear your information before the photo coloured it,' Carrigan said. 'I need you to make a good copy and set up a press conference. We have to get this photo out as soon as possible. We need to find these other girls.'

'What are you going to do?'

'I'm going to find out where it was taken.'

Carrigan waited until Karlson had departed before flicking through Anna's passport. He had a digital copy onscreen but it only told half the story. The passport smelled faintly of tanning lotion and coconut oil, a lingering reminder of past holidays and blistering beaches. He remembered Geneva mentioning the multitude of stamps, a chronology of Anna's trip laid out page by page, and he started at the beginning – Anna's arrival in Singapore.

The entry visa told him she'd landed in the island-city on a Wednesday and the exit visa showed she'd left three days later. She was in Australia for two weeks, then spent a week in New Zealand. From there she flew to Bangkok. The Thai entry visa seduced him with its cursive script and he felt an unexpected longing for foreign shores.

Anna left Thailand a week later, spent four days in Cambodia, six in Vietnam, one in Laos then flew to Bali. The Indonesian stamp was the last in her passport. She'd arrived in Bali on 4 August and left two weeks later.

Carrigan checked through his inbox and found the file containing Katrina's passport which Forsyth had emailed over. Like Carrigan, he'd also made several copies of the entire passport after seeing the carefully snipped-out photo.

Katrina travelled before Anna. She went to more places and was more adventurous, crossing the bandit-ridden highlands of Dagestan and sculpted wastes of the Karakum Desert, through the folded Caucasian hills and the huge expanse of the Kazakh Steppe, across plains and mountains and forests and into China. From there she'd dribbled down the South Asian archipelago and visited Vietnam, Laos and Cambodia. Carrigan flicked between passports comparing dates. The two girls had both started their trips in Europe and crawled up opposite sides of Asia. He knew they'd met on a beach somewhere.

He clicked open his digital calendar and printed out blank pages for July, August and September. He began to go through each passport chronologically, this time writing the girls' arrivals and departures in the calendar's tight square divisions. He made notes, correlated dates and checked atlases and local maps.

Katrina had left Cambodia a day before Anna had arrived in Phnom Penh. They'd missed each other in Laos, Vietnam and Australia. Carrigan filled in squares until there were no more stamps left.

He laid out the calendar pages side by side on his desk. There was only one place where the girls' journeys coincided – Bali.

Katrina had arrived a week before Anna but both girls had

left the island on the same day. They had overlapped for nearly a fortnight in mid-August. It was the only time they were both in the same place and it was the last place they'd visited before heading home.

Carrigan got up, made another coffee and thought about this and what it could mean.

The two girls had both spent the third week of August in Bali. It was not so unusual, the island was a hub for backpackers traipsing across the wilds of South East Asia, a place to recuperate and party, to meet others and discuss plans and escapades. Carrigan tried to imagine the scene, the way in which the two girls might have met, the things they would have had in common. He googled photos of beaches in Bali, trying to recognise either the beach behind the group of girls or the beach in the final tweet Anna had received, but all beaches looked the same. He saw a link to an English-language Bali-based newspaper, catering to expats and ravers, and used his credit card to gain access to their archive. He plugged in the dates of Anna and Katrina's visit and searched through the two editions that bookended it. He started reading, forcing himself to slow down, to pay attention, going through every story, paragraph and sidebar.

There were elections coming. There was violence and insurgency in the remote islands, bombs going off in the jungle and a story about a priest who'd been boiled alive. Carrigan read about drunken Brits getting into fights with locals, women being arrested for wearing skimpy clothes outside the designated tourist areas, drug smugglers receiving the death penalty for an ounce of weed – and then his eyes focused on a small column in the bottom right-hand corner.

The body of British tourist Lucy Brown was found by a fisherman on Balangan Beach early this morning. The beach is well known for its 'Full Moon' parties and it is believed that the victim had been attending one the night before. Her body was discovered ten metres from a migrant workers' camp on the beach. Witnesses report seeing the girl wandering around intoxicated and naked the previous night. Jokar Mahinidi, the fisherman who found her body, said, 'At first, I thought she was sleeping it off, she looked so peaceful, but when I got closer I saw what had been done to her.' The initial report from the coroner states that Brown had been repeatedly raped and that her throat was cut. Bali police raided the migrant camp this afternoon and two Laotian migrants were taken into custody.

Carrigan read over the piece twice. He plugged Lucy Brown's name into the paper's search box and found two more follow-up articles. The first was dated a month after the murder.

TWO MIGRANTS SENTENCED TO DEATH

Two unnamed Laotian migrants pled guilty today to the rape and murder of British tourist Lucy Brown. The judge, in his remarks, condemned the crime and, unsurprisingly in a place where tourism is the major source of income, sentenced both men to death. The sentence will be carried out at Indonesia's notorious Nusa Kambangan island where the two will be executed by firing squad.

The second follow-up article was from a couple of months later, the story by now reduced to one column, stating only that the two men had been executed for their crimes.

35

The next morning, Carrigan burst into the incident room impatient to tell them what he'd found – but Geneva and Neilson had news of their own.

Carrigan took a seat and stared at the flickering bank of screens.

There were far more Ratting forums than he'd expected. Neilson and Berman had managed to narrow the search to ones based in the UK or with significant UK traffic. They'd spent the night logging in under some of Neilson's previously established accounts and running image recognition software through the files. When that hadn't worked, they'd scanned them by eye, playing each video on the large monitor above their heads, a rolling inventory of the missing and lost.

They had mugs of tea, biscuits and bottled water on the table. They had the slitted eyes common to those who spend their waking hours staring at screens. Neilson and Berman had been working for twelve hours straight, logging into forums, folding back into fake identities, scanning and scouring the web for images of Anna.

They found her on a forum called whatyoudontknowcanthurtyou.com.

Carrigan looked at the plain homepage. Nothing to indicate what lay beneath. He thought about the Bali information and how it fitted in. He knew what Geneva would say. He had too little to go on and decided to keep it to himself for now. There were a couple of things he needed to check first. 'How did you manage to find Anna?'

'A mixture of logic and software.' Neilson had a box of wet wipes by her side and she pulled one out and quickly rubbed it across her hands.

'You can just google this stuff?'

Neilson shook her head and tilted a screen packed with tightly bunched code towards Carrigan.

'Deep web, the Internet's subconscious. All the stuff Google and other search engines can't find. The searchable web's only ten per cent of the net, and the really nasty stuff, the stuff we're looking for, is often found within that, on the dark web, but it's all connected – everything can be traced back to everything else. You just need to know what you're looking for.'

They watched footage of women walking across rooms. Women typing or staring into screens. Women kissing boy-friends, women crying, women applying make-up. Some clips were as boring and uneventful as life, played out in real time, while others were highlight reels of late-night undressings and naked walk-bys. This was how people behaved when they thought no one was watching.

Geneva pumped her stress ball, Neilson by her side, her own Virgil guiding her through this binary inferno. 'Warhol would have loved this,' she said, a weak attempt at distancing herself from the reality of what they were seeing. Someone had filmed these women without their knowledge and posted it online. Others watched and got their kicks.

The site they were on was a Ratting forum, password protected, based on a UK server. The thread containing the clips hid behind the innocent banner *Check This Out!*

There were twenty-three clips of Anna. The user had not uploaded anything else. They watched them in chronological order, an escalating narrative etched out in fear and binary code.

The first clip showed two minutes and twenty-three seconds of Anna staring at the screen, her face in close-up. It was unsettling to finally be face to face with Anna but unable to do anything to help her, separated by both time and space. Geneva thought of stricken families crammed into small steamy living rooms watching hostage footage of their loved ones. The mute agony and impotence. How image becomes merely another form of torture.

There were forty-nine comments below the clip. They ranged from *Hilarious, bro!* to *That bitch deserved everything she got* to things much worse – each successive poster bragging what he'd like to do to Anna, torrents of fantasy and humiliation lashed in pain and sex.

The user who'd uploaded the clip had also uploaded twenty-two other clips, all of them featuring Anna. The entire batch had been posted over a week ago, four days before she'd disappeared.

The clips were low-lit, fuzzy and distorted but, Geneva had to admit, there was something compelling about them. Some showed Anna typing, others Anna walking around the dorm, singing or trying on clothes, examining herself, squeezing different parts of her body and making faces at the mirror. The early clips all ran four or five minutes and nothing much happened.

The first intrusion was recorded on Clip 13.

Anna Becker clicked the mouse and began reading. She had no idea she was being watched. She had no idea she was being filmed.

The camera was located on the top bar of her laptop. You could see a slice of bright green poster behind her. Light streamed in from the dorm windows and highlighted her hair as she idly surfed away her evening.

And then it began.

Anna was staring at the screen, reading something, when she started blinking rapidly and her mouth fell open. A yelp crackled through the speakers. Anna pushed her chair back. She reached for the laptop lid and the video cut to black.

The next intrusion came two days later.

Anna stared at the screen. Anna typed. Anna bit her lip and scrunched her forehead. Anna resumed typing. She looked up and jumped almost an inch off the chair. Her eyes grew wide and wet. The webcam caught two minutes and twenty-three seconds of Anna sobbing and shaking. There was no question of it being fake. If Anna had been that good an actress she wouldn't have had any problem getting a place at RADA.

They continued watching in silence, uneasy at their complicity in viewing but unable to take their eyes off the screen.

Clip 18 showed Anna sleeping, the image pixelated and tinted blue. Anna tossed and turned, the sheets rippling and folding like waves. All of a sudden Anna sat bolt upright and screamed. She scanned the room wildly, her chest rising and falling, then buried her head in the pillow.

Clip 20 depicted Anna on hands and knees, searching for something on the floor, her head jerking up every few seconds, her eyes quick and alert as any hunted animal's.

Clip 21 caught Anna crawling into the wardrobe, crouching beneath her clothes and shutting the door on herself.

With each successive clip, Anna's appearance deteriorated. Dark swollen pouches showed up under her eyes. Her hair lost its lustre and hung limp and frayed. She'd stopped putting on make-up and her lips became chapped and cracked.

Geneva remembered the destroyed laptops in Anna's locker. She couldn't begin to imagine the panic and hope which came with booting up each new laptop, only to be crushed a couple of days later by the next intrusion.

'They get progressively worse,' Neilson said, her face strained and lined by the hours and by what they'd seen. 'It's rare to get this level of sophistication and organisation in a Ratter. He's calibrated his torments precisely so they'd be most effective.'

'You've not seen this kind of thing before?' Carrigan hunched over the desk and squinted at the screen.

'No. Not this organised. Most Ratters tend to cut out the boring bits. They're only interested in naked walk-bys. This is something altogether more complex and planned. Kids don't have the patience for this. This is someone older. Someone used to setting a trap and lying in wait.'

When they'd finished watching, they turned to the comments below the clips, a repository of sickness, rage and bitter entitlement. Each clip had nearly fifty comments. They were on the fourteenth clip when Carrigan pointed to the bottom half of the screen.

Geneva scanned the comments. There were the usual gripes and raves and boring rants, flame wars and digressions that spiralled out into the far reaches of obsession and madness, but it was the last set that drew her attention.

More!

This chick is spooky!

Fake!

I want me some of her!
> So do I, but she's been claimed.

36

Neilson caught the startle in Geneva's eye. 'That last one means something to you, doesn't it?'

Geneva reread the comment. 'It's what two of the women said before they disappeared. That he was coming to *claim* them. But I don't understand its context here.'

'It's a common term in Ratting,' Neilson explained. 'It means she's a slave.'

'A slave?' Geneva said.

'That's what they're known as,' Neilson replied. 'The hackers get into your computer or phone and install the RAT software. Once that's done, you become their slave. Hackers collect them.' Neilson seemed pleased by the expressions of shock she'd managed to elicit from Carrigan and Geneva. 'We're coming across it more and more. Reality TV opened the gates, it conditioned us into thinking the recorded life was the only one worth living. RAT tools are easily available online. They even come in packages so you don't need to know anything about computing apart from how to install a program.' Neilson clicked on an icon and the screen in front of her divided into six equal squares. Each square displayed a room. Two were empty but the other four contained women looking directly into the screen.

'These are just some of the slaves currently available for general viewing on this particular forum,' Neilson said. 'Anyone who has a username can access them at any time. They're streaming in real time so what you're seeing is happening right now in someone's flat or house.'

'Why don't you stop them?' Geneva said as she watched women pounding keys, talking to loved ones, crossing empty rooms in the nude.

Neilson laughed. 'It would require at least a week to hack even one account and trace it to a real-world address. It's too time-consuming and as soon as we've cracked one system, the hackers will develop a better one. It makes more sense to watch what they're doing, learn their tricks and collect information. Everything you see is being recorded for later use.'

'So, basically, they just get away with it?'

Neilson shot Geneva a sharp look. 'If this was a perfect world and we had a hundred times more personnel and a fuck lot more money, we could do something about it – but this world isn't even halfway to perfect. It's only when they step across a certain line that we bring it to the attention of other squads.'

Geneva knew that what Neilson was saying was right but she also knew it was wrong. 'How often does it spill over into the real world?'

'Very rarely in terms of violence. These are teenagers. Cowards, geeks and nerds. This is their preferred battleground. What we mainly see is extortion, or sextortion as the press love to call it. The Ratter gets into your system, pokes around until he finds jpegs or videos, the ones you took of yourself naked and sent to your boyfriend one drunken night so long ago you don't even remember they're on there. The Ratter then contacts you and threatens to upload the photos to all your

Facebook friends if you don't deposit a certain amount in his PayPal account. Or they demand payment in kind.'

'And women fall for that?'

'What would you do?' Neilson said. 'Imagine you had some compromising photos on your hard drive and someone accessed them and threatened to send them to your parents? Imagine you're an eighteen-year-old girl. Imagine your reputation is staked on this. You do what you have to do. Unfortunately, like all blackmail, it never stops. They take the money, shut up for a while, but eventually they contact the person again or sell the slaves on.'

'Sell them to who?'

'There's a big market for slaves. If you happen to have someone who is either very good-looking or spends a lot of time naked in front of their laptop you can sell or trade her to someone else. These are teenage boys, remember. They get bored very quickly so they swap a lot.'

'But we're still talking virtually, right?'

Neilson nodded. 'There's entire wikis on the forum expressly for the trading of slaves. Ratters spend a lot of time seasoning their slaves so they'll fetch the highest price.'

'Do I even want to know what that is?'

Neilson shook her dreads back and hunched her shoulders. 'Generally speaking, the more broken down a slave is, the more they fetch. The more compliant they are, the more they're worth.'

'Can anyone view these?' Carrigan looked down at the trailing tangle of wires snaking out the back of the screen.

'Anyone who's a member.'

'Shit,' Carrigan said as the pieces clicked into place. 'This is what Farouk must have seen. He said she was fully clothed and that it had nothing to do with sex – which means anyone who saw these clips could have become fixated with Anna and tracked her down.'

Geneva shook her head. 'That's highly unlikely. It's far more probable that whoever made the clips followed it through to its conclusion. It fits the profile. This is exactly what he would do. It's the logical progression – first he intimidates her on Twitter, then he starts Ratting her, slowly breaking her down through these intrusions. It's a campaign, a war of attrition. This is what he has to do to them before he can snatch them. It's as much his signature as it is his MO.'

'I agree,' Neilson said. 'Ratters are very territorial in that way and for someone else to find out Anna's real-world address would be very difficult and time-consuming – it makes much more sense if it's the other way around.'

Carrigan thought about this. 'When were these clips posted?'

'Eleven days ago.' Neilson smiled and pointed to a line of spidery text. 'The person who posted them goes under the username PANOPTEASE.' She switched back to the Anna videos. 'He's quite a presence below the line.' She pointed to a running list of comments under the username.

I think I scared the shit out of her. LOL

Hey, more please. This one really got me going. Yes.

Some of these girls are pigs but, hey, a slave's a slave, right?

'These guys are real charmers,' Geneva said but Carrigan wasn't listening. He was reading a comment from PANOPTEASE in reply to someone asking if they could post the Anna clips on another forum. He pointed it out to Geneva.

PANOPTEASE: Anyone, and I mean ANYONE who rips off my stuff or posts it elsewhere or tries to capture it, I will find what you love most and take it away from you. That is my word and guarantee. So, please, before you do anything rash, take a moment to think about whether you really want me inside your life?

'Lovely.' Geneva looked over at Neilson. 'That definitely sounds like him and it fits the profile, but how the hell are we going to find him?'

'We're not.' Neilson smiled for the first time that afternoon. 'He's going to find us. We're going to sell him some slaves.'

37

They were closing in – he could feel it. A sensation he couldn't put into words, it was all nerve and hunch, yet over the years he'd learned to trust it. The technology the killer had used to ensnare the girls was now being turned against him. Like any weapon, its power lay only in the direction in which it was pointed.

Neilson had told them that this stage of the operation would take several hours. Carrigan had retreated to his office and tried filling out another report but his eyes kept drifting back to the photo. Anna and Katrina still alive, smiles and suntans and white teeth in the setting sun. If PANOPTEASE went for the bait, they had him. It was as simple as that. But the photo complicated things. The photo didn't fit. It turned what they'd assumed was a territorial serial killer into something else. Of course, it could mean nothing. The random often confused us by hiding under the cloak of purpose and every investigation had its own peculiar anomalies, clues they never understood even long after they'd solved the case. The law of unintended consequences was entropy in action. Seepage and chaos were inevitable and secrets always found a way out.

Carrigan fired up his laptop and reread the Bali news articles. Questions popped and rattled. How did the death of an English tourist connect to this? Did it even have anything to do with the case outside the coincidence of geography and time?

He searched through the national newspapers' coverage of the death. None of the articles gave him what he needed. None of them told him anything new. He looked up the beach, the town closest to it, and checked police and Interpol databases until he found the sub-station responsible for the region and the name of the acting police chief. It never failed to amaze him how much information was available at the click of a button. Everything was now logged and itemised, the entire world encapsulated in anonymous servers hidden deep inside the elephantine legs of abandoned oil rigs. The problem was that there was too much information. The digital Enlightenment was in danger of blinding us.

Carrigan clicked the browser shut and looked at the name and number he'd written in his notebook. He rechecked dates and entry visas against his calendar. Anna and Katrina had left Bali three days after the murder of the British girl. Had it frightened them off the island?

The phone rang for a long time, the tone languorous and hypnotic. A gruff man answered in a language Carrigan couldn't make sense of.

'Do you speak English?'

'Yes, of course.'

Carrigan told the police chief who he was and why he was calling. The man didn't say anything but Carrigan could hear the stutter of his breath and knew he was still on the line. 'The article says that the girl, Lucy Brown, was found naked on the beach.'

'Yes, that is so.'

'That she'd been raped and murdered.'

'Yes, yes. Why are you asking this now? The case is closed. We found the killers. Two migrants admitted to stumbling on the girl. She was out of her mind like all the tourists and they couldn't help themselves. We charged them, they went to trial and received the death penalty and were executed. What else is there to say?'

'There were a couple of details in the report that didn't make sense.'

'Well, that is your problem, then. Thank you for calling, detective, but there's not much else I can help you with and I need to get back to work.' The chief cut the call and Carrigan listened to the dead tone for a few moments then phoned Geneva. Berman told him she'd popped out for a cigarette. The sergeant reported no online developments. Carrigan put down the phone and, as soon as he did, it rang.

'Geneva?'

There was a brief burst of silence at the other end and Carrigan thought he'd caught her in the act of lighting a cigarette but the voice, when it came, wasn't Geneva's.

'You called here a minute ago?'

The woman on the other end of the line had the same sing-song accent as the man but none of his gruff wariness.

'Yes. Yes, I did.'

'I can't talk long. I heard my boss speak to you. I heard the name Lucy Brown.'

'Why did you call me back?'

'I wanted to know why you wanted to know about her.'

'And why would that be?'

'Perhaps because I'm curious why a London detective should call several months after the case was closed?'

Carrigan cleared his throat. 'I read the reports and there were a couple of things that didn't make sense to me. Your boss declined to discuss them. I'm guessing the reason you're calling me is they didn't make sense to you either?'

'You should be a detective,' she said and laughed, a lovely high-pitched sound that made Carrigan feel a curious thirst for languages he couldn't understand, the caress of foreign air on bare skin. 'Tell me what you know about the case.'

Carrigan looked over his notes. 'Only what I've read. That the body of Lucy Brown was found in the early hours of Sunday morning. That she'd been repeatedly raped then killed. That the killers were found the next day, two migrant workers who were squatting in a refugee camp by the beach. That they confessed to the murder, were tried and executed.'

'So, you know all the facts. Why then are you calling?'

'The facts don't add up. You were on the case?'

There was a slight hesitation and Carrigan knew this was the moment he could lose her.

'I was taken off it.'

'Why?'

'Probably because I asked the same questions you're about to ask.'

Carrigan smiled. 'It says she was discovered naked. Did you ever find her clothes?'

'That is a strange question but no, we didn't.'

'And that didn't strike you as weird?'

'No. You should come down here in the summer. These kids get so out of it on drugs, they often tear their clothes off. Or perhaps the migrants, once they'd realised what they'd done, got rid of the clothes?'

'Why go to all that trouble when they could have left them on the body?'

'Exactly.'

'Did you do a tox test to see what drugs she was on?'

'No, there was no need. Several witnesses reported seeing her before she disappeared, walking around in a daze, naked, singing to herself.'

'And they didn't try to help her?'

'They didn't want to ruin their evening.'

'Did you ever suspect she'd been spiked? As in date rape?'

There was a pause. 'No, we didn't and perhaps that was a mistake, but everyone who comes here, comes here to do drugs. Finding out which ones is not standard procedure for us.'

Carrigan scanned his list of questions. 'She was discovered with her eyes closed. Why would these migrants who'd raped and killed her bother doing that?'

'How do you know he closed her eyes? We kept that from the papers.'

'The fisherman who found the body described her as looking as if she were asleep. He wouldn't have said that if her eyes were wide open.'

'Very good. But why are you asking this question?'

He knew it wasn't fair to hold back and so he told her about Anna and Katrina – the beach photo, the hostel, the abandoned house.

'Yes,' she answered. 'The eyes always bothered me too. The eyes didn't fit.'

'What were the migrants like?'

'Big, rough men. Uneducated, from poor farms out in the

Annamite mountains. The kind that treat their wives worse than their dogs.'

'But they confessed?'

There was a slight pause. 'I interviewed them first. After we presented the evidence, they admitted to raping the girl but not to killing her. I said maybe she slipped and cut herself and we can call it manslaughter and still they refused to admit to killing her. Ten hours me and my partner worked on them but they wouldn't admit to the murder. At the end of my shift, my boss took over the interrogation and two hours later they'd confessed to everything.'

'He beat them into a confession?'

'No, there were no marks on them. Maybe they couldn't tell a woman this and waited until a man came along. Maybe they had a sudden return of memory.'

'These things are known to happen,' Carrigan replied cautiously. 'What position did you find her in?'

'Position?'

'How was she lying?'

'She had her arms and legs out, like a starfish.'

Carrigan felt a current running through his hand, the phone hot against his ear. 'Do you know if she was part of a group? Travelling with other girls?'

'No. She was with her brother.'

'Did you interview any Western witnesses?'

'Nearly a hundred. There was a full moon rave that night. So many people dancing and having fun while a few metres away someone raped that girl and took her life.'

'I don't suppose you could email me those files? The names of everyone you interviewed?'

'It would be traced. You'd have to make a formal request and it would take weeks.' She paused. 'But, if you said a name to me, I can look the files up on my screen . . .'

'Was Anna Becker one of the girls you interviewed?'

A moment's hesitation. The sound of a distant ceiling fan slapping the hot wet air. 'Yes.'

'Katrina Eliot?'

Another pause. A slight exhalation. Then: 'Yes.'

38

Carrigan found Geneva and Hoffmann in the cafeteria. Officers were downing cups of tea or eating crisps and sandwiches before their shifts. A muted TV showed Syrian cities reduced to rubble, more ruin than the ancient Roman ones surrounding them.

Carrigan noticed they stopped talking when they saw him and he quickened his step.

'We were just wondering where you'd got to,' Geneva said. 'We thought it better to come down here and keep out of Neilson's way for the time being.'

Carrigan nodded and sat down. The table was covered in stacks and fans of print-outs. Carrigan saw PANOPTEASE's avatar on every one.

'Stupid name.'

'No, not so stupid,' Hoffmann replied. 'It's a pun on Panoptes. In Greek mythology, Panoptes is a giant with a hundred eyes, the God of surveillance if you will. Jeremy Bentham later appropriated the name for his concept of the Panopticon.' Hoffmann picked up one of the files. 'I've been going through his interactions on various forums, comparing it to the profile and it's definitely him. This fits the profile to a tee.' He shoved a stack of papers into Carrigan's hand. 'His need to taunt, to overcompensate, to dominate and subjugate – it's all here. This is exactly how I'd expect a hunter-type like him to behave.

Calm, controlled, controlling. He's obviously educated and shows a certain maturity – the patience to take his time and drag it out and the knowledge that in this very patience lies the ultimate reward. Furthermore, his presence on these forums is evidence he has all the requisite knowledge and capability to do what he did to Anna.'

Carrigan flicked through the print-outs. 'That's a circular argument.'

'Nevertheless, it's true.'

Carrigan put the papers aside. He updated them on the beach photo. He showed them the newspaper articles on Lucy Brown's death and explained what led him to call Bali.

'She knew the migrants hadn't killed her,' he said, remembering the soft rolling voice of the policewoman. 'She couldn't come right out and say it but it was there.'

'Yes. Of course! Why didn't I see it earlier?' Hoffmann slapped his forehead. 'We didn't find any previous victims because we were looking in the wrong place. The wrong country.' Hoffmann drained his coffee. 'The positioning. The drugs. Closing her eyes after she was dead.' There was a note of triumph in the profiler's tone as he tabulated the evidence. 'He might be able to change his MO as suits the circumstances but he can't change his signature. The positioning and closing their eyes mean something to him, something he feels he needs to enact and re-enact until he's got it right. Of course, he never will, and he senses this deep inside, which is why we see his rage surfacing further with each subsequent victim. The more he comes up against the truth of himself, the more he blames the victims and the worse he treats them.'

Carrigan took a sip of Geneva's tea. His back and shoulders

yearned for the oblivion of pills but he resisted. He wasn't going to let either Hoffmann or Geneva catch him at it again. 'I don't buy it. There's just as many differences as there are similarities between the Bali killing and Anna's murder.'

Hoffmann acknowledged this with a nod. 'Yes, of course, but it's knowing which are important.'

'Lucy Brown was raped. We don't know about Katrina but Anna wasn't. I'd say that's a pretty significant shift in both MO and signature.'

'Of course you would,' Hoffmann said. 'But the rape may tell us nothing. These migrants may have raped her, even if they didn't kill her. Or it may be that our guy raped Lucy and found the experience unsatisfactory to what he needed so, the next time, he forgoes it.'

Carrigan didn't agree but he had to admit it was possible. 'You think he started over there?'

Hoffmann smiled. 'Yes, I believe so. Maybe because it's easier – large groups of unsupervised girls, the wide open beaches and sudden darkness of the islands, the way we do things abroad we'd never do at home. It's not unusual behaviour. Look at Lucian Staniak and the Vienna Woods Killer. Many murderers get their start on holiday.'

'Then what?' Carrigan said. 'He followed the girls here?'

'Precisely.'

'That still doesn't explain how both Katrina and Anna ended up at the Milgram.'

'Maybe they arranged to meet up in London,' Hoffmann replied. 'Maybe they talked about the Milgram. It's only a coincidence because we haven't seen the pattern yet.'

Geneva's phone buzzed. She checked it and a grin spread

across her face. She looked up to see Carrigan and Hoffmann still arguing. 'Neilson was right. You two *are* like dinosaurs. You can talk about possible connections between the girls and behavioural indicators another time. None of that matters now – we've got him.'

Hoffmann waited until Geneva was out of earshot then leaned across the table, his voice dropping down to a whisper. 'A minute?'

Carrigan shrugged and sat back down.

'I know this isn't the time nor the place but we're both stuck here so—'

'What is it you want to say?'

Hoffmann's eyes slid away from Carrigan. 'I'm sorry. I'm just so sorry about everything. The way it all turned out. Christ, that's not what I ever intended . . .'

Carrigan was about to reply when he realised the profiler wasn't talking about the case. 'You made a choice. You went with someone else's wife.'

'But the illness? That was something . . . fuck. I'm so sorry.'

Carrigan studied him for a long moment. 'So, what you're saying is that if she hadn't got sick you would have continued seeing her?'

'That isn't what I meant.'

'But that's what would have happened?'

Hoffmann hung his head and didn't deny it. Carrigan reached out his hand and brushed the profiler's shoulder. 'I would have preferred that, you know. At least I would have known she was happy. It's those last few hours that keep coming back to me, the utter blackness she must have been feeling, all the thoughts spinning through her mind . . .' Something struck Carrigan and he looked up. 'All along? You knew that I knew about you?'

Hoffmann nodded. 'Louise guessed you'd worked it out. That you were going to leave her. That's why she did what she did.'

Carrigan's cup rattled against the saucer. 'What the fuck do you mean? She killed herself because she couldn't face the coming months.'

Hoffmann cradled his head in his palm. 'She did it for you. She did it so *you* wouldn't have to suffer, wouldn't have to see her screaming in pain every day. She knew you'd found out about us and she felt it was unfair to put you through all that. She was too weak to leave you by then. She thought about it for several weeks. It wasn't some spur of the moment thing, a sudden low spell, nothing like that. You knew Louise. She would never do anything without thinking it through.'

'She told you all this and you didn't try to stop her?'

'She sent me a letter. It arrived . . . after.' Something had gone from Hoffmann's eyes, a spark that had previously animated even his grimmest comments. 'I know it's dumb and irrational but I keep thinking if I hadn't been with her, if none of that had happened, would the rest have?'

'You made her happy. I'm glad she was happy. Let's just leave it at that.'

39

Carrigan made his way up to the small cramped space off the main incident room, his brain still reeling from Hoffmann's confession. He forced himself to shut it down and concentrate on what was in front of him.

On the screen next to Neilson – an empty room.

They sat and watched. Time ticked off in rain splatter and thunder crack.

Then they saw her glide across the screen, a willowy suggestion of a figure, nothing more than a slight disturbance in the colour field, too fleeting to fully apprehend. 'All good on our end,' Neilson said into the mike.

As Carrigan watched, the figure came back, stopped halfway across the room and sat down in front of the computer. DS Singh's face filled the screen. Neilson nodded, pressed a key and the screen flipped to another angle, another room, another woman. This was DC Roth, one of Nielson's constables. She was standing in front of a mirror directly in the computer's sight-line. She was straightening her blouse and smoothing down her trousers.

'We're all set,' Neilson said, crumpling up the chocolate wrapper and pulling out a wet wipe. 'Singh's in our room downstairs. It's made up like a bedroom for exactly this kind of procedure. Roth's on her day off but she agreed to help us from home.' Neilson turned to Carrigan. 'You ready to start?'

Carrigan tried to shake away Hoffmann's words, the deep vaulted ripples they were spreading through his stomach, the fact he'd got everything wrong, including his own life. 'How do we know he's going to go for it?'

Neilson hitched her shoulders. 'We don't, not for certain, but luckily for us, PANOPTEASE is a compulsive slave-trader. In the last three weeks alone, he's acquired thirty-two new slaves. We spent a couple of hours analysing the clips he's posted and working out his preferred type.'

'Singh?'

Neilson nodded. 'He likes thin women with long hair. So, that's what we have for him. Whether he goes for it or not depends on whether his libido trumps his paranoia. He's online at the moment and posting on several boards since late last night so we know he's active. He's been arguing with other Ratters, trolling and flaming for hours.'

'It doesn't get him thrown off?'

Neilson laughed. 'In this place? It's a badge of honour. More importantly, he has the goods. No one's going to throw him off as long as he posts content like those Anna clips.'

Neilson went back to the keyboard. She started typing, the words appearing in a small box at the top left-hand corner of the screen. 'I'm posting a general message to all board users,' she explained. 'It would be too obvious to target him directly.'

'Won't it seem weird anyway? You not being a regular member?'

'People from other forums always cross-post. I've used one of our identities from a stalking forum, one we've had a presence on for a while now.' She resumed typing and the small box filled up.

Hey! Popped over from allyoucanhunt.com, heard good things about you guys here. Need something a little new. Got some stuff to share – enjoy!

'Now, we wait.' Neilson reached for another bar of chocolate. 'I've uploaded two twenty-second clips of Singh and Roth. You've got to post original stuff on these forums or they kick you out. These are just ones of Singh and Roth typing, nothing too explicit, but it shows I have some goodies in my hard drive.'

They sat and clock-watched and typed into their phones. Geneva composed a long text to Jim then deleted it. She wrote to her mother to say she'd call later. She looked over and saw Carrigan frowning over his phone, reading something, his mouth taut and strained.

'There he is!' Neilson rocketed her chair forward as a red light went on in one of the consoles attached to her mainframe. She smiled. 'He's had a look at the clips.'

Geneva rushed over to Neilson's desk. 'You can tell?'

'We've got the board cloned in real time on our servers. Means we can see what people are watching and when.' Neilson pointed to the screen. 'He's just watched the clips again for the second – no, third time.'

Carrigan and Geneva looked at the sidebar. A list of usernames was scrolling down its length, each one currently accessing the Singh/Roth videos. PANOPTEASE's name appeared three times in the last five minutes.

'He's definitely interested. Time to reel him in.' Neilson began typing. Words appeared in the small blue box.

Got these slaves I'm tired of. Anyone want to take them
off my hands?

They waited. Carrigan fielded calls and ignored others. Geneva
briefed uniforms and kept checking her phone. Over a hundred users had now watched the clips and twenty-one of them
had asked for more footage but Neilson ignored them. She was
busy on another computer, studying long rolls of code, and
then Carrigan saw a smile crack her face.

'He's just posted on another forum, an extreme porn one,
asking if anyone's heard of me. He's checking my bona fides,
which means he's definitely interested.'

'Won't that give the game away?' Carrigan said.

Neilson shook her head and typed fast. 'He's just had me
confirmed as a genuine member by three other users of that
site. They all vouched for me.'

'They don't know you're a cop?'

'*They* don't exist. I control all three accounts. Remember
that *New York Times* cartoon? *On the Internet no one knows
you're a dog*? – well, no one knows you're a *pig* either.' Neilson
smiled at her own joke and hit the Return key. 'Good. He's
watching them again.'

'He's not going to suspect it's a trap?'

'Desire always wins out over logic for these guys. If it didn't,
they wouldn't be here in the first place.' She looked up at the
screen. 'And here we go.' A line of text appeared in her blue box.
It was in a different font.

PANOPTEASE: I like what I see.

LOOKATYOU: I only have the highest quality. None of that skank meat here.

PANOPTEASE: You have a live feed?

LOOKATYOU: That and much more.

PANOPTEASE: You should post it, then. You shouldn't play games. That's not the way it works. You're making a choice and you should be aware that for every choice there are consequences and that those consequences will sit on your shoulders and no one else's.

LOOKATYOU: Bad boys don't get to see nothing.

PANOPTEASE: How do you know I can't see you now?

Neilson looked up from the screen. 'Let's give him a couple of minutes to stew.'

'That exchange won't have put him off?'

Neilson laughed. 'They thrive on it. These boards, it's nearly all male – teenagers to boot – and so it's all about insults and what I'll do to your mother.'

They waited and watched the blue box. Nothing happened for five minutes and then PANOPTEASE couldn't hold back any longer.

PANOPTEASE: I want to see more. You wouldn't have posted those clips if you weren't ready

to share. So, please, for your sake, stop
playing games.

LOOKATYOU: £

PANOPTEASE: You aren't even remotely aware
of what I can do to you, are you? You don't
realise I can destroy your entire life in
five minutes. Without moving from my seat.
If you have a wife, I will turn her against
you with what she finds on your computer.
If your parents are still alive, I'll send
them a message saying all the things you've
always been too scared to say. How much you
detest them. How they are small and stupid and
wrong. And if you have children, I'll show
them things that will make them no longer
children.

'He's just tried to get into our system,' Neilson said as she
continued typing. 'Trying to steal the images and fuck up our
hard drive. Good luck to him with that.'
    'Switch off the Singh/Roth clips,' Carrigan said and Neilson
immediately saw what he was thinking and did it.

PANOPTEASE: I know where you live. I've
already learned more about you than even
your closest friends know. Don't let me use
it to hurt you. I don't want to do that but
I will.

LOOKATYOU: ff

PANOPTEASE: How do I even know you've got
what you say you've got? How do I know you
didn't rip those clips off some other site?
You're lying. Don't waste my time. Don't
think you can outsmart me. You'll never be
alone again. If you use a phone or computer
or TV, I'll be there with you.

Carrigan smiled. Neilson turned to one of the other computers and told Singh and Roth to get ready, then switched on
their feeds. Roth was quietly eating dinner on the sofa, feet up,
a short skirt revealing long legs. Singh was typing and biting
her lips.

'He's watching them,' Neilson confirmed.

Roth was the better actress, Carrigan could tell. She was
teasing PANOPTEASE with the way she sat, the way she
moved, the way she got up and took off her sweater. Neilson
cut the feed at that exact moment.

They sat back and waited. Seven minutes later, text appeared
in the blue box.

PANOPTEASE: How much?

Neilson silently punched her fist in the air. Carrigan and
Geneva looked at each other. They hadn't thought the RAT
trap would work – most criminals were too cagey and paranoid
to fall for something like this – but Neilson had understood
their prey better than they did.

LOOKATYOU: 20 each. You get access codes exclusively.

PANOPTEASE: Okay. Bitcoin.

LOOKATYOU: No. Don't trust Bitcoin. Silk Road, duh? C/C only. Use secure Tor site.

Neilson keyed in a long string of commands. There was no reply for a while. She explained to Carrigan and Geneva that the electronic currency favoured by most hackers, Bitcoin, had taken a series of blows when sites such as the drug marketplace Silk Road had been shut down, resulting in millions of Bitcoins being wiped off the map. Many still preferred to use credit cards on untraceable sites. It was how most child porn was funded. Done through Tor, the onion routing network, it was completely untraceable.

'If that's the case, how are we going to trace him back to a real-world person?'

'I said the pay sites were untraceable. I didn't say the one PANOPTEASE will pay us through is. We've been developing fake sites for the last two years. What's called phishing in the hacker world. You go to a site that looks identical to your Barclays one but it's actually a copy set up to harvest passwords. Same here. We have a site that looks and reads identical to the one they use. By now he'll be too impatient to get the goods. He won't bother to run proper checks, too time-consuming. And as soon as he puts his credit card details into the site, we've got him.' Neilson allowed herself a smile as she typed into the blue box.

LOOKATYOU: You want to buy? I have others expressing an interest.

PANOPTEASE: I've warned you.

PANOPTEASE: Last chance.

PANOPTEASE: Okay.

40

They had a name, an address, an occupation. They knew where the killer lived, the type of car he drove and what he spent his money on.

PANOPTEASE had entered his credit card details into Neilson's fake site. Neilson punched the numbers into a reverse directory. The credit card was registered to a Michael Hart. Geneva put the name into the PNC as well as council and inland revenue databases.

'No hits on the PNC,' she told Carrigan. 'He's clean.'

'That doesn't mean anything,' Carrigan replied. 'Everyone's clean until they're not.'

Geneva and Neilson exchanged a glance, then Geneva switched tabs and resumed her search. 'Now, this is much more interesting.' She tilted the screen towards Neilson. 'Hart teaches at an all-girls' school in Camden. Been there fifteen years.'

They looked at each other. In the post-Savilian age, anyone whose job gave them unsupervised access to children was immediately suspect. Carrigan skimmed the scant facts on offer. He couldn't help but think how useful InfoCatcher would have been right now.

Hart lived on Highland Avenue, a narrow and extremely exclusive street cresting the heights of Holland Park. Carrigan studied the house on his computer screen. As soon as they'd got the address they'd plugged it into Street View and surveyed the area. The road climbed up towards the park at a steep angle, unusual for London, a city of mainly flat plains and low hills. Trees striped the street in shadow and hid the houses from casual scrutiny. Hart's house was huge and set back from the road, ringed by high hedges and tall oaks. A small drive jutted out from the property and a shiny black BMW stood idle on the flagstones. They used Street View to check all angles of approach and escape. There was no need to do preliminary surveillance. All they needed for the task was right here on screen. Carrigan had already notified Branch. The warrant would be ready by morning.

'Zoom in there.' Carrigan watched as the front door of the house filled the screen. A silver security camera sat perched gargoyle-like above the lintel. 'He's going to see us as soon as we make the gate,' Carrigan said. 'We don't know what weapons he might have in there with him. We do know, from everything we've learned about him, that he will have prepared for this eventuality. We've got a surveillance team watching the house. If he makes a move during the night, they'll grab him. If not, we'll pay him a visit nice and early. Either way, we end this tomorrow.'

41

The back-up team were suited up in black, with dark visors shielding their faces, looking more like a futuristic army fighting on another planet than a group of public servants deployed in one of the leafier parts of the capital. They made their way to Holland Park in the pre-dawn blur, approaching the house from three directions to triangulate their target. The street was quiet and deserted, the first rays of sunlight bleaching the eastern sky. Birds perched on telephone poles, slick with last night's rain. Carrigan watched as heavily laden figures scurried through the underbrush, a few birds exploding out of the road in stark surprise. He signalled them to wait. They were only to be deployed if needed. Carrigan hoped that words, not guns, would secure Michael Hart.

The BMW was parked in the drive. Carrigan put his hand to the bonnet but it was cold. His skin chafed against the bullet-proof vest and his head was pounding. He hadn't taken any pills this morning – had actually got to the point where he was about to swallow them when he remembered his vow and reluctantly put them back in the drawer.

He was approaching the front door when he heard the sound of someone running. Carrigan turned to see Hoffmann coming up the drive, in a half-jog, his forehead mottled with sweat and his breath short and snatched.

'What the fuck are you doing here?'

Hoffmann wiped his brow. 'I've been going through the transcripts all night,' he said. 'And I think I was wrong.'

'You *think* you were wrong?'

'But I'm not sure, which is why I want to sit in for this. I have a theory.'

'Are you going to share it with us?' Carrigan said, a snap entering his voice.

'No,' Hoffmann replied. 'It'll influence your questions. And, as I mentioned, I may be wrong.'

'That's good to know.' Carrigan wanted Hoffmann gone but there was no point in arguing. The longer they stood outside the house, the more likely they were to tip off Michael Hart to their presence. 'Just make sure you stay behind us. We don't know what he's got in there or how hard he's prepared to fight.'

Carrigan pressed the buzzer. There was no answer and he was about to press it again when the door opened, releasing a wash of heat and steam.

'Yes? Can I help you?'

The woman was wearing a large red bathrobe, a towel cinched around her waist. She was tall and slim, streaks of white snaking through her hair, her face sharp-boned as a bird.

'We need to speak to Michael Hart.'

'I'm Valerie Hart. His wife. You can speak to me.'

Her tone brooked no argument, a woman used to getting her way, Carrigan thought, not scared by the sight of policemen at her door in the early morning. He handed her the warrant. She squinted and brought the paper closer to her face.

'You can read it when we're inside.'

Her eyes shot up. 'No. Let me finish. I know my rights.'

'Good,' Carrigan replied. 'Then I don't need to explain that you have no choice but to let us enter.'

She continued reading, and when she was done, she turned and without a word disappeared back into the darkness of the hallway. Carrigan, Geneva, Hoffmann and two officers from the search team followed her in.

'What do you want with my husband?' Valerie Hart lowered herself onto an overstuffed Chesterfield, the robe tight around her waist, her eyes watching their every move. In the corner, reading a book, sat a skinny boy, fourteen or fifteen years old, with black hair neatly parted at the side. He wore a button-down shirt, khaki slacks and serious shoes. He glanced at the policemen for a moment, then went back to his book. Above him hung a painting of the crucifixion, except that Jesus's face had been replaced with Che Guevara's. Carrigan couldn't tell whether it was meant to be ironic or not. He sat down on a chair directly opposite the Chesterfield. 'Your husband teaches at The Camden Girls' Boarding School?'

'Yes, but you already know that.'

'What's his subject?'

'History and Technology. How the computer changed the twentieth century.' Valerie Hart looked up, a sudden animation in her expression. 'Imagine the Second World War without Turing and Enigma? How do you think we would have fared? Or imagine how hot the Cold War would have been without the threat of mutually assured destruction?'

Carrigan nodded politely. 'That's all very fascinating, Mrs Hart, but I'd rather hear it directly from your husband.'

'He's not here.'

'What do you mean?'

'What do you think I mean? He's not here, in the house – do you understand that?'

'But we've had surveillance throughout the night. No one saw him leave.'

Valerie Hart smiled. 'That's because he doesn't use the front door. His bike's out back and that's how he always goes to work.'

'Shit.' Carrigan looked down at the coffee table, immaculate and smudgeless and so unlike his own. He checked his watch. 'He'll be at school by now?'

Valerie Hart smiled. 'No. Not today. He left early because they're taking the girls on a trip.'

'Where to?' Geneva asked.

'Somewhere in the north of Scotland. They caught the train this morning.'

'How long is he away for?'

'Six days.'

'Fuck.'

Carrigan heard Geneva swear under her breath. Their main suspect was on a train heading to the remote north of the country with a group of young women. It didn't bear thinking about.

'What is it you're blaming him for now?'

The question surprised Carrigan and he had to fight the urge to glance over at Geneva. 'You say that as if he's no stranger to trouble?'

Valerie Hart's smile turned off as if a switch had been flicked. 'He's a schoolteacher, for God's sake. Don't you have better things to do than harass people whose thinking you don't agree with? His politics have nothing to do with you.'

'I'm not here about his politics.'

'Yeah, yeah, yeah, but somehow it always comes down to that. You'd think we live in a totalitarian country the way you lot go on. He warned me this day would come.'

'He did?' Geneva said.

'He said one day you'd be smashing down our door. Ever since that protest march last year. He told me all about the lists.'

Carrigan looked over at Hoffmann but could not read his expression. 'Lists?'

'Don't play ignorant. There are always lists. All the meetings and protests he goes to. All the petitions he signs. He knows you guys film everyone who attends, tap phones of anyone whose thinking you don't agree with.'

'I'm afraid they keep all that stuff from me,' Carrigan replied. 'I don't think they trust me. But I'm not here about that. I haven't got the slightest interest in his politics.'

Valerie Hart blinked twice. 'This isn't about Saturday's march?'

'No,' Carrigan said. 'This is about Friday night. Do you know where your husband was between 7 p.m. and 10 p.m. last Friday night?'

'He was right here with me.'

'Anyone else who can verify that?'

Valerie Hart shook her head.

Carrigan thought about how close Holland Park was to Queensway and the alley where Anna had disappeared. 'How proficient is your husband with computers?'

'I told you, he teaches Technology.' She looked at him and

Carrigan thought he saw something new in that look, a slight stumble of recognition, the growing disorder in the weave of her past.

'Has your husband been to Bali in the last twelve months?'

'Bali? No, of course not.'

'We're going to need his computer, both laptop and home. His phones, too.'

'His computer?' Something struck her and she looked away. 'Why would you want those?'

'Because they're in the warrant,' Carrigan replied. 'And because your husband's credit card was used in an illegal transaction last night.'

'Anyone could have done that. You read about ID theft all the time.'

'You do, indeed,' Carrigan said, watching Hoffmann out the corner of his eye. The profiler had sat up, suddenly animated, something in the conversation sparking connections in his brain. 'Which is why we also checked the IP address the credit card was used from and it originated here.'

'You're out of your mind.'

'These are facts, Mrs Hart. It has nothing to do with me or my mind.' Carrigan turned to Geneva. 'We need to stop that train. Once he's in Scotland—'

'Don't bother.' Hoffmann got up from his armchair, his eyes bright and alert. 'It's not the train we're after.' He took a couple of steps forward, briefly looking over at the boy. 'Mrs Hart, I was wondering whether your husband's ever taught Classics?'

'What? No.' The question seemed to unsettle her and Carrigan could see how the profiler's presence was working to their advantage.

'Perhaps ...' Hoffmann continued, the words trailing off. 'Perhaps he studied it at university?'

'He studied History. That's why he teaches History.'

'I understand that, Mrs Hart.' Hoffmann looked over at the boy again. 'But surely he'd have a basic understanding of, say, Greek mythology? The Greek pantheon? Figures like Zeus, Panoptes, Poseidon?'

'What? I don't understand?'

Hoffmann smiled. 'No, I don't believe you do, but I think your son does.' Hoffmann turned to the far corner but the boy was already up and running.

He almost made it to his bedroom. He was opening the door when Geneva reached him. He looked up at her, something in his brain clicked and his shoulders slumped.

'How did you know?' Carrigan stopped Hoffmann at the top of the stairs.

'I was watching him,' the profiler replied. 'His eyes weren't moving across the page. He was only pretending to read while he was listening to us. And every time you mentioned computers, he gripped his book a little tighter. He also fits the profile better than his father does.'

Carrigan thought about it but there wasn't much to think about, the boy's flight had confirmed Hoffman's theory.

'You shouldn't have run,' Carrigan said as he entered the room. 'It would have taken us a few hours to have chased up that train and work out you used your dad's credit card and by then who knows what you might have been able to erase from your hard drive?'

'You can't talk to him like that.' The woman grabbed Carrigan by the elbow. 'How dare you?'

Carrigan pulled himself free. 'Your son's been up to things he shouldn't have been up to. Maybe you ought to ask him why we're here?'

She glanced at Geneva and sighed theatrically. 'This is typical of you lot. Just barge in and bully and intimidate everyone. I'm going to call my solicitor.'

'Please do that,' Carrigan replied. 'Your son will need him.'

The woman's expression shifted as she looked over at her son. Nothing was said for a few moments. Carrigan kept his mouth shut.

'What did you do, Hugo?'

'Nothing, Mum. I wasn't doing anything.'

The woman turned to Carrigan. 'You need to leave before I get in touch with your boss.'

'I'm not leaving without your son or his computer.'

'He's only fifteen, for God's sake. What can he have possibly done?'

Carrigan turned to Hugo. 'Show her. Show her what you've been up to.' When the boy didn't respond, Carrigan added, 'Show her or I will.'

Hugo blinked. Carrigan waited, giving the boy a chance, and then nodded to one of the techs. The tech swiped the mouse and the monitor came to life.

'Oh my God!' Hugo's mother put her hand up to her mouth as she took in the screen. It was divided into twelve squares. Each square held a live feed, three-quarters of them populated by young women staring back out. 'What . . .?'

The girls onscreen typed, or hummed, or did their hair.

Hugo tried to disappear into his chair.

Hugo's mother frowned. 'Tell me this has nothing to do with you?'

Hugo didn't reply.

She turned to Carrigan. 'You did this. You set this up, didn't you?'

Carrigan glanced over at Hugo. 'Perhaps you should tell your mother what username you go by, show her some of your comments?'

IV

42

'Your suspect is fifteen?'

Branch was standing in front of the whiteboard, his bulk blocking out the photos of the missing women. A thin line of sweat glossed his forehead as he used his pipe to stab punctuation marks into the air. 'I sincerely hope this is some sort of practical joke because, otherwise, it suggests an incompetence that is staggering and exactly the kind of thing we don't need at this particular time.'

They were alone in the incident room, everyone else gathering evidence or securing testimony but most of all trying to understand how all the clues they'd followed had led them to a fifteen-year-old boy. There'd been confusion, disbelief and stifled anger when they'd brought Hugo in. Everyone wide-eyed and pissed off as they'd watched their suspect and his mother being marched to an interview room.

'We followed the evidence.' Carrigan felt a swirl of emotions rattling through his chest. He tried to get comfortable on the chair. 'This is where it led us.'

'Then I suggest you review the evidence again.'

'We have.'

'Are you telling me a fifteen-year-old boy spiked two women, then abducted one and drove her away in a bloody van?'

'No. But he—'

Branch tapped his pipe against the desk. 'Then let him go

before we're up to our necks in lawsuits and more fucking internal investigations. Quinn's probably laughing his head off
right now, having heard you arrested a fifteen-year-old for our
murder – laughing and working out how he's going to use it
against you.'

'I didn't arrest him. I asked him to come in so he could answer some questions. His mother agreed. I went by the book.'
Carrigan held his hand up before Branch could interrupt. 'I
know what you're saying, I know how this looks, but I can't let
him go.'

'He's a minor, for God's sake.'

Carrigan took a deep breath, trying to concentrate on the
space behind Branch, the faces of Anna and Katrina silently reminding him why he was doing this. 'A minor who was running
234 slaves on his computer, some of them as young as twelve.
With all due respect, sir, children are not what they used to be.'

Branch sighed and took off his glasses. 'Do you really think
the boy has anything to do with these murders?'

'He posted the Anna clips.'

'It's the Internet, Carrigan. Even I know he could have taken
it from a million different sites and reposted it.'

'I don't think so. These clips aren't on any other sites and the
metadata tells us it's very close to the source.'

'But you admit he isn't our killer?'

'I don't know. It's complicated. We're pursuing another line
of investigation which might help us clear things up. The
profile led us away from the facts. Hoffmann led us straight to
the boy.'

'You're blaming him for this?' Branch rocked his head from
side to side as if trying to dislodge a particularly stubborn knot

in his shoulder. 'What exactly is going on between the two of you?'

'Nothing.'

'Fine. Have it your own way. But keep in mind that all this time you're chasing false leads, Patterson and his goons are collecting data on you, gathering information that will fuck you up in court.'

'Do you think I don't know that?'

'And you still mean to interview the boy?'

Carrigan nodded. 'He's a teenager. He'll be terrified. I'll get what I need in no time.'

43

'This is the wrong Coke. I can't drink this.'

Carrigan looked at the can. 'You asked for Diet Coke?'

Hugo held it up. 'Does this say Diet Coke? No. It says Coke Zero. It's a different colour. It's a different drink. If I'd wanted Coke Zero, I would have asked for Coke Zero.'

This wasn't their regular interview room. This room looked like a conference suite in an elegant but slightly down at heel airport hotel. It was the one they reserved for debriefing sensitive witnesses and sexual assault victims. It was where they told relatives they would never see their sons or daughters again. The carpet was deep and stifled every sound, a soft neutral grey like a bed of ash. Posters from bygone theatre productions dotted the walls. The chairs were upholstered and comfortable and not bolted to the floor.

Hugo Hart sat slouched on a chair, one leg draped across the armrest, playing with his phone. His mother kept telling him to put it away, then finally prised it from his hands and deposited it in her handbag. They shot each other looks long rehearsed, an entire history of disagreements, sulks and petty estrangements in a single glance. A social worker sat between them, long-legged and lost in a world of his own.

Carrigan looked over at Geneva and nodded. They'd developed a pattern to interviews. They could tell as soon as they met someone which of them should take the lead. The giveaway was always there, in the split-second hesitation of a handshake or the slant of a wayward eye. Carrigan activated the recorder. He was halfway through stating his name when Hugo interrupted.

'You've got a camera there, right?' The boy was pointing at the small black bauble in the top left-hand corner of the ceiling.

'And another behind the glass.' Carrigan gestured to the large mirror on the opposite side of the room.

'Of course.' Hugo brushed his fingers through his hair. It was a gesture meant to appear nonchalant and casual but it only had the opposite effect. 'There's always one more camera in any given room than you think there is.'

'I like that,' Carrigan said.

Hugo tried to mask his smile.

'Where did you read it? A blog?'

'A book, actually.' Like most teenagers, Hugo was pitch perfect in that particular blend of confidence and sarcasm. His face was narrow and craggy, all planes and bones, the kind of face that would get him a lot of attention from girls in a couple of years but which only looked awkward and lopsided now. 'You're recording everything, right? Video and audio?'

Carrigan nodded.

'I want copies. Before I leave. That's my right, isn't it? To make sure you don't tamper with the tapes and make me say things I didn't say.'

'We don't tamper with the tapes, Hugo.' Carrigan took a sip of coffee. 'You know why? We don't need to. The people we bring into this room are the right people and, most of the time, they're intelligent enough to realise they can't lie to us and get away with it, so they tell us the truth.'

'Detective Inspector!' The social worker sprang forward. He was tall and twitchy, every knuckle and joint seemingly moving of their own accord, his eyes shot a deep red. 'You can't harass the boy, this isn't your normal—' He stopped and hacked his way through a coughing fit, his face blushing bright red.

'You should think about investing in a vaporiser,' Carrigan said, catching a strange look in Geneva's eye as the social worker tried to reply, only to double over into another coughing fit.

'I want you to know you're simply here to answer a few questions,' Carrigan told the boy. 'We haven't arrested or cautioned you – do you understand?'

'You mean, I can walk out of here any time I want?' He glanced over at his mother with a triumphant grin. She looked away.

'You could,' Carrigan replied, glad she was here. It would allow him to read the boy through her expressions. 'But then you'd leave us no choice but to arrest you so we can ask you those same questions. Either way, we get our answers, but one way you get to go home tonight and the other, you don't.'

Hugo placed both hands flat on the table and leaned forward. 'What's your IQ?'

'I have no idea.'

'Mine's 155.'

'That means nothing to me.' Carrigan checked his watch, hoping the social worker wouldn't end the interview before he got what he wanted. He could see the man sneaking looks at him and writing furiously in his notebook.

'It means I'm much cleverer than you or anybody in this room,' Hugo said. 'So you're not going to beat me by playing word games or trying to trick me into saying something.'

'You're absolutely right.' Carrigan was happy to see he'd managed to wipe the smirk off Hugo's face. 'It's not going to be my brain or logic that's going to nail you – it'll be facts. No matter how clever you are, you can't argue against facts.'

Hugo shifted in his seat. 'What facts?'

Carrigan drained his espresso and wiped his lips with the back of his hand. 'Your computers are whispering all your secrets into our technicians' ears at this very moment. So, enough. Your mother wants to go home, you want to go home and I want to go home, so let's make it easier for ourselves and start by telling me what you know about the clips you posted on whatyoudontknowcanthurtyou.com.'

Hugo crossed his legs. 'And what if I decide not to say any-thing?'

'This isn't a film and this isn't America. You do not have the right to remain silent. Not here. So, the sooner we talk, the sooner you get out of this room.'

'You just want me to say something so you can keep me here for good. You have no intention of letting me go.'

'Hugo, for God's sake!' The boy's mother was halfway out of her seat when Carrigan held his hand up.

'Mrs Hart, please don't interrupt.' He looked over at the boy. Hugo was grinning. Carrigan rubbed his head. Spiky tendrils swarmed behind his eyes. His skull pounded in time with his pulse. He felt the strip of pills weighing down his pocket. 'You need to tell us about the Anna clips, Hugo.'

'Who?'

Carrigan slid over a series of screen shots, each bearing Anna's face.

Hugo picked one up and carefully studied it. 'She's cute.'

Carrigan snatched the photo away. 'She's also dead, Hugo. This isn't some computer game. Someone kidnapped her. They cut her throat and let her bleed to death. At this moment our most logical suspect is the person who filmed and uploaded these clips, and that's you.'

'Murder?' Hugo glanced at his mother. 'What are you talking about?'

Carrigan fanned the photos. 'You posted these videos on the forum.'

'You can't prove that.' As Hugo's tone became more petulant, he sounded closer to his real age, callow and dismissive and slightly pissed off.

Carrigan sighed. 'We already did, Hugo. How do we think we found you? You made these clips and you posted them on that forum to show everyone how clever you were. But that's not all you did, is it? You trolled Anna on Twitter, sent her nasty photos, somehow rigged her computer to make those "voices" in the walls. Is that really how an intelligent boy like you gets his kicks?'

Hugo didn't reply. He stared down at the table and remained mute throughout Carrigan's further questioning.

They took a break. The social worker led Hugo to the canteen while Carrigan conferred with Geneva outside the interview room. Then, Hugo was back and Carrigan, having reached a dead end, tried a different tack.

'You say you're good with computers, right?'

The boy shook his head. 'A lot of people are good with computers. I'm way better than that.'

'I'm glad we've got that cleared up.' Carrigan wrote something down in his notebook. He was trying to work out which buttons to press and which to avoid if he wanted the truth out of this boy, how far he could go and how far he should go. 'How long have you been doing this?'

'Doing what?'

'Please stop playing games.'

'I'm not playing games,' Hugo replied. 'You need to be more specific if you expect me to answer you. I could have said forty minutes, the *this* you refer to could easily have meant answering your questions. How am I supposed to know what's in your head?'

Carrigan clenched his fist. If this were a normal interview he would turn to other strategies now, increase the pressure, but this was a boy, and his mother and social worker were watching, as was the constant eye of the camera. Carrigan took a deep breath. 'How long have you been running slaves?'

'I have no idea what you're talking about.'

'Hugo, listen to me. I know you're an intelligent boy, more so than most. So, just take a minute to think about your position. We've seized your computer and we know you had 234 slaves on tap at any hour of the day. We can even look and tell exactly when you logged on and to whom. Now, you could choose to insult me by telling me you downloaded the RAT program by accident, that you were trying to download a song and got this instead but I wouldn't advise that course of action and, I think, if you consider it, you'll realise it will only get you into deeper trouble.'

'Detective Inspector. Please?' The social worker said it more quietly this time, his voice trailing off on the last word.

Carrigan ignored him. 'Can I ask you a personal question, Hugo?'

'Sure. I guess.'

Carrigan took his time, studying his notebook and nodding to himself as if he'd just come to some important decision. 'Is there something wrong with you, Hugo?'

'What?'

'Because you're not a bad-looking kid,' Carrigan continued. 'You're smart, you've told me yourself how smart you are and so I assume there's something I'm not seeing because, otherwise, you'd be out in the real world with a flesh-and-blood girlfriend and not wasting your time glued to a computer screen. You should leave that to dirty old men.'

Hugo sat upright in the chair, a knotty tautness focusing his features. 'Maybe I don't want a girlfriend? Have you even considered that? Perhaps the world's moved on, old man.'

'You can tell yourself that, Hugo. You can even kid yourself into believing it but deep down you know you're lying to yourself. We always do.'

'You wouldn't understand.'

'Oh, believe me, I do.'

'It's not like you think,' Hugo said, all the sass and strut quickly draining out of him. 'I was lonely. That's all. I just wanted some company. It's hard to find girls to talk to and, anyway, it's easier to talk to people online. People lie when they know you're watching them. They never tell the truth to your face. Online, you don't have to be defined by how you look, how people choose to see you because you have red hair or zits or can't pronounce a word properly. It's more like your real self talking.'

'There's a big difference between Facebook and what you've been doing.'

'You still don't understand, do you? Facebook is too much like life – cliques and hierarchies and who you know. I didn't want to be alone in the evenings. You don't know what it's like to be alone.'

'Hugo, this is not the time or place.'

'Mrs Hart, please. Let him speak or I'll have to ask you to leave.'

Hugo turned to his mother with a smirk on his face. 'They're never there,' he said, looking directly at her. 'I get home from school and go straight to my room. Mum's always on the phone, Dad's never back from work in time, so I switch on my slaves. They keep me company while I do my homework. I can see them out the corner of my eye and, sometimes, it's almost like they're in the same room with me. Like they're doing their homework or something and so am I.'

Hugo's mother shook her head repeatedly. Geneva kept her jaw clamped shut. Carrigan scribbled down notes. 'How did you go from watching them to Ratting them? That's a big leap.'

Hugo shrugged and Carrigan realised that for a teenager it wasn't.

'You have to if you want to stay on the good boards. I got bored of the one I was on, it was just short clips – I wanted live feeds, real-time, but on those boards if you're not posting original content they won't let you join. I wanted more control. I wanted to be able to look into every corner of their lives and see if it resembled mine.'

'And you worked out how to do it all by yourself?'

'There was nothing to work out. The programs are everywhere. Just type in *RAT tools* and see how many results pop up. They're a piece of shit, though. Very basic and unimaginative. I had to modify the code to get it working just right. I got a string of IP addresses off another forum member and started to actively trawl for women to add to my collection.' Hugo's eyes lit up and flashed a dark green. 'It was different. I knew it immediately the first time I went into someone else's computer. She was mine in a way the previous ones could never be.'

Geneva scraped her chair forward. She'd let Carrigan talk and he'd managed to wind Hugo up and get him to drop his defences but she couldn't keep silent any longer. 'And you never, not even once, felt a twinge of guilt at intruding into these girls' privacy?'

Hugo shrugged. 'Not really. It's just images on a screen. There's no harm in that.'

'Try telling that to Anna Becker.'

'Who?'

Geneva frowned. 'The dead girl whose clips you posted to show everyone how clever you are. Where did you get those clips, Hugo?'

'The net. I plugged into her laptop off Facebook.' The boy scratched his jaw, a tell Geneva had picked up on midway through the interview.

'That's interesting, since Anna wasn't on Facebook. How about I tell you what we know and see if it changes your mind? Because the person who made those videos of Anna, that's not all he did. He also stalked and trolled her on Twitter. Unlike the videos, the trolling consisted of making threats against her and the law's pretty clear on that. You're what? Fifteen? That's only three more years till they let you out.'

Hugo scratched his jaw again. 'What do you mean?'

'I mean that if you really did make those videos like you said, then we have a problem, but I don't think you did.'

Hugo's eyes flicked from his mother to the social worker.

'I looked at some of your other captures and they're very different in style from the Anna sequence. I've seen your work. You like it when they're naked. You edit out the boring bits.' Geneva's voice rang out across the table, a steely tremble underlying each word. 'Tell us where you got them from, Hugo, and all this will be over.'

'Okay, okay,' Hugo replied, his voice drawn down to a whisper. 'So they're not my work. So what?'

'Where did you get them from?'

'Where do you think? I stole them off someone else's computer.'

44

'You claimed her?'

'Claimed? What do you mean?'

Carrigan studied the boy's face. There was no discernible re-action to the word *claimed*. 'Whose computer did you steal the clips from?'

'How am I supposed to know? It's all automated. I have a program set up to do that for me.'

'What kind of program?'

'I told you. When I downloaded the RAT software off the web, I immediately saw it was shit. Just basic Ratting tools with a few add-ons – no one had taken the time to refine it. That pissed me off. I started fiddling with the code. I had to rewrite the entire program. It was clunky and inelegant. It had too many glitches and vulnerabilities. It wouldn't let me do what I wanted. I streamlined it and added all sorts of tools to make it more fun.'

'Like what?'

'A button that makes your start menu disappear or one that pops open your CD tray. That's always good for a scare.'

'Nice to know your high IQ is being put to good use.'

'You're so backwards.' Hugo shook his head in mock dismay.

'That I may be,' Carrigan replied. 'But you're the one in trouble here, not me, and you still haven't answered my ques-tion – how did you get hold of these clips?'

Hugo rubbed his shoes against one another. 'When I finished developing my Ratting program I posted it as freeware on the forum. But I also put in a backdoor so anyone who downloaded the program, I could sneak into their computers.'

'Why would you do that? I thought you were only interested in live girls.'

'I wanted the things people didn't post. The stuff they keep to themselves, the interesting stuff. So, I created an algorithm. Every morning it automatically searches through all the hard drives that have downloaded my Ratting program, trolling for image and video files and saving them onto my server. That's how I got the Anna videos. You pick up so much junk doing a data trawl but I could tell immediately this was different, that whoever Ratted her, his work was far superior to anything else on the board.'

'And so you pretended it was your own?'

Hugo's smile flickered. 'It got me some good trades. I thought it'd be cool.'

'Cool? Do you realise how much of our time you've wasted? Fuck.' Carrigan punched the table.

Hugo flinched and moved his chair back. 'There'll be a record.'

Carrigan looked over at the boy. 'What kind of record?'

'On my laptop, if I can access my server. It keeps a log of all the IPs it snatches data from.'

'I need you to find it.'

Hugo asked for his laptop. As soon as he got it, he became transformed, all the awkward edges of the past few hours tunnelled into an intense engagement with numbers and code. They watched as he ran a program through his hard drive.

They saw him smile as he turned to Neilson and pointed to a long string of numbers.

Neilson copied the numbers down and plugged them into her system. Hugo had accessed the Anna clips from this IP address. Neilson converted the numbers into a real-world location. She read out the street name and number and saw Carrigan and Geneva exchanging glances.

'What?'

Geneva double-checked the screen to be certain. She turned to Neilson and said, 'That's the address of the cleaning agency Anna worked for.'

45

There was nothing to be gained by holding Hugo any longer and they released him once he'd signed his statement. Carrigan went to his office, flicked on the coffee machine, and let his mind empty to the sound of hissing water. He closed his eyes and saw Anna on hands and knees, her body starred in supplication. He remembered the martyred penitents and combustible saints of his youth, their faces bathed in ecstatic torment. He drained the coffee in one gulp, made another, and escaped to the roof as the phones began ringing.

He stared out at a landscape obliterated by mist and drizzle, the mere suggestion of a city, and thought about the recent list of reversals and revelations. They'd double-checked the IP address on a different database but the result was the same. Hugo had downloaded the Anna clips from a computer located in the offices of Sparta Employment Agency. Carrigan had skimmed Geneva's report of the Eleanor Harper interview but there was frustratingly little to go on. Could a woman have done it? Hoffmann had ruled it out and, for once, Carrigan had to agree. This was a man's crime and Madison had seen a man carry Anna away. Carrigan shivered and pushed his hands deep into his pockets, a part of him welcoming the cold and soaked fabric, the way temperature can snap you back into your body, and made his way back downstairs.

Geneva was waiting in his office when he got there.

He switched on the overhead lights, dissipating the late-afternoon gloom, and headed straight for the coffee machine. 'You want one?'

Geneva nodded. 'We need to send a team over to Sparta as soon as possible.'

Carrigan passed her a cup. 'I read your notes. But they don't say much. Tell me, how did Eleanor Harper strike you?'

Geneva started to speak, then realised what he meant. Facts and theories came tumbling down and collapsed into one singularity. 'She was rude and stand-offish but I didn't get any vibe off her if that's what you mean?'

Carrigan nodded and wrote something down. 'Which is exactly why sending in a full team could be counter-productive. Someone like her will only clam up.' Carrigan sipped his coffee. 'We don't know for certain that she has anything to do with this. We know the killer is good with computers, he could have sat in the Sparta waiting room and piggy-backed their IP or he could have done it remotely.'

'Let me come with you. If she lied to me, I want to be there.'

'If she lied to you, she'll find it that much harder to change her story in front of you.'

Geneva nodded, realising he was right. 'I'd love to know what Hoffmann makes of this.'

Carrigan snorted and Geneva decided she'd had enough of these games, the petty boundaries men erect between themselves and the world. 'I need to know, Jack. Who is he to you?

And please, don't lie to me this time. Not again. You know you can trust me.'

Carrigan squeezed the coffee cup between his hands. He didn't answer for a long time. Finally, he put the cup on the table and cradled his head. 'He was my wife's lover.'

Geneva tried not to let the surprise show on her face. Then something else struck her. 'That's one hell of a coincidence.'

'It's not a coincidence,' Carrigan replied. 'Hoffmann's golf buddies with Quinn. It's why he gets all the top assignments. He probably told Quinn he fucked my wife and Quinn couldn't resist.'

Geneva shook her head. 'Shit. Was he still seeing Louise at the end?'

Carrigan saw his own face dimly reflected in the porcelain curve of the cup. 'I was going to leave her. I had it all prepared and then she came back from the doctor and everything had changed. Suddenly the affair didn't mean anything – not in the light of what was coming and the years we'd spent together. I fell in love with her all over again and I don't think she could handle that. Not with what was happening to her.' Carrigan looked down at his empty cup. 'I thought I was okay with it and then Hoffmann reappeared and I realised I'd been kidding myself all along.'

'And now?'

'Now? I don't know. It feels different.'

Geneva leaned over and brushed a flurry of crumbs from his lapel. The phone rang. Carrigan picked it up, muttered *Yes*, and put it back down.

'We got a hit on the Bali beach photo. Downstairs just got

a call from someone responding to our TV appeal. He recognised one of the girls.'

Geneva pushed her chair back. 'Which one?'

'That's the thing. He doesn't know her name. He's a doctor in the secure mental health unit at St Charles. He says the girl is one of his patients.'

46

'Frankly, we don't know if the story she told us is something that happened to her or something she imagined.'

'And you're not interested in finding out?' Geneva said, her trousers clinging to the chair's sticky leather skin.

Dr Brian Hunt shook his head. 'It's not relevant. What matters is that she believes it was real. It's these memories, regardless of their actual veracity, which are the cause of all her anguish and terror.'

Geneva was sitting in Hunt's office at the St Charles Hospital in North Kensington.

'She checked herself in six months ago,' Hunt continued. 'In a terrible state. Having paranoid delusions and seizures. We thought it was due to whatever drugs she was on and that it would wear off but it never did.'

'What condition am I likely to find her in? Will she be able to understand my questions?'

Hunt frowned. 'She has some memory loss. She can't remember her name or much of her childhood. By tomorrow, she won't recall meeting you. It's like her brain wipes itself every morning, but she can't forget the attack. She goes through long periods when she's almost what you and I would call normal and then something inside her snaps and her memories of the assault drag her back under. It's always inside her head, never an outside trigger. She's in one of her better states at the moment but talking about her ordeal is not something she's come to terms with yet. If it wasn't for the fact you've impressed on me how serious this is, I would have grave reservations about potentially upsetting her like this.'

'And you're not in the slightest bit interested in what really happened to her or who she is?'

The doctor shook his head. 'It's what she thinks happened to her that counts. The rest is up to you.'

Hunt led Geneva down a long corridor reeking of bleach and soap, through two locked doors and into a large, open-plan ward. He pointed to a woman hunched over a desk in the far corner then disappeared back down the hallway.

The ward was filled with the sound of screaming, moaning and weeping. The smell of institutional meals, bleach, urine, and bodies slowly rotting from the inside out. Two orderlies sat behind a desk, deep in gossip, totally unruffled by the bedlam surrounding them. A large TV hung on a wall, muted children's shows flashing across the screen.

Geneva felt her shoes stick and suck at the linoleum as she crossed the room, avoiding the manic stares and outstretched hands. She neared the woman and stopped a couple of feet away from her. Before coming here, Geneva had studied the Bali photo, committing to memory the faces of the girls, speculating on which one she would find. But she needn't have bothered.

She was facing a strikingly composed young woman hunched over a sprawling and intricate jigsaw puzzle. The woman was so focused on her task she didn't notice Geneva's approach. She was holding a beige square in her hand, two pegs protruding, weighing it in her palm and examining the scene in front of her. 'You always think this time you'll manage to complete it.'

She made no move to acknowledge Geneva's presence nor turn around and Geneva couldn't be sure if the words were addressed to her or to some imaginary companion perched atop the woman's shoulder.

'But you never do,' the woman continued, her voice scratchy and hoarse and slightly slowed down as if someone had placed a finger on the turntable. She was dressed in a bathrobe and grey felt slippers. Scars from several unsuccessful suicides crisscrossed her wrists. 'You never get to see the full picture. The pieces never fit, never quite fit, always one too many or one too few.'

She turned around and Geneva came face to face with a ghost.

47

He found Eleanor Harper alone in the empty waiting room, lost in a private waltz of tidying the scattered magazines and discarded application forms. Her eyes shot up and she froze midgesture as Carrigan's knock intruded into the room's silence. He saw her clutch the top of a chair, her hand wrapped tightly around the crossbar, whether for comfort or as potential weapon, he couldn't tell. He took out his warrant card and flicked it open.

'I already told the woman detective everything I know.' Eleanor walked towards a squat oval coffee table and dropped the magazines.

'I know you did,' Carrigan replied, watching her carefully. 'And I appreciate your co-operation, but I like to hear things for myself. It's my responsibility to the investigation to make sure I get as much as I can first-hand. I'm sure a woman in your position can understand that.'

Eleanor finally looked up, her eyes taking in the rumpled raincoat, crumpled trousers and untrimmed beard. A faint smile turned up one corner of her mouth. 'I don't imagine you're the kind of person who takes no for an answer?'

Carrigan laughed, then caught himself. 'This won't take up much time. And then you'll have us out of your hair for good.'

Her shoulders dropped slightly. 'Fine by me.' She edged the magazines with her hand until they were even and she was satisfied. 'I told your detectives, I have nothing to hide.'

'We all have something to hide, Ms Harper. Determining whether it has anything to do with the case is all I'm interested in.'

Her eyes darkened as she considered Carrigan's statement. Her face was severe and striking in the slightly unreal way of old paintings or silent movie stars. Her smile was cold and precise as if she'd measured out its exact width in the mirror. Her fingernails, glossy as jewels, clicked on the surface of the table. Carrigan realised he must stink of stale coffee and felt a curious schoolboy squirm behind her glare as they entered the office.

He took off his jacket and pulled out his notebook and pen. 'Some new questions have come up.' Carrigan flicked back a few pages until he found his notes from the Hugo interview. 'Were you here, in your office, on the evening of 12 May?'

The question surprised her. The metronome of her fingernails stopped and her forehead twitched as she realised this conversation wasn't going to be quite the same as the one she'd had with Geneva. She picked up a tub of hand cream and spun the lid. The city was a faint hum outside, like static from a detuned radio, everything muffled and made distant by height and glass. Eleanor scooped out a small snake of lotion and rubbed it into her palm. 'I don't like the way you're phrasing these questions.'

'I'm sorry about that, but I still need your answer.'

'Is this some sort of game? First that woman comes barging in here and now you?' She got up and reached for her handbag.

'Sit down,' Carrigan said. The smell of hand cream was cloying and chemical and way too sweet. 'You'll have to excuse me if I sound a little brusque, but I have two women dead. At least one of them got work through your agency in the weeks prior to her disappearance. Before she was killed, she was being filmed without her knowledge. Whoever did that was in your office on the evening of 12 May.'

'I have no idea what you're talking about and if you don't leave this minute, I'll—'

'You'll what?' Carrigan interrupted. 'Call the police?'

Eleanor took off her horn-rimmed spectacles, her eyes losing their fierce temper for a brief moment. 'Why should I tell you anything? Especially as you insist on being so rude.'

'Because he's already killed three girls we know about. Because he won't stop. This is simply him warming up. And if you're keeping anything from me and he goes on to kill again, you won't be able to live with yourself.'

'Three? I thought a moment ago you said two?'

'His first victim was in Bali. We're not—'

'Bali?' She spat the word out as if it were a piece of food that didn't taste quite right. 'What are you talking about? Why are you mentioning Bali? When did this happen?'

'Last summer. We believe it's likely this was his first. A girl called Lucy Brown.'

Eleanor shook her head and, for a brief moment, Carrigan caught sight of the trapdoor that had just sprung open beneath her life. 'I don't understand.'

'What don't you understand, Ms Harper?'

'They caught the men who did it. Caught them and executed them.'

Carrigan couldn't keep the surprise out of his voice. 'You know about Lucy Brown?'

'Is this some kind of sick joke? Of course I know about Lucy. Lucy was my daughter.'

48

Katrina Eliot looked like an older sister of the smiling sun-lit girl in the Bali beach photo. Her eyes were grey and worn and there was a fine hatchwork of lines radiating across her face. It was as if her youth had completely vanished in a matter of a few months. They'd feared she was dead or captive in some benighted basement but no one, not even Hoffmann, had predicted this.

Geneva took a step forward, ignoring the rest of the patients. 'Katrina?'

At first, there was no response, but when Geneva repeated the girl's name, Katrina froze.

'No one knows who I am,' she replied, pronouncing each word slowly and clearly, the sibilant hissing like steam.

'We can get you out of here.' Geneva glanced down at the table. The puzzle seemed to describe a network of labyrinthine rooms but Katrina had only completed a few unconnected fragments and it was impossible to tell what the piece was supposed to represent.

'What makes you think I want to leave?' Katrina said, her skinny body rocking back and forth in the chair. She glanced over at the orderlies. 'He sent you here, didn't he?'

'Who are you talking about?'

'You know who.'

'I'm here to make sure you're safe from him.'

'Where? Out in the world where he can find me just like that?' Katrina picked up a puzzle piece. 'Why do you think I'm here? I can leave anytime I want. Why do you think I never gave them my name?'

Geneva pulled out a chair and sat down. The seat was slightly wet but she ignored it. 'You checked yourself in so you could hide from him?'

'It's worked, hasn't it?'

'That's the only reason you're in here? To get away from him?'

'That and the fact I can't function out there any more. I try. I try so hard, but something always happens, something he did to me, and I find myself waking up in a hospital room, a doctor stitching my wrists or pumping my stomach.'

Geneva kept the Bali photo in her pocket for now. She wanted to hear Katrina's story untainted by knowledge of subsequent events. 'The man who did this to you is still out there. He's doing it to other girls. Whatever you can tell us, no matter how small, will help us stop him.'

Katrina stared at Geneva for a long time, a silent reckoning in her gaze. She put down the puzzle piece she'd been clenching and scraped her chair forward. 'I wasn't the type of girl this happens to,' she said. 'I wasn't one of those girls you see on a Saturday night, so drunk they can't even walk, spilling out of their clothes or passed out on the pavement.' She closed her eyes for a few seconds. 'But it doesn't matter, does it? Whether you're naive or drunk or wary?'

'No,' Geneva replied, thinking that for someone residing in a mental health ward, Katrina seemed surprisingly sane. 'Not if he's already singled you out.'

'I still blame myself.' Katrina tried to laugh it off. 'I keep thinking that if I hadn't left the bowling alley at that precise time, if I'd stayed for another round, if I'd stopped to buy those cigarettes ... there were an infinite number of ways I could have avoided walking past that alley at that exact moment but only one possible route to lead me there. How does that make any sense?'

'I don't know,' Geneva admitted. 'The things that should make sense rarely do.'

Katrina reached out and picked up one of the many pieces in front of her and unerringly fitted it into the puzzle. 'I left the bowling alley, I was feeling sick, thought maybe I'd had too much to drink or a dodgy curry. I was nearly home when I heard a baby crying, crying really hysterically, that annoying way babies do when you think they're never going to stop. It was coming from inside this alley. Look . . .' Katrina held up her hands. 'I know this is the point where you say I was crazy to go in there, a dark alley at night, right? – but the baby was crying and no one was doing anything about it.

'It took my eyes a couple of seconds to adjust but by then it was too late. There was no baby. There was only a man holding a mobile phone in his hands. He pushed a button on the phone and the baby stopped crying. Then he attacked me.'

'Do you remember anything after that?'

Katrina nodded. 'One minute I'm in that alley, the next thing I know I wake up and my head's pounding like crazy, there's this terrible taste in my mouth and I can't move, literally cannot move. Panicking. Thinking I'm paralysed. The room starts to spin and I turn my head and realise I'm tied down to a large wooden table. The wood is rough and I can feel it chafing against my skin and it's then I notice my legs are bare. I can tilt my head up just far enough to see I'm wearing a miniskirt that isn't mine.' Katrina stopped, counted to ten and back under her breath.

'Did you see him?'

'No, not his face. He was standing in the shadows,' Katrina said as Geneva tried to hide her disappointment.

'Did you notice if he spoke with an accent?'

'I only heard him breathing.'

'Breathing?'

'When I was strapped to the table, he was standing behind me, breathing heavily as if he had a really bad cold. Then I felt a sting in my right arm.'

'He injected you?'

Katrina nodded and started to turn over all the unused puzzle pieces. 'The first wave came about ten minutes later. I was short of breath, there was this awful buzzing behind my eyes like they were going to pop out of their sockets, the room rushing past me, my head splitting with pain, all these streaks of mad colour, being sick over and over again.'

'What happened next?'

Katrina laughed. She laughed for about thirty seconds too long. 'There was no next. Whatever he'd given me made me lose all sense of time. Time slowed down until there wasn't any difference between one minute and the next. I later found out I'd been missing for only three days.'

'How long did you think you'd been gone?'

'A year.' Katrina looked down at the table. 'I was certain a year had passed. I'd counted and lived through all those days and weeks. How could it have only been three days when I'd been in that room for months?' She paused and counted under her breath. 'Some days I'm convinced these past six months have been an hallucination and I'll wake up and be back on that table and only five minutes will have gone by.'

Geneva placed her hand over the girl's. 'You're here. This is real. I'm real.'

Katrina pulled her hand away.

Geneva sat back and waited for the girl to settle down. 'How did you manage to escape?'

'I didn't. I couldn't have escaped. No way. After some time passed, maybe weeks, maybe hours, I don't know, the door opened again. Something covered my eyes and I couldn't see.' She picked up one of the facedown pieces and flipped it and placed it in its rightful place. 'I felt the sting in my arm again and woke up on a bench in Hyde Park.'

'Did you report it to the police?'

Katrina searched Geneva's face for any hint of accusation. 'I barely knew where I was. I felt sick and spaced out. I lay down on the park bench and closed my eyes and I was back in that room again and I could taste the drug in my mouth, hear him breathing, feel the grainy wood scratching the back of my knees. This went on for what felt, to me, like weeks. I later discovered it all took place in less than ten minutes.'

She looked down at the floor and crossed her legs at the ankles. 'It comes back every now and then. I'll be in the middle of something else and then snap, I'm back in that room again and I don't know if I'm a patient in a mental institution who's having a flashback or if I'm still in that room, dreaming of being a woman who's only dreaming this.' She took Geneva's hand, her fingers bony and sharp, and squeezed, the pressure turning

Geneva's skin white. 'But the drugs couldn't still be in my system? Not after a year? No way. Not unless it isn't really a year and I'm still in that room and this entire conversation is only a dream I'm having.'

'This isn't a dream and this isn't the first time he's done this. It began in Bali.'

Katrina shot back in her chair. 'Bali?'

Geneva took the beach photo from her pocket and laid it flat on the table. Katrina's eyes turned wide as she grabbed it and brought it up close to her face. 'Why are you showing me this? Where did you get it from?'

'Do you recognise the girl on the far left?'

'Of course. That's Anna.'

'The man who abducted you murdered Anna Becker several days ago. He also killed a girl in Bali – Lucy Brown. We think he followed you back to London.'

Confusion wrinkled Katrina's brow. 'But the police, they said Lucy was killed by migrants. There was a trial.'

'We have reason to doubt that version of events but we need to know what happened in Bali. He's almost certainly stalking the next girl. I want to stop him. I want to make sure he can never do this again.'

'You can't stop him,' Katrina said. 'He'll find you. It doesn't matter where you hide.'

Geneva pointed to the photo. 'Tell me about Lucy Brown and I promise I will do everything I can to make sure this man gets exactly what he deserves.'

Katrina bit down on her bottom lip. 'What's Lucy got to do with it?'

'We believe she was his first. You were interviewed by the

police over there. You can help us. Your friend was murdered.'

'She wasn't my friend.'

A flutter in the girl's tone made Geneva look up. 'Who was she?'

Katrina glanced at the photo and shrugged. 'She was just this girl, that's all. Always hanging around. It's awful what happened to her but we had nothing to do with it.'

'We?'

Katrina picked up a puzzle piece. 'There was a bunch of us girls – we weren't even friends or nothing, just partied together. You know how it is on holiday – you're not there for very long so you make friends quickly. Anna ... Anna was part of our group.'

'What about Lucy?'

'Poor fucking Lucy. She always had the worst luck. She was. Fuck. She was a little, okay, slow. She was there with her brother. She should have been splashing in the kiddie pool or making sandcastles but instead she used to hang out, or at least try to hang out, with us.'

'Try?'

'She was, God, this sounds terrible now but you want to know what happened, right? She was always asking us to take her to clubs and parties, to let her join our group. She was sweet, but. You know. A couple of girls were a bit nasty to her. This Serbian girl would tell her to scram, leave us alone, go find something more suited to her mental age, but Lucy never quite got the message.'

'And you didn't try to stop this?'

Katrina looked down at the table. 'I was drunk, high, stupid. It seemed a bit of harmless fun, the kind of thing we'd experienced every day at school. It was just a silly game that got out of hand. We never intended for anything like that to happen.'

The number of times Geneva had heard that. But the world didn't give a shit for anyone's intentions. 'What took place the night of the full moon rave?'

Katrina scratched behind her ear and crossed her arms. 'Lucy was at the beachside bar as usual that afternoon and she kept pleading with us to take her to the rave. It was the biggest event of the season and tickets were sold out but we had a couple spare. We were all extra-fucked that day, drinking and doing other shit in preparation and the Serbian girl said sure and gave Lucy one of the tickets.' Katrina picked up a peg and left it hanging in empty space near the middle of the puzzle. 'The rave was a big deal, DJs coming over from Brooklyn and the Balearics. A lot of us were going home in the next few days. We were drinking a lot, partying on the beach. We got Lucy drunk and I don't think she'd ever had booze before because she didn't take it well at all. She was sick and stupid but all the time pretending to enjoy it.

'We went skinny dipping at sunset. A bunch of Aussie boys had showed us this hidden lagoon the previous day. This Swiss girl made a special full moon punch. There was MDMA, Ketamine and coconut water in it. We all drank it knowing full well what it contained, we'd all done plenty before and knew what to expect – but Lucy didn't have a clue and in her eagerness drank far too much. It only took about fifteen minutes. She started to scream *What's happening to me? What's happening to me?* Hitting herself in the head, scratching her legs, crying and panicking. Some of the girls laughed and took photos.'

'And again, you didn't try to stop this?'

Katrina looked away.

'What?'

'I did. I did try to stop it. I suggested we go for a swim, a swim would cool Lucy off and bring her back down but, fuck, why did I say that? We tore off our clothes and plunged into the lagoon. The Swiss girl thought it would be funny to hide Lucy's clothes.

'Lucy was last out the water, crawling over the sand, and we all watched as she tried to find her clothes, stark naked and senseless, scrambling and slipping over the rocks.'

'And you left her like that?' Geneva couldn't believe the casual cruelty of it. Had too much reality TV and the Internet stripped the world of consequence for this generation? She thought about the theft of the clothes and what it might mean to the investigation. 'You didn't think leaving a mentally challenged girl naked, with a head full of drugs, might be a bad idea? That someone might take advantage of her?'

'We just ... no, you're right, there's no excuse. I haven't stopped thinking about it since I got here. All the things we could have done to stop it but we were so high by then we had no idea what was going on. We could barely take care of ourselves. We only found out what happened to Lucy when the police started interviewing everyone the next day.'

'You gave him his first taste.'

It had shocked her as Geneva had intended. Katrina scowled and turned back to the puzzle. She picked up one of the few remaining pieces and scrutinised it, then broke off a peg and slid it into place where previously it hadn't fitted. It matched perfectly and you couldn't tell it wasn't meant to be there at all.

She ran her hands across the surface of the puzzle and when she spoke, she spoke so quietly Geneva had to lean in to hear her.

'If you find him . . .'

'Yes?'

'Kill him,' Katrina said and upended the puzzle onto the floor.

49

'Lucy Brown is your daughter?'

'Was, Mr Carrigan. Was.' Eleanor Harper frowned. 'Why are you bringing this up now?'

Carrigan sat back and thought about what Eleanor had just said. This particular scenario had never occurred to them and he knew it was his fault for narrowing the investigation's parameters and that he'd missed a crucial link somewhere along the way. He could feel cogs turning, this new information reaching out and making connections, one more piece slotting into place, and he could almost see the shape of it now and understand how it had come to be.

'You're divorced?'

'No. My husband died thirteen years ago.'

Carrigan saw the loss briefly flare back behind her eyes. 'Can I ask how he died?'

Eleanor tapped her fingernails against the table. 'He fell down the stairs. Pathetic, I know, but.'

Carrigan acknowledged this with a tilt of the head. 'What was Lucy doing in Bali?'

Eleanor scooped hand cream from the jar and rubbed it into her skin in small circular motions. 'My daughter had learning difficulties but that doesn't mean she can't go on holiday.'

'I'm sorry.'

'I'm used to it.' Eleanor smiled, but her eyes were another

matter. 'It was my fault. I was supposed to go with her.' She glanced down at the papers and files, the meaningless debris of her days. 'But the evening before our departure we had a crisis at the office, a client was suing us because items had gone missing from his flat, and I had to stay behind.

'My son, Robert, was spending the summer in China. I got in touch with him, explained the situation and told him to meet Lucy off the plane the next day. He complained a bit, of course, but he was already in the region, all he had to do was hop on a plane. It wasn't a big deal.

'I spoke to Lucy after she'd arrived and she sounded happy. And that was something I didn't hear very often. I'd been so worried about sending her out on her own but she'd insisted. Two days later, I get a call from the Bali police chief.' Eleanor stopped and rubbed a stray drop of cream from her thumb. 'I remember it so damn clearly. I was leaving the office when the phone rang. I thought about whether to answer or let the machine pick up. People always talk about a mother's instinct but it wasn't that. It was just one less thing to do in the morning.

'As soon as the man on the other end explained who he was, as soon as I heard the tone in his voice – polite and businesslike, but as if he wanted to be anywhere else but on the other end of the line – I knew. He didn't need to say it but he did and every hope I had that this was a mistake, a wrong number, vanished. He told me they'd found her that morning on the beach. That she'd been killed the night before, had wandered off in a druggy stupor and stumbled into a migrants' camp. He said they were interviewing suspects. I didn't say a word. Language seemed impossible. A week later he phoned back to tell me the killers were in custody and to arrange shipment of

Lucy's body back home.' Eleanor wiped her cheeks. 'Why are you asking about this now? The case was closed. They caught and executed the men who did this.'

'I'm afraid it's a little bit more complicated than that.'

'What's that supposed to mean?'

'We believe they may have arrested the wrong men.'

'Are you saying the man who killed Lucy is free?'

Carrigan nodded. 'Yes, and he hasn't stopped. We think he was another tourist and he met this group of girls on the island. We don't know exactly what happened but he obviously became fixated with them. He killed your daughter and he's continued targeting them now he's back home. One girl is missing and presumed dead, the other is Anna Becker.'

'The girl who worked here?'

'Yes. We're still trying to understand how he got both Katrina and Anna to stay at the hostel. We think he might have emailed them discount vouchers. He knew once they were inside, he could keep an eye on them.'

'Hostel? Which hostel?'

'The Milgram.' Carrigan explained about the Ratting and Twitter trolling. 'We need to find out what happened in Bali, Ms Harper. Is your son still in China? We need to talk to him to see if he remembers anything. Maybe he knew this man? Maybe he met him at some bar or club?'

Eleanor frowned. 'I don't understand? He told me you'd already spoken to him.'

'We did? Where?'

'At the hostel, of course. That's where he spends most of his time.'

50

Geneva watched as Katrina got down on hands and knees and started to pick up the scattered puzzle pieces. When she offered to help her, Katrina ignored her, focusing on her task with a furious precision. Geneva felt torn between sympathy for the girl and a hot burning anger at what she'd done to Lucy Brown. She knew how cruel kids could be in groups, the anonymity shielding them from guilt and agency, but it was no excuse. She turned her back on Katrina and headed for the desk. The orderlies directed her to the main reception where, after showing her warrant card and explaining the circumstances, a nurse came to talk to her.

'She seemed very sane to me,' Geneva said.

The nurse nodded. 'Yes. She's very good at that. She can keep it up for several days at a time and we encourage her to do so but, after a while, she begins to break down – she loses the thread of her conversation and lapses into a catatonic state. A few times she's tried to injure herself and we've had to put her under observation.'

Geneva wondered what horrors hid behind that euphemism as she wrote down the details in her small, cramped handwriting. 'She thinks the drugs are still in her system. Is that possible?'

'We've run several tests and there's nothing there. But the drugs may have rearranged parts of her brain and who knows if that kind of damage is repairable? Her short-term memory's only good for a few hours. It's such a shame because when she's okay, she's very bright and extremely personable as you've seen. But then something sweeps her up and it's like she disappears from the world. It's even worse for her boyfriend. I can't imagine the—'

'Boyfriend?'

'Yes. At least I assume that's what he is. I never actually asked but he comes in quite regularly. He seems lovely too, very patient and devoted, unlike a lot of the visitors we get here. Some days he reads to her for hours at a time. She's very lucky to have someone like him.'

'What does he look like?'

The nurse paused to think. 'Skinny with long black hair. Otherwise unremarkable. Young people all start looking the same after you get to—'

'Do you know his name?'

'No. But it'll be in the visitors' book. Everyone has to show ID to get in.'

The nurse retreated behind her desk and retrieved a large visitors' book bound in spill-proof plastic. Geneva sat down on a nearby bench. She flicked through the crinkly, yellowed pages. The entries were organised by date. In the next column was the name of the visitor and, beside it, the patient they were visiting. Geneva ignored her phone and the pervasive smell of urine and started going backwards through the entries. She felt herself falling into that familiar spell that always overtook her when she plunged into paper lives, the persistent buzz of the present giving way to the silent words on the page.

The name of Katrina's visitor snapped her back to the room.

Katrina had only one visitor during the past six months but they had been conscientious and reliable, appearing twice a week, every week, since she'd been admitted.

Geneva looked at the name in the small white box. She ran through the investigation in her head and checked her notes but couldn't recall where she'd heard it before, yet it was naggingly familiar.

She thanked the nurse and walked out into a dark cleansing storm, the rain splashing the pavements and jewelling the surface of the road into glassy drizzle. She stood under the NO SMOKING sign and lit a cigarette, trying to remember where she'd come across that name. She needed to go back to the station, plug it into the HOLMES system and see what it would spit out. The cigarette fizzled and died and Geneva headed for her car.

As she opened the door and slid into the seat, the name came bouncing like a bomb, exploding in her brain with all it meant and she pulled the door tight against the rain and took out her phone to tell Carrigan the news. Her breath fogged the windows and the outer world disappeared. Rain streaked the glass, turning it opaque. Geneva lit another cigarette, the flame hot against her thumb and dialled the number. It went straight to voicemail. She was about to leave a message when the figure rose from the backseat.

Geneva felt a shift of light and then his hand was clamped across her mouth as he plunged the needle softly into her neck.

51

It was raining. A steady soothing rhythm that lulled her back and forth. It felt good to be indoors, lazing in bed, the world dissolving beyond the windows, nothing to do but listen to the rain and gently drift. She swayed in and out of drowsy sleep, the rain marking time, drip, drip, drip, a constant and irritating punctuation that held her back from surrendering completely to the dark.

Drip. Drip. Drip.

Geneva's eyes blinked open. The sound was sharper now, tiny percussive footsteps. It couldn't be raining inside her bedroom and yet it was. She blinked away motes of dreamstay and sleep gunk.

Drip. Drip. Drip.

She tried to suppress all the stray thoughts and hectoring panics trying to make themselves real on her tongue and focused instead on the rain, listening out for the soft detonation as it kissed the floor.

It was raining inside her bedroom but it couldn't be raining inside her bedroom which meant this wasn't her bedroom.

A burst of palpitations rumbled through her chest. Geneva opened her eyes and saw a cracked, unpainted ceiling. A pipe running a few inches below it. Water sliding along its surface. A single drop forming around an imperfection in the metal, so close she could see the room reflected in miniature across its surface. She watched the drop bulge and strain, pregnant with run-off. She thought she'd been watching it for hours but she couldn't be sure. And then it was gone. Her brain registered the sound as it collided with the floor and it came to her all at once – the complete where she was and what was about to happen.

She couldn't put the bits in the right order no matter how hard she tried. It was like that puzzle. What puzzle? It didn't matter. She was here and the how she got here wouldn't help her.

The room tilted abruptly as if it were a ship hit by a massive swell. Closing her eyes only made it worse. Images from her past shot out at random like bingo balls. Her stomach cramped and spat up a hot stream of bile. She counted to five and the room was back on its axis. The air tasted sweet and dry but there was no telling when the next wave would hit.

She'd had a boyfriend, a few months out of university, who'd been obsessed with survival documentaries. They'd watched countless ordeals, men with broken legs dragging themselves down impossible mountain moraines, men freezing to death in snow caves, men forced to amputate their own limbs in gloomy canyons. She'd always thought there was something a little silly about it. How it was always men. Men trying to prove themselves against God and nature. They were idiots for getting into those situations in the first place was what she'd always thought – but here she was.

A damp brick basement. Strapped to a chair. Her arms were pulled back behind the chair and held to it by some form of restraint. She shuffled her wrists, the cold roughness of the metal immediately familiar as the encirclement of handcuffs. Her feet were tied to the chair's legs but the ligature was soft, a fabric of some sort, and the knots felt looser.

She was surprised to find that her primary emotion wasn't fear or panic but a hot raw anger at herself for getting into this situation. All the rationalisations in the world didn't help. With everything she'd seen and read in the past few days, how could she have been so stupid? Those grizzled survivors hovered like disappointed ghosts. Art Davidson trapped in a snow cave high on Mount McKinley. Krakauer on Everest. Shackleton seesawing through the Drake Passage. Scott's final foray into endless white.

The spinning returned and Geneva gripped the chair for support. She thought about Hoffmann's breakdown of the various drugs the killer had used and then she tried not to think about it. She hoped this was merely a concussion. She wanted to find any other explanation but the one that logic kept insisting on. Were these the first signs of what was to come or was it just her mind playing tricks on her? It didn't matter. All that mattered was getting out of here or, failing that, into another position so as to add a small element of surprise when he came back.

Opposite her was a door made of dark wood, the handle and keyhole glinting in the meagre light. Geneva focused on it and tugged as hard as she could at the handcuffs. She bit down the hot spasm of pain that ran through her elbows and rattled her collarbone. It was no use. She had no leverage from this position and she would only succeed in tiring herself out or dislocating a shoulder. The drugs made her feel alternately hot and cold. Sweat stung her eyeballs. She stared at the door, so tantalisingly within reach.

There was only one option.

She needed to get her arms over the back of the chair. She could then work at the knots on her legs. Geneva relaxed her diaphragm and took several deep breaths, letting her muscles unwind. She began to rock – slowly at first, finding her rhythm, correcting any divergences, then using the tips of her shoes to push down and accelerate. She felt the momentum building and the slow hiccup of gravity the split second before the chair reached its tipping point. Geneva exhaled slowly as it tumbled over and she hit the cement, taking the full force of the fall in her shoulder, jaw and hip.

She kept her eyes closed and waited for the worst of the pain to subside. She was lying on the floor, her face against the wet cement. She could see the door, the handle glinting like a promise, and she began to work herself up the chair, pushing her feet against its legs, the knots around her ankles sliding up bit by bit. After what seemed like hours but was probably only minutes, she kicked one final time and her wrists cleared the top of the chair.

A spider crawled next to her face, its legs huge and endless from this vantage. Her arms were free of the chair but she was still cuffed and her legs were still tied. She slammed the handcuffs against the cement in frustration. The shock juddered through her wrists but when she heard the cuffs rattle she ignored the pain and raised her arms and struck them once more against the floor. She felt a muscle tear in her back, electric arrows torqueing her spine, and the unmistakable crack of metal as a fleeting weightlessness jumped into her wrist.

Geneva cried out in surprise. Her heart beat thickly in her neck. She hadn't thought for one moment she'd be able to break the handcuffs, she'd been certain her chance would come later, in those final moments when he took off his clothes and made her stand up next to him as she knew he would – but there was no time for congratulation or relief. The door could open at any moment.

She pulled her arms to her chest and rubbed the blood back into her wrists. She examined the handcuffs and saw the ridge where they'd been previously broken and inexpertly welded back together. She didn't want to think about that so she left them on the floor and reached down and undid the leather straps that bound her feet to the chair. She remembered something Milan had said and pocketed one of the straps.

The door was only five feet away.

Either it was locked or it wasn't.

The room began to spin again and she knew she hadn't been imagining it. She'd taken enough drugs back at university to recognise the distinctive sensation of coming up. Her knees trembled, not an altogether unpleasant feeling, warmth coursing up and down her thighs like a million tiny fingers. There was no point fighting the drugs. The more you resisted, the more your mind broke against their will. The room span to the left but she knew its tricks now and continued unabated. She focused only on the handle, the silvery lock beneath it, this small part of the door that would render it gift or curse.

She let her hand rest on the handle and caught her breath. It felt warm as if another's touch had only recently departed it. Geneva pushed down, waiting for the inevitable click that would signal the lock engaging, but it never came.

The door swung open and, when Geneva saw what lay behind it, she collapsed to her knees.

52

She was staring at a brick wall. She could see the zigzag pattern of scratch marks left on the bricks by the room's previous occupants. A door that opens onto a brick wall. She should have expected something like this when she'd seen the weakened handcuffs. She should have known this would be his style.

'You've done well.'

Geneva turned suddenly. The voice came from somewhere behind her. She could just make out the mere suggestion of a figure in the fuzzy distance.

'It took Madison eight hours to get out of the chair. She never did get the handcuffs off.'

Geneva blinked the hallucination away but it refused to disperse. 'You're lying. I spoke to Madison. She's safe on the other side of the world.'

She heard him laugh, a small strangled choke of sound coming from the centre of the room. 'You "spoke" to her? It's funny we still say that when we mean texts. *About to get on a plane. Sorry. Don't feel safe. Thank you for listening to me and keep me informed. Please find Anna.*'

Geneva resisted the urge to curse, cry or betray any hint of feeling in front of him. She knew it would only make him stronger. 'That was you?'

He took out his mobile and tilted it so she could see the screen.

Madison stared back at Geneva. Madison tethered to a chair in this same basement. Madison screaming and fighting her restraints.

'I couldn't let her go home. I didn't know what she'd remember when the drugs wore off, or what she'd told you.'

'You bastard.' Geneva tried to push herself up from the floor but it felt like her arms were made of sand.

'Don't bother.' His voice bounced against the low ceiling and brick walls, making it sound as if there were a multitude of him encircling her. 'It won't make a difference. You should save your energy. It's only just beginning.'

'What the fuck did you give me?'

'A mixture of things. Knowing their names won't help you, though. It's in their combination where the magic happens. You'll see. What you're feeling now is only the first of many rungs. I designed it so each drug will kick in sequentially.' He flicked his head to the side and swept back his hair. 'You're going to be spending a long time down here. The DMT will make it seem like you're on that floor for ten years. What are you going to do? How are you going to keep your mind occupied so you don't go mad? And the things I'll do to you? They'll feel like they're taking for ever.'

His voice was so calm he could have been talking about the football results or a movie he'd watched the night before. He moved closer to her and she began to discern the shape of his body, the details of his face but, at first, her brain refused to accept what she was seeing. She blinked and rubbed her eyes.

'You?'

His hair was no longer in a ponytail but hung down either

side of his shoulders. She'd seen him sitting in Eleanor Harper's office three days ago. She'd been only a couple of feet away. 'You were at Sparta when I interviewed that woman?'

He reached out and stroked a wayward strand of hair from Geneva's forehead, tucking it neatly behind her ear. 'My name's Bob, not *You*, and that woman happens to be my mother.'

Geneva pulled away and tried to speak but the words got stuck in her throat. Memories, images and facts spun through her brain. A page from Carrigan's report on the hostel. Something Eleanor had said. 'I don't understand? If she's your mother . . . You led us right to her? You told us about the man harassing Anna.'

'You would have found out about Anna's job soon enough.' Bob flicked his hair back and Geneva was struck by how young he was, only a few years older than his victims. No wonder he'd been able to blend in so effortlessly. 'By telling you about a client who tried it on with her, I knew you'd waste valuable resources pursuing that particular line of inquiry.'

He was right. They'd been so eager to see a pattern, they'd accepted the first one that had come along. It meant everything they'd thought and profiled was wrong. The last few hours came back in a kaleidoscopic rush – Katrina on the floor picking up puzzle pieces, the visitors' book, the shadow in the back of her car. 'Why did you follow me to the hospital?'

'Why would I need to follow you? Your phone tells me where you are. No, as it happens, I was on my way to visit someone. Imagine my surprise when I saw you go in.'

'You were there to see Katrina?'

'Someone has to. Poor girl has no one since her parents died.' Geneva clamped her jaw tight, a spike of adrenaline momentarily clearing the drug from her brain. 'You went to the hospital to gloat.'

'Got me there.' Bob held up his hands. 'I like to check in on her every so often, see how she's doing.'

'You never intended to kill her,' Geneva said, only realising this as she spoke. 'You fucked her brain with drugs so you could come and watch the results, knowing she would never remember your visits?'

'See? You could have worked it out by yourself all along.'

Geneva heard the soles of his shoes scrape against the floor as he moved closer, the sharp metallic tang of his sweat flooding her nostrils. She used the flat of her hand to prop herself up. 'Who's the next girl? There's four other girls in that photo. Which one are you currently stalking?' It took all her effort to force the words out in their rightful form, her jaw chattering as if she were bivouacked in deep ice, but there were also fleeting moments of clarity, the first for a while, and she understood her body was fighting the drugs.

'The next girl?' Bob grinned. 'You haven't worked it out yet? *You're* the next girl. You always were.' He took out a palm-sized digital camera and flicked it on. A rectangle of white light shot out the front. He fast-forwarded through a collection of clips. Geneva saw footage of herself over the last few days – at home, on the job, in front of her computer. Bob aimed the device at her and switched from playback to record. 'A little souvenir for your partner. It'll prove you once existed.'

She tried to ignore the camera and meaning behind the words and concentrated instead on his every movement, following the curve of his arms, anchoring herself to the moment and its geometry. She knew how easy it would be to slip away.

The drugs came in ebbs and massive rushes that felt as if a hundred light bulbs had been switched on inside her skull. Time had stopped its ticking. It could have been minutes and it could have been days. Memories and facts reasserted themselves. The gravity of consciousness and guilt took over.

'We're in the hostel, aren't we?'

'In the basement, yes.'

Geneva scanned the room. 'But we checked the entire building?'

'Not this bit. This is the north wing. You were on the other side of that brick wall.' He pointed over her shoulder to the door she'd placed so much hope in. 'This building has many strange features, rooms that don't make any sense. It's far more fun when you're in an altered state, as I'm sure you'll soon discover.'

She glanced over at the damp walls and concrete floor. 'This is where you brought the girls?'

Bob pointed to a faint striping of scratch marks scored into the brick. 'As you can see, they left their mark.'

She tried not to think of Anna and Madison captive in this dank basement, both awaiting equally terrible fates, but it was all she could think about. 'Why kill Anna, then? Why not leave her impaired like Katrina?'

'Because of you.'

'Me?'

'Because Madison came to you. Madison fucked it all up. She drank from Anna's drink and once she'd been to see you, keeping Anna for any longer was too risky. You were now actively searching for her. It was much easier to get rid of her.'

Geneva remembered the photo of Anna spread-eagled on

the floor, her dress perfectly arranged. The blood on the wall and the defaced passport. 'You knew when Anna's body was found we'd start looking at her life and that eventually we'd come to you, so you staged it to appear like a serial sex slaying. The blood, the positioning, the passport photo – it was all a bluff, wasn't it?'

'It's a shame you didn't work it out before. But then you were looking for patterns and I provided them – only they happened to be the wrong ones. I knew, once you saw Anna like that, your brains would start to work in one way, you'd see what you were hoping to see and ignore the rest.'

Geneva's eyes had adjusted to the darkness and she could make him out clearly now, surprised at how slight and unprepossessing he was. The kind of person you could talk to for an hour and instantly forget the moment you got up. 'My boss suspected all along. He never believed the profile.'

'Which is why it was lucky you were there to steer him towards it.'

Geneva knew he was trying to goad her but she also knew he was right and that her insistence on a serial pathology, along with Hoffmann's, had made them blind to certain clues and anomalies that might have led to Bob sooner. 'I don't believe you,' she said, the drug alive and hectic in her blood. 'You say you did this to put us off the scent but that's bullshit – you used the same MO in Bali and you weren't trying to mislead us then.'

Bob leant forward and brushed his hand against her face. She felt the sting of his fingers and then he changed his mind and pulled his arm back. 'You still don't understand, do you? Lucy Brown was my sister. Those girls were never punished for what they did to her.'

Geneva stared mutely at the floor as her brain caught up to the words. It was something they'd not even considered and yet it made perfect sense. 'So you decided to punish them by recreating the murder scene?'

She heard him suck in a deep draught of air and felt a charge take hold of his body, an unsettling that caused his chair to creak rhythmically against the floor.

'The Twitter trolling and intrusions? Was that more punishment?'

'It was justice,' Bob snapped back, his voice catching on the last syllable. 'They needed to see what it was like to be bullied, to be picked on and picked apart, how your entire life telescopes down into this one thing. Their parents deserved to suffer the way my mother did. That was only fair.'

'Fair?' Geneva said, wondering how many times Bob had watched the footage of Anna's parents. 'You're out of your mind.'

'And yet look where you are.'

She had no answer for that. Somewhere time was still ticking at its normal pace but down here it had slowed to an almost imperceptible crawl. She knew she had only one card to play and she would have to play it carefully. 'You're very good at making up stories. You should have become a proper filmmaker instead of this.'

'What stories?'

Geneva smiled. 'The one about Bali, for instance.'

'What the fuck are you talking about?'

'You see, I used to be an English Lit student so I'm very good at pulling stories apart and there's something about yours that doesn't add up.'

She saw him flinch and continued. 'You say you killed Anna and Katrina because of what they did to your sister in Bali. That it was revenge. And I can understand that. Who wouldn't feel that way? The part that doesn't make sense to me is you were Lucy's big brother. You were supposed to be looking after her.'

She heard the faint crack of his teeth grinding against one another, his shoes scraping the floor.

'This didn't happen in a split second, Bob. Between Lucy being spiked and her murder there were four hours when you could have saved your sister, and the fact you didn't makes me wonder.'

'Shut up.'

'Makes me wonder if maybe you were somewhere else. Perhaps you met someone and thought you could have the night off from being the ever-present guardian – but no, I don't think that's it either. I don't think you'd neglect your duties and abandon your sister for some girl you'd just met.'

'I said shut up!'

'I think you were there. I think you saw it happen. You could have stopped it at any time but you didn't because you were enjoying it too much.'

'Shut the fuck up.' Bob swerved forward and raised his left heel and stamped it down on Geneva's fingers.

She pushed the pain to the back of her mind and tried to recall more details from Hoffmann's profile, words the only ammunition she possessed. 'It's not easy to care for a mentally disabled sibling, I'm sure. It takes up your entire life. You were probably looking after Lucy from the moment she was born and it's made you resentful. You can't keep from imagining what your life would be like without her. All the failures and disappointments you blamed on her, because that's what we do, isn't it? Otherwise, we have to accept that our lives are our own fault or that the world is random and capricious. And Lucy was always going to be your burden, you could never be free while she was alive – so, tell me if I'm wrong, but I think a part of you enjoyed what Anna, Katrina and the others were doing to her. After all, you were stuck on this island with all these beautiful girls and wild parties and instead you had to spend every last minute looking after your sister.

'So, I think you got a kick out of Lucy being humiliated and I can understand that too – we all occasionally have those feelings towards the people we're tethered to – but what I can't understand is why you didn't intervene after they hid her clothes? When she was naked and terrified on the beach? Or why you didn't stop her when she was wandering around in a daze?'

'You don't know what you're talking about.' Bob pressed down with his heel and electric arrows shot through Geneva's fingers.

She bit her tongue and warm blood flooded her mouth. She swallowed it down and continued. It was too late to stop now. 'The only thing which makes sense is that watching her turned you on. That's what I get from your online activity and the crime scene. You can cover up a lot of things but your behaviour will always betray your true motivations. You've convinced yourself you're doing this out of revenge but you're not – you just haven't realised it yet.'

Geneva stopped, caught her breath, and continued. 'Watching Lucy awakened something in you. Something that was always there but which you've denied and suppressed your entire life. The things you did to Anna – the drugs, the clothes, the positioning – you weren't avenging Lucy's death. You were recreating it.'

She paused and waited for a reaction but there was only the sound of his breathing.

'I bet seeing her body on the beach gave you an unexpected thrill? That's why you didn't try to intervene when the migrants took her or call for the cops. Did you hide behind some bushes and film it? Of course you did. I'm sure you've replayed the footage countless times. You saw your sister being taken and you filmed it on your phone and you couldn't control yourself. Watching her struggle and cry. Knowing you had the power to stop it if you wanted. And when it was over, you went up and closed her eyes. That's what gave you away. The migrants didn't care enough about her to do that.' Geneva forced herself up on one leg, the chair she'd been strapped to taking the weight of her arms. 'And you know the funniest thing? We might never have caught you if a fifteen-year-old brat hadn't outwitted you with his Ratting program. That's how it ends for you, Bob. Pathetic and pointless. It's time for you to accept the truth of your life. You've been lying to yourself for far too long.'

He didn't respond for almost a full minute then something shifted in his expression. He reached out and gently stroked her hair. 'It doesn't matter. Even if you catch me, there's hundreds of thousands just like me all over the world, cruising the web, looking for prey, and it's only going to get a whole lot worse. You think the things I've done are bad, just wait and see what the next generation is capable of. You'll have nowhere to hide. You'll never feel safe again.'

Bob stood up and kicked the chair away. He crouched down beside Geneva and lifted her up by the throat. She felt his fingers pressing down on her windpipe but she didn't struggle. She knew her one chance would also be her only chance and that it would come in that moment before the end, that precise instant when he lost control. She felt the first tingle of the next wave of drugs coursing through her. The heat radiating off his body. She waited for him to begin but instead he pulled a small silver scalpel from his back pocket.

'You're not going to take off your clothes?' She'd been planning for this, knowing it would be her best and last chance, and she couldn't hide the disappointment in her voice.

'That was far more hassle and much less fun than I expected.' He pushed the blade against her neck. It was all happening too quickly. Geneva's head snapped back and hit the wall. She felt the icy kiss of metal as he thrust the knife below her jaw and slid it into place. He pressed lightly to test the skin and was about to make his incision when the phone rang.

Bob looked down at his waist in surprise but he recovered quickly, shooting his fist out, the knuckles connecting with Geneva's forehead and sending her sprawling to the floor. He rubbed his fingers with his other hand and took out his phone. He saw his mother's name on the caller ID and put the receiver to his mouth. 'Not now. I'm busy,' he said, about to hang up.

But the voice on the other end was not Eleanor Harper's.

53

'What the fuck are you doing with my mother's phone?'

Carrigan could hear a strange reverb bleeding from Bob's voice as if he were speaking underwater. After listening to Eleanor's story, Carrigan had called Hoffmann. They'd conferred and considered and come to the same conclusion.

'You need to let DS Miller go. It's over.'

Bob laughed. 'It's not even begun. You think I can't get away and reach the Continent before you have your warrants and teams set up? There's four more girls out there who haven't come to terms with their actions yet. Two in Cologne, one in Bern and another in Belgrade I'm saving for last. You really believe your jurisdiction will stretch that far? In the meantime, DS Miller will spend years trapped down here even if you get her out today.'

'I understand that, Bob,' Carrigan replied. 'But we know where you are. We have the hostel surrounded. You're not going to get away.'

'I don't believe you. There's no way you could know that.'

'You're right. Which is why I had to ask your mother. She told me you like to spend time in the basement of the abandoned section, that it reminds you of your room at home when you were a kid.'

'She would never have willingly told you that,' Bob replied, a slight hesitation in his voice. 'What the fuck did you do to her?'

'Nothing. Nothing at all. In fact, she'd very much like to speak to you.'

Carrigan handed the phone to Eleanor. She took it mutely, the revelations of the last hour still rattling through her head.

'Robert? You told me Lucy ran away. You said you tried to find her?'

'I did it for you.' There was a long pause, punctuated only by the sound of Bob's breathing. 'I was waiting until it was over. I was going to tell you about it then.'

'What on earth are you talking about?'

'You don't know the things they did to Lucy. How they humiliated her. And they got away with it. That wasn't fair. It was their fault. They killed her more surely than those migrants did and they were enjoying their lives oblivious to what they'd put you through. It was all for you, Mum – can't you see that?'

'Are you out of your mind?'

Geneva tensed her body, waiting for the right moment. Bob kept shaking his head at the phone, ignoring her, his attention completely focused on the conversation, the scalpel dangling from his fist.

'I remember how happy you were after Dad died. I only wanted you to be happy again.'

'God, you're just like him. Your father was a weak man and a bully and so are you. None of this has brought Lucy back. How could it? The only thing it's done is make me lose you.'

'What . . . what do you mean? I'm still here.' His voice trailed off and Geneva noticed the way his posture changed to accommodate the words, the coiled tension in his limbs and wild disturbance in his eyes.

'No. No, you're not. I don't recognise you. The boy I raised

332

would never have done this. All you've managed to do is hurt their families the way ours was hurt.' Eleanor was crying but her voice betrayed no sign of it. 'Is that what you call fair? I can't believe that you – of all people – would do such a thing. You know better than anyone what it means to lose someone close. I don't understand you at all and I'm not sure I can speak to you again. Not after this.'

Eleanor hung up. Static buzzed across the basement. Bob shouted into the receiver, 'No!' He lifted the phone up to his face. 'Mum? Mum? Speak to me. Please.'

Geneva moved quickly, while he was still off-balance. She wrapped her hands around his ankles and pulled. He tried to resist, but gravity was on her side for once and he crashed to the floor in a series of delayed stumbles, the scalpel flying from his hand. Geneva tried to reach for it but he was surprisingly quick, grabbing her by the thigh and squeezing hard. He got to his knees and punched her in the stomach, the air exploding from her lungs, black stars swarming her vision. She tried to shake him off but his grip was too fierce. She pivoted her hips, spun her legs, and went for his head but missed, her fingers snatching at his long black hair instead.

She grasped the hair and wound her fist around it and used it to pull herself up. He screamed and his head jerked back. Geneva twisted the hair tighter, reeling him in. He shot his arm out and punched her in the chest. She held on and pulled until there was no more slack, then rotated her fist and slammed his face into the floor.

Blood streamed from his eyes and nose. He flapped his arms wildly, his legs kicking out underneath him. His fingers grappled and flailed and found her shirt and he began to slowly pull her towards him. She tried to kick him off but she had no leverage. Any moment he would be above her. Her fist was still clutching his hair. She cocked it and twisted his head and brought it down hard on the floor, a sickening crunch filling her ears. All resistance immediately disappeared. His body began to spasm. Geneva uncoiled her fingers and pushed herself away until the cold wall was at her back. She felt light-headed and drugsick, on the verge of passing out.

Bob lifted his head. There was a dent where his skull had caved in. His right eye rolled back into its socket, leaving only a milky blankness. He began to speak but it was in no language she could recognise and she saw the raw panic in his face when he realised what was happening. He tried to reach out for her but lost his balance, his body convulsing one final time before it surrendered to the floor.

Epilogue

'I've made my decision.'

Carrigan sat across from the doctor discussing the thing you hope never to have to discuss. His head swarmed with hesitations, guilt, and the smell of fresh raisin cake. The call had come an hour ago. He'd driven straight to the emergency room. His mother's heart had stopped during the night. They'd broken two ribs resuscitating her.

'You tell me she'll never recover. You say all her brain function is gone and even if she woke up she'd be in a persistent vegetative state. What other option do I have?'

The doctor shrugged, small sloped shoulders caving in towards his chest. A man not given to grave pronouncements spending his life dispensing them. 'Some people, regardless of the prognosis, choose to have faith we're wrong.'

'And are you ever wrong?'

'Sometimes, yes,' the doctor admitted. 'But not in cases like this. The facts I gave you are just that – facts. We've scanned her several times and what's gone isn't ever coming back, I'm afraid.'

'What if she's conscious underneath it all and going out of her mind staring at the ceiling?'

The doctor folded his hands. 'We still don't know what happens in the brains of coma patients, no idea how much of

335

the world they can perceive or what's going on internally. We only have the facts. Without the machines supporting her, she wouldn't be alive.'

Carrigan rubbed his beard. 'Does that mean she's actually dead?'

The doctor thought about this, a frown settling on his face. 'That's where definitions tend to get a bit slippery.'

'Even between life and death?' Carrigan stared at the back of a picture frame propped up on the desk, wondering if the other side held a wife and family. 'When can it be done?'

The doctor pulled out a large desk diary and flicked through it, much more comfortable with data and action than abstract speculation. 'How about later today?'

*

The machine beeped every five seconds. Carrigan had been sitting here for the last half hour watching the spikes and lines on the heart monitor flutter and falter. Geneva was beside him, quiet and crouched low in her seat. She'd been released from hospital only the night before but had insisted on being here.

Bob Brown had not regained consciousness. Three minutes after Geneva knocked him out, the assault team had entered the basement. His brain continued to swell in the ambulance and he was dead by the time he got to St Mary's. Carrigan looked over at Geneva but her expression was unreadable. She would have to spend the next few weeks mired in paperwork, counsellors and review boards and he wondered how and in what shape she would emerge from it.

The door opened and a young doctor entered, followed by

a jowly white-haired priest. Several nurses and other medical staff filed in and surrounded his mother's bed, charts and tablets in their hands. A video camera was recording the procedure. The priest stunk of whisky and week-old sweat. He spoke to Carrigan briefly then went over to the bed.

'Are you ready?' the doctor asked.

Carrigan took one final look at his mother and nodded.

The priest gave her the last rites and gently placed the tips of his fingers over her eyes. The doctor performed a sequence of tests on the machine, the assistants helping, each responsible for a specific function like the integrated parts of some fleshy contraption.

All of a sudden, the beeping stopped.

The doctor's expression changed and he pressed more buttons. The nurses and assistants ceased what they were doing and stared down at the bed.

'What's wrong?' Carrigan said.

The doctor pushed another series of buttons, the lights blinking and flashing, tubes and pumps suddenly springing to life. He looked up, his eyes unable to meet Carrigan's, and said, 'She died.'

'Isn't that supposed to be the point?'

'No. You don't understand.' The doctor became more frantic as he ran a battery of tests on his machines. 'I hadn't finished the checks. She died before we could switch her off. She died of her own accord.'

*

Carrigan sat next to Geneva in the hospital cafeteria. Discarded cups of coffee ringed the table. Faint muzak leaked

337

through the ceiling. The clock on the far wall had stopped nearly a year ago but no one had bothered to replace it. All around them were men and women adrift in their own private gloom. Everyone looked stunned, as if they'd just heard the worst news of their lives, which they probably had. It was there in the way they stirred their drinks and nibbled their food, the father on the fifth floor, the wife in ICU, the baby clinging to life under heated glass. Their lives had been put on pause. They'd abandoned holidays, jobs and children to rush here, in the middle of the night or at two in the afternoon, not knowing what they would find, only that the moment they stepped through the hospital doors their lives would change for ever.

Geneva took a sip of coffee and turned her head. It was weird to be sitting side by side but the seat opposite had been soiled by a previous occupant and no one had yet come to clean it. 'I'm so sorry about your mother.'

'Thank you.' Carrigan cradled his cup, the hot ceramic stinging his palm. 'I feel awful saying this, but, in a lot of ways, it's a relief. She was never going to regain consciousness. Maybe deep inside her coma she knew that. Maybe her last act was willing her body to shut down. She's no longer stuck in limbo. She has a chance at heaven now.'

'You believe that?'

Carrigan glanced at the tables surrounding them. 'In this place, not so much, but sometimes, yes.' He saw the cuts, nicks and stitches on Geneva's face, her left eye yellow and fat, a gash across her top lip that would leave a scar and her chipped front tooth. 'How are you doing?'

She shrugged. 'Better, thanks. Valium and two days in bed and I feel almost good as new.' It wasn't the entire truth but, for now, it would do. Bob only had time to give her the preliminary round of drugs and for that she was grateful. As bad as she'd felt these last few days, she knew Katrina, Anna and Madison had suffered worse. She would get over it. That was life. You either got over it or you didn't.

'That's good to hear, but I was talking about what happened in the basement.'

'You mean how do I feel about killing Bob?'

'Yes.'

'I don't feel good about it.' She took another sip of coffee. 'But I don't feel that bad about it either. I wasn't going to die down there.'

'I wasn't going to let you.'

They both turned at the same time and suddenly they were facing each other. A beat passed and their fingers collided. Their faces were only an inch apart. Geneva closed her eyes and let her body sway forward. She felt Carrigan's lips brush hers . . .

'Isn't this nice?'

Geneva snapped her eyes open to see two men standing either side of the table. They both wore suits and one of them was waving a piece of paper in his hand.

'We have a warrant for your arrest, Carrigan.' Patterson placed the document on the table. 'I'm sorry to break this up but you're going to have to come with us.'

It took Geneva a moment to process what was happening but by then it was too late. Patterson was reading Carrigan his rights. She tried to object but the other man held her back as Patterson finished the formalities and, with great deliberation, snapped the handcuffs shut on Carrigan.

Acknowledgements

This book came to be under the most difficult of circumstances. It probably wouldn't have seen the light without the following:

Angus Cargill – I mention this every time, but what else is there to say except he's the best editor any author could wish for and, if you enjoyed this book, a lot of that is down to him.

Sophie Portas, Katherine Armstrong, Andrew Benbow, Katie Hall, Miles Poynton, Lisa Baker and everyone else at Faber & Faber who do so much to bring these books out into the world.

Everyone at Aitken Alexander Associates, for spreading my words around the globe.

Kent Carroll for the always entertaining breakfast chats and for everything he's done at Europa Editions to get my books published in America.

All those reviewers and bloggers who took the time to read and comment on my previous novels. Without you, this would seem a very pointless job.

My mother, for always being there.

Jane, for everything that is not contained within language.

And, of course, most importantly, to all the readers who have followed me through the years – thank you so much! Without you, none of this would have a reason to exist.

The phrase, 'There's always one more camera in any given room than you think there is,' was kindly borrowed from Matt Thorne.

Also by Stav Sherez

ff

A Dark Redemption

THE FIRST CARRIGAN AND MILLER NOVEL

Shortlisted for the Theakston's Old Peculier
Crime Novel of the Year 2013

A Dark Redemption introduces DI Jack Carrigan and DS Geneva Miller as they investigate the brutal murder of a young Ugandan student. Plunged into an underworld of illegal immigrant communities, they discover that the murdered girl's studies at a London college may have threatened to reveal things that some people will go to any lengths to keep secret . . .

'Masterful.' *Daily Mirror* ****

'Fast-paced and slick.' *Guardian*

'Sherez is superb at evoking the unfamiliar world of immigrant communities . . . Although there is nothing more conventional than an unconventional cop, Sherez has beaten the odds and created an original detective in Carrigan.' *Daily Telegraph*

Available in paperback and ebook now

ff

Eleven Days

A CARRIGAN AND MILLER NOVEL

*Shortlisted for the Theakston's Old Peculier
Crime Novel of the Year 2014*

Eleven days before Christmas a suspicious fire rages through
a small convent in West London. DI Carrigan and DS Miller
are called in to investigate. As they try to tread carefully amid
the politics of the force and of the Catholic Church, their investigation seems to uncover more questions than answers: why
did the ten nuns not try to escape the fire? Where is Father
McCarthy, the last person known to visit them? And who is the
mysterious eleventh victim?

'Sherez belongs in the top league
of British crime writers.' Eva Dolan

'Powerful . . . Sherez is emerging as a very interesting
crime novelist indeed, pursuing dark themes with
impressive authority.' Andrew Taylor, *Spectator*

'Addictive.' *Financial Times*

'Strikingly modern.' *Sunday Times*

Available in paperback and ebook now